# THE
# MESSENGER
# MUST DIE

# THE MESSENGER MUST DIE

## Kjell-Olof Bornemark

DEMBNER BOOKS
New York

DEMBNER BOOKS
Published by Red Dembner Enterprises Corp., 80 Eighth Avenue New York, N.Y. 10011
Distributed by W. W. Norton & Company, Inc., 500 Fifth Avenue, New York, N.Y. 10110

**Library of Congress Cataloging-in-Publication Data**
Bornemark, Kjell-Olof, 1924–
    The messenger must die.
    Translation of: Legat till en trolös.
    I. Title.
PT9876.12.076L413   1986      839.7'374     86–6252
ISBN 0–934878–75–7

Legat Till en Trolös, the original edition of this novel, was published by Norstedt Publishing, Stockholm.

The Messenger Must Die was translated from the original Swedish edition by Laurie Thompson.

Design by Antler & Baldwin, Inc.

## ❧ I ❧

The greeting card lay on the doormat along with a few brown envelopes. He saw it dimly through his steamed-up glasses and realized immediately what it meant. He was not surprised. On the contrary, it confirmed his suspicions. The insecurity he had felt and the doubts he had entertained these last few weeks, ever since that first newspaper report, could now give way to certainty. Actually it came as a relief. All that time, he had avoided drawing conclusions or making decisions. It was not his responsibility, not up to him. Now that the message had come he was ready—as he had been for over thirty years.

As he bent down to pick up the card, snow dripped from his fur hat down his neck, and he paused with a smile. Ten minutes, he thought. It can stay there for ten minutes. If it were time to move out, he could allow himself ten minutes before getting ready to leave. To do what, though? Take a last look around the apartment? Think about what he would miss? He felt no curiosity, no excitement; no more excitement than usual. He was always on his guard against any sign of self-deception.

1

He took off his shoes in the hall and went in stockinged feet into the bathroom to hang up his fur coat and hat. Even though it was freezing cold outside, at least 35 below, he was sweaty. He had spent the last quarter of an hour angrily shovelling away an enormous heap of snow a plow had piled up around his car. His next door neighbor in the apartment block, a Dane, had stood at his window watching all the time.

It must have looked odd. No sane person shovels out his car shortly before eleven on a frosty winter's night. But he had no choice. He knew that unease, not fear but unease, must always be kept at bay. If the alarm came that night, every second of the first few minutes would be of vital importance. A snowed-in car could not be allowed to impede his getaway. It would have been negligent not to set to work with a shovel, for as the night wore on his unease would have gradually taken possession of him, developing fatally into unnecessary and dangerous fear. He would not allow that to happen.

There had been a time when he worried about the Dane, whom he had noticed all too often standing like a guard at his kitchen window. It was certainly possible the Dane had been recruited by the opposition, even though they usually arranged for watch to be kept in a more discreet and professional manner. History could provide many instances of chauffeurs, waiters, and housekeepers taken on as extra informers. Nobody was so insignificant that he was beyond suspicion. When he had discovered why the Dane kept watch at his window, however, he had a good laugh to himself. In fact he celebrated solving the riddle by touring most of the city's bars, but he did not regret for one moment the apparently unnecessary suspicion he had directed toward the Dane for the past three weeks.

The reason the Dane diligently watched the street from his kitchen window was Clothilde, a frizzy white Persian cat—the only company the Dane had in the world. Clothilde blithely carried out her nightly raids while the Dane loyally stood at the window, waiting for his faithless friend. That very evening the cat had followed Tragg in through the front door when he had finished shovelling snow. Clothilde had behaved arrogantly in the elevator, avoiding contact with his stiff, frosty trouser legs. By way of revenge he had left her alone out on the landing, after ringing the Dane's doorbell.

The ten minutes were almost up. He had changed into something dry and comfortable and fetched a beer and whiskey. Before going back into the hall to pick up the card and the rest of the mail, he had switched on the lamp by his armchair.

The greeting card was handwritten and addressed to Mr. *Greger Tragg, Attundavägen 17, Stockholm*, postmarked West Berlin. The picture had a turn-of-the-century air, two hands grasped in a handshake surrounded by a wreath of white, yellow, and red roses interspersed with greenery and lilies of the valley. The text was in German, and looked most elegant:

**Many Happy Returns**
**on your**
**——birthday**

Someone had written "50th" in the space provided. The same person had signed it in clear, old-fashioned handwriting. Two names:

**Max and Bertha**

At the top of the card, between the fancy bronze-colored frame and the flowers, was a thought-provoking verse in smaller print:

**May happiness and cheer galore**
**Be what the future has in store**

3

That was all. Slowly and solemnly he raised his whiskey glass to the empty room. "Cheers!"

He emptied the glass in one gulp and waited patiently. It should go away now. The chill in the pit of his stomach, like the after-effects of a kidney stone attack, had first hit him three weeks ago. A lieutenant, or was it a colonel—Tragg was well aware the press always got it wrong—had defected to the West. Among his papers was a list of names. Half a dozen men and women, all connected with the Insurance Company Tragg worked for himself, had been arrested the next night in various parts of West Germany and West Berlin, probably at exactly the same time. One of them managed to get away just a few hundred yards away from the police headquarters in Pullach, the intelligence center in southern Germany. The paper said the man had drawn his pistol from a shoulder holster, forced the driver to stop, disarmed the driver and the two security officers who had arrested him, pushed them out into the street, and with screeching tires raced past the police headquarters before disappearing into the night. It could well be true. West Germans are so much in awe of ministry officials that even if a person were arrested in the middle of the night on strong suspicion of espionage, it is quite likely he would not be subjected to the humiliation of a body search, at least not by low-ranking officers. Tragg also knew it could be a fabrication, a bold attempt to plant an established counterspy, this time on home territory.

That same week the headlines in Stockholm announced the arrest of a Swedish spy, a high-ranking police officer who was said to be working for more or less all the powers—Russia, the United States, and the Arabs. Then, a few days later, the Israeli security services returned a Swedish ex-army officer to Stockholm, handcuffed to be on the safe side, and accompanied by stony-faced Shin Beth men. He was taken straight from Arlanda airport to the high-security block in Bergsgatan. This was the worst case of espionage in Sweden since the days

4

of Colonel Wennerström, and had been leaked to the press by the Swedish secret service, SÄPO.

Greger Tragg sat at home that first week, taking it all in. He read the newspapers in great detail and was careful not to miss any news bulletin on the radio or TV. Despite poor reception, he sat by his radio set every night and listened to agitated German commentators expounding at length on the decadence of their government administration and the treacherous infiltration by fellow-Germans from the East whose views differed from their own. When it came down to it, they had little more to say than the succinct Swedish reports.

He spent most of his time waiting for the telephone to ring. He left his apartment reluctantly three times a day; eight o'clock in the morning, four in the afternoon, and twelve midnight, for half an hour at a time. It was the cold that forced him out. The temperature remained constant at about 25 below during the day, and sank to around 35 below at night. He cursed the fact that he had tried no harder to get one of the few available free garage spaces in the building. Of course, he could have rented one, but it might have drawn attention to him, and attention was one of the things Greger Tragg always tried to avoid. As a result, his Volvo was parked out in the open alongside all the other snowed-in and iced-up cars, at least half a dozen of which looked exactly like his own. Many of the owners had given up the unequal struggle with winter, having failed to start their cars despite such ploys as spare batteries and tows. Tragg knew that the only solution was to run the engine often so the oil had no chance to thicken.

He was drinking less than usual, and only went to the liquor store once to restock with whiskey and beer. His suitcase stood in the hall, ready packed. It contained only the bare necessities: underclothes, shirts, money, and passport. Next to his suitcase was a spare car battery, permanently on

5

charge. He had bought the charger for a few hundred kronor. Even if he was asleep when the call came, he would be able to leave the apartment within five minutes.

The telephone rang on four occasions that first week. Each time, he started breathing again after the third ring. The agreed procedure was simple: two rings, a pause of forty-five seconds followed by two more rings and a pause of thirty seconds. He then was to lift the receiver, and a totally unknown voice would give him the crucial order. Five different meeting places had been arranged, each with its designated code-word. The most distant one was in Årjäng, not far from the Norwegian border. The nearest was the stableyard at the Solvalla racetrack in Stockholm.

After a week, Tragg decided to return to his normal routine. He signed off at the health insurance office, and took up his newspaper contacts once more. He wrote freelance for several weeklies, supplying them mainly with popular scientific articles. No one had missed him, in fact. His type of material was regarded as a useful space-filler, and he was retained because the editors found it convenient to have a number of regular features, and because he was cheap. He used a pseudonym, and was the only one whose articles did not have a picture of the author.

Greger Tragg felt it was clear by now that the Berlin defector had only a limited amount of information to sell, and the immediate threat to his own person was past. He was even more convinced, but also somewhat confused, when he read in an evening psper a few days later that according to a so-called reliable source, SÄPO suspected there was still a leak in the organization at a very high level, and that the latest arrests, serious though they might be, were insignificant compared with the one they had so far failed to make. The writer indicated official fears that a foreign power had access to material at such a high level that the two agents exposed so far could not possibly be the source.

Someone had deliberately leaked this information, pos-

6

sibly to defuse the interest of the press and the general public in the latest revelations. After this remarkable article, which could also be interpreted as a warning to a very small number of people, the mass media carried very little on the two spy affairs. Someone had put the muzzle on, and it would only be taken off, very cautiously, when the prosecutions began. Such cases were still heard in public in the Kingdom of Sweden.

If anyone had hit upon the idea, unlikely though it might seem, of asking Greger Tragg if he thought there was a leak at the top in the Swedish defense and security forces, he would not, of course, have received a direct answer. Tragg would have shrugged his powerful shoulders and said that in the first place he had no idea about such matters, and in the second place he couldn't care less. Both claims would have been untrue. Tragg was not the leak. However, he was one of only three people who knew the identity of the person concerned.

The silence in the apartment was broken by a long, drawn-out noise from his neighbor's bathroom. The TV was off the air and it was time to go to bed. His mind made up, Greger Tragg emptied his whiskey glass and took out his diary from his jacket pocket; it was a traditional diary with each day of the year dedicated to a particular Christian name. Today was the nineteenth of January. Max's nameday was the first of February, and Bertha's the eighteenth. He had been given two alternative arrival dates, and this generosity together with the picture of the firm handshake on the card was the decisive, calming indication that all was well.

He decided on Max straight away. On the first of February he would be in Berlin and meet Ulrich Langer. The number 50 on the greeting card did not only mean

*Come!*

but also

*New instructions*

7

For a moment he wondered whether he should pour himself another whiskey, but desisted. He did not really miss it. He was going to have a lot to do in the near future. A quarter of an hour later when he turned off the bedside lamp after setting the alarm clock for seven o'clock, he smiled for the second time that evening. Just like an ordinary citizen, he thought.

Five minutes later, he was asleep. The last trace of unrest had gone, replaced by firm resolution and reaffirmed motivation for what was in store. Several days later, while he was waiting for the green light at a pedestrian crossing, Tragg became momentarily aware that the chill feeling in the pit of his stomach had disappeared. He was surprised it had ever existed.

# ❧ II ❧

The pungent smell of ammonia hung in a haze over the stables at the Solvalla trotting track. It tickled the nostrils like a drug, inspiring dreams and foolhardiness, hopes and self-deception. The weather had improved during the week, but the thermometer on the wall of the check-in still indicated 20 below and the horses returning from the warm-up lap had ice on their muzzles and in their manes. Despite the cold there were plenty of people milling about in the open space between the stables and the newly built Traverna.

It was half past five, an hour before the first race was due to start, when Greger Tragg came in through the stables gate. Despite the wintry weather the track was clear and well-raked; lit up by powerful spot-lights, with the snow piled up on all sides it looked as well-tended as a garden path. Out of the glare, more and more people were beginning to drift toward the restaurants and stands.

Tragg joined them. Now and then he nodded to familiar faces, knowing nothing of their owners except that he had happened to sit near them in the stands on some occasion or other, and exchanged a few words. There were faces he had

9

been greeting for fifteen years, watching them grow older but knowing nothing about the bettors themselves. Racing crowds are made up mostly of regulars who turn up faithfully at every meeting. They are part of a closed society, and new members are admitted only after many years of compulsory attendance. Tragg occasionally bumped into such a face in town. Away from the horses and the Tote, without a program in their hands and binoculars around their necks, smelling of aromas other than the seductive scent of ammonia, it could well take several seconds before he recognized them. Such meetings generally culminated in a hasty nod and an introspective smile, an acknowledgment that as far as a racing man is concerned the only meaningful thing in life is the races, nothing else.

He could not avoid being known at the racetrack, but very few people actually knew his name. The closed society had unwritten laws and one basic principle: all acquaintanceships came to an end the moment one passed through the gates. Nowhere are anonymity and integrity as jealously protected as among gamblers. Every undue question from an outsider is met with scornful silence or speechless incomprehension.

As he passed on through the biting wind toward the old restaurant, Tragg missed the coal-burning braziers that used to stand there. There had been winters when he used them as a meeting place. Among the mass of frozen fingers thawing out over the smoky coal fires, rapid exchanges of particularly informative racing cards had taken place, but the information they held was by no means the names of horses and jockeys running that day. It was a classic procedure, but had now been replaced by a much more reliable method.

Solvalla had changed. It had been modernized and asphalted, and Tragg did not like it. Soon, the old restaurant would disappear as well, to be replaced by a new concrete block with plenty of steel and glass. As yet there were no TV cameras keeping an eye on the spectators, but they would soon come once they started to knock down the ramshackle old wooden buildings with all their little passages and hiding places. To the detriment not only of all the pickpockets, but also of himself.

The state is the only certain winner at the races, and every day during a Solvalla meeting at least a million kronor are earned for the benefit of society. Somewhat less secure and, moreover, branded as criminal by the state authorities, is the business of bookmaking. The bookies are well-established and more or less untouchable by the police, who seem to have given up long ago the battle against this particular branch of financial crime, even if they make a raid every year or so for the sake of appearances. One reason for the lack of interest on the part of the police is that it is almost impossible to prove anyone is keeping a book, Swedish style. A few words exchanged with a neighbor in the stand or over a drink in the restaurant, a whispered message to someone who likes to stand at a particular bend, or at most some barely decipherable squiggles in a racing program is not much to put before a court as evidence. Everyone bets on credit, and debts are settled in town. The police also understand that even if bookmaking is a crime in the eyes of the law, it is in no way immoral as far as the bettors themselves are concerned. The bookmakers always give higher odds than the state-owned tote, sometimes as much as nine per cent more after rounding up the decimals. Moreover, the police can never count on any help from informers. The surest way of getting into trouble is to interfere in other people's business. In racing circles a particularly grave case can result in a crippling injury for life, or an early death. At the very least it means the cold shoulder, not only on the course but at all the other venues where gamblers gather, an exclusion that lasts forever.

Piero Svanberg was a bookmaker, a Swedish-Italian aged about twenty-five. He had his regular table in the far corner of

11

a bar behind the old restaurant. The table was stained and badly cleaned, but years of spilled beer and nervously stubbed-out but still burning cigarettes had given it a resilient quality which not even a disinfectant firm could have dealt with. It had been new as far back as the days of Frances Bulwark, the famous winning trotter. Now it exuded a smell of stale beer like the toothless mouth of an old man.

Piero Svanberg could not see the racetrack from where he sat, but his view of everyone who entered the place was all the better for that. When he caught sight of Greger Tragg his face lit up, and he stood up politely.

"What a surprise!" he said, shaking his hand. "It must be months since I last saw you. Let me get you a beer."

Tragg nodded and sat down. As he polished his glasses he watched the bookmaker shuffling his way with considerable difficulty back into his favorite place right in the corner. The young man was a strange mixture, offspring of a lively, talkative, and totally unreliable Sicilian who made a short but much appreciated guest appearance in Stockholm at the beginning of the fifties, and a peasant woman from Ytterhogdal, tall as a Swedish spruce, cool and blond as a buttercup meadow in June, and sufficiently sensible to resist with pride the Italian's proposal to take upon herself the role of princess forever more. The Sicilian took the train back home to Palermo and was never seen again; the mother remained single, unapproachable and regal as ever over the years. The son could not speak a word of Italian. He was tall and scraggy in stature, his broad shoulders hunched as if from bearing heavy burdens in the forest. He had inherited a lot from his mother's father, but his head was Italian. Shiny black curly hair, a Roman nose, and bright black eyes with a dash of melancholy from the waters of a Swedish lake.

"I'd like to talk to you alone for a few minutes," said Tragg.

The bar was barely half full, and the men behind the beer

bottles were without exception engrossed in their racing cards or busy filling in betting slips. In the pale, nicotine-yellow light they looked like dozing seals on a rocky outcrop.

"Of course."

The waiter served their beer in response to a slight nod from Svanberg, who took out his binoculars case and stood it upright on the table.

"We're closed, Augustson," he told the waiter with a smile.

"Make sure no stupid jerk comes bursting into the office. The customers know."

"How's business?"

"Good. I could expand if I liked, but I don't want to. Not now at any rate. Three days a week I work as a cabby. I make a bit of cash and that explains why I don't starve to death. I live with my mother. Even the tax authorities must regard me as well-behaved."

"I need your help," said Tragg.

They drank in silence. Svanberg looked his companion calmly in the eye. Like all bookmakers he had a good memory and a well-developed ability to listen without forgetting. He waited. There was a smile in Tragg's light-blue eyes, but his voice was deep and tempered with seriousness.

"I'm going away. It could be for quite a while, and I don't want it known. Here is a set of duplicate keys to my apartment. I'd like you to go there once a week to check everything. Make sure there have been no visitors. Use dust and the hall carpet. The hall is quite badly lit and the carpet is red. Don't overdo it, but make quite sure you can't possibly make any mistakes. Do you drive your taxi on Thursdays?"

"That's the only day I'm on the day shift."

"Good! On Thursday afternoons the whole place is deserted. Most of the men are at work, and the women are doing the cleaning. They do the shopping on Fridays. The risk of bumping into someone in the elevator or on the staircase is a hundred to one. There's only the Dane. He's curious. You know, the neighbor with the white Persian cat."

Svanberg nodded. "He'll remember me all right. I once asked him what the cat was called."

"Clothilde. Talk to him if need be. Answer his questions. Tell him you're watering the plants, that I've gone away. . . . But don't try to make excuses for yourself. . . ."

"I'll cope. There isn't a Dane in the land who can resist my Italian charm. It's sometimes a positive advantage to be a half-breed."

That was true. When Piero Svanberg switched on his Sicilian smile, he was a changed man. It was compelling without being overwhelming, and hard to be suspicious about. Just now he looked like a polite young man from the Italian middle class. Or like a volunteer in the Sicilian Mafia.

"All right. If you suspect the apartment is being watched or you're being followed, make sure you're right. Don't try and shake off anyone who's following you. Don't slink away if you think the entrance door or the apartment is being watched. Act openly and normally."

"And if . . . ?"

"Tell me about it when I call."

"When will you call?"

"Every Tuesday. How about some time between ten and half past?"

"Suits me fine. What do I do if anything has gone wrong?"

"You answer by saying, 'Good morning, Mr. Editor.' And then you don't need to wait for me to call any more, nor to go to the apartment. I'll contact you some other way. What's your cab license number?"

"1582."

"When the taxi intercom tells you one Thursday that you have to get in touch with your father at home, drive to the Central Station and wait in the line. I'll be there."

14

Svanberg nodded. He had understood. "What do I do if you don't call?"

"I could be otherwise engaged. Wait for me to try again the following Tuesday."

Svanberg hesitated a moment. Then he asked almost timidly, his shoulders hunched and his head bowed, "Are you in trouble?"

"No more than usual," answered Tragg.

By now most of the tables in the bar were more or less full. March music blared out from the loudspeakers, indicating that the buggies were doing a preliminary circuit before the first race. During the last half-hour, several people had come in through the door, shaken off the snow that had started to fall, then left again when they saw the stop signal on the corner table. Ten more minutes, and they'd be off. Tragg called the waiter over and ordered another round of beer.

"You can take away your binoculars case now."

Svanberg smiled. "The worst part of this job is all the beer. Did you know I don't really like beer?"

"Industrial injury is a cross we all have to bear," said Tragg. "There's nothing you can do about it."

A man in a black trenchcoat with a puffed-up face and an unhealthy looking pasty complexion was approaching the table cautiously. After a nod from Svanberg he sat down on one of the empty chairs.

"I think I need a swig," said the newcomer, his listless eyes checking his race-card. "A hundred green ones on number three, I fancy. Uffe's bound to win this one."

"Done."

"I've got to go now," said Tragg, emptying his glass. "Many thanks."

"Look after yourself," said Svanberg. "I'll be seeing you."

"Yes," said Tragg. "See you."

• • •

15

Loyalty grows out of either love or gratitude, and should not be confused with the straitjacket known as dependence. Genuine loyalty cannot be betrayed. It lasts until one of the people concerned dies. On the other hand, betrayal is always a consequence of dependence, and this dependence is sometimes so ruthless that betrayal is punished by death.

The friendship and loyalty between Greger Tragg and Piero Svanberg were genuine, because Tragg had once rescued the young Swedish-Italian from an awkward situation which could have cost him his life, or at least deprived him of his bookmaking activities. Fired by the rashness of youth and innocent of the realities of the power game, he allowed himself to be tricked into a gambling session financed by the really big boys. They wanted to teach him a lesson and make it clear to him once and for all that unless he had their permission, he was a dead man on the racetrack. The game cost him all his capital and in addition a debt of forty thousand kronor. He was given a strict ultimatum and had a fortnight's grace before he could expect the first and only visit from the heavies. No one would or could help him. In desperation, he happened to tell the whole story to Greger Tragg, who had long been an occasional client of his.

Tragg let Svanberg live in his apartment—in complete safety. Within a week Tragg had produced the necessary cash. Relations with the big boys were restored after hard negotiations, with Tragg as an advisor in the background. Not without a certain amount of surprise and admiration, Svanberg's creditors were forced to admit the young bookmaker had not only managed to honor his commitment, but had also displayed astonishing toughness. As a result, they allowed him to carry on. His territory remained small, but it needed looking after and if Svanberg were to disappear, somebody else would turn up immediately and take over the corner table in the bar; he might be less easy to handle and less good at the job. Part of the agreement was that no competitor should be allowed to disturb him at his place of work.

Afterwards, Svanberg used to refer to the time spent in Tragg's apartment as his university education. For the first time, someone had taught him the rules that apply when one lives outside the apparently secure world of wage-slaves. It was primarily a question of assessing one's own position and weighing one's strengths. The basic rule was never to trust anybody. Svanberg put his activities into perspective and was intelligent enough to see that there are exceptions to every rule, and that he had Tragg to thank for the fact that he had a future at all. Greger Tragg was therefore the only person he trusted, and he had repaid the borrowed sum a long time ago, without being asked for interest. Ever since, he always responded positively when Tragg asked him to do odd jobs now and again. He immediately put everything else to one side, and it never occurred to him to ask questions.


If Solvalla was bread and butter for Piero Svanberg, for most people who went there it was a stimulus giving rise to dreams of a new life. Small-time bettors hoped for the big win that would liberate them from their daily grind. Deep down, they knew their stakes were too small for them ever to achieve that goal. In fact, it was not so much the goal they were looking for as the intoxicating effect of the dream. The big gamblers, some of whom were out to launder money while others were desperately trying to cover up hitherto secret embezzlements or tax fiddles, were also dreaming about the big win which would solve all their problems at a stroke. But no win could ever be big enough to induce them to leave the racetrack for good and give up gambling. For them, neither alcohol nor drugs, a secure and idle existence in Switzerland or Spain, nor a guaranteed index-linked pension could replace the unbearable stimulus, the incomparable kick experienced by every genuine gambler when the horses round the last bend and head for the finish.

It was only Greger Tragg for whom Solvalla was a letter-box.


In one respect Tragg was unique in the eventful and checkered history of the Eastern bloc intelligence services. He was the only one who had managed to persuade his masters to invest in the purchase of a trotting horse. When he first suggested it in Berlin, Ulrich Langer choked over his beer and looked as if he were going to strangle the Swede. It was several hours before Tragg's logical arguments and overtly expressed threat convinced his host of the necessity of the investment. There was a further delay of three months before Tragg received a surly communication to the effect that the comrades responsible had given the venture the go-ahead. He sometimes fantasized about whether the decision had been made during a closed session inside the Kremlin. He would like to think the matter was so controversial it could only be dealt with by persons of the highest ideological competence.

The horse was two years old when it was bought, and cost 20,000 kronor. Although it ran in red colors, it had no idea it was financed by socialist funds and had highly placed people in a country where trotting was regarded as bourgeois decadence to thank for its oats and its monthly training fees. Without giving a thought to the contradictions of its existence, it developed steadily and proved to be well above the average in talent. The socialist investment had paid off. The horse even made a profit, which Tragg was allowed to keep.

The doorman at the entrance to the owners' stand gave a nod of recognition as Tragg showed his member's pass. They were under orders and the horses were in the start formation. The last bettors, slow to make up their minds, came rushing

18

up the stairs from the betting windows down in the club-rooms. Also downstairs was the entrance to the Jockey Club's exclusive rooms, a remnant of the upper-class world from the turn of the century. Not without difficulty, Tragg managed to find a seat right at the top of the stand. He nodded to his neighbors. Everyone here knew everyone else. Not necessarily by name, but everyone knew the name of the horse owned by his neighbor. Down at the entrance, a strict watch was kept and an unknown face would often have to answer searching questions about the name of his horse, its pedigree, and its trainer. Very few non-owners succeeded in getting into this carefully guarded room, and there had been cases of intruders actually being thrown down the stairs. That was why Greger Tragg had been obliged to become a horse owner.

Just before the start of the sixth race, Tragg went down to the clubrooms for a cup of coffee. Everyone who had seen him here over the years knew that he always did this. The sixth race was often the least interesting one on a given day, and it was sufficient to watch it on the TV screens. Moreover, there were no lines while a race was actually being run. Most betting men are inveterate creatures of habit, and more attention would have been aroused if Tragg had failed to go for his cup of coffee and remained in his seat.

As the horses raced towards the stables curve for the first time, and the disappointed mumbling from those who had bet on the stragglers that had already lapsed into a gallop mingled with the agitated bluster of the commentator, the club's betting shop was empty, apart from the staff at the windows. Tragg went up to the only window where winnings were paid, and presented two slips from previous races.

"I'm going home," he said quietly. "It might be a few weeks before I'm back."

The woman behind the glass panel eyed him up and down closely. As always, he noticed the small wrinkles emanating from the corners of her eyes. Sometimes there was a foolhardy glint in those nut-brown, still young eyes of hers which occasionally worried him but more often confirmed why she was the only woman in the world he ever gave a thought to. She was serious today, and he noticed a line running down from the corner of her mouth, suggesting nervousness.

"Is it that bad . . . ?"

"No," he said quickly. "On the contrary. The insurance is paid up. I received guarantees the day before yesterday. There is no need at all to worry."

"I must see you," she said urgently. "Alex . . . is worse than ever."

"We'll have to wait till I get back. I'm going tomorrow."

"Should we start cleaning up?"

"Certainly not," answered Tragg firmly.

He got forty-two kronor for one of the slips. He noticed a blue-colored voucher among the ten-kronor notes, and without comment put it into his wallet, together with the money. He should have said something to cheer her up. He was not worried that she might go over the top, panic or turn hysterical; but she needed support, something to look forward to and help her withstand the strains of the coming weeks. Before he could stop himself, he heard himself saying, "I promise we'll be taking the Finland boat together within the next month."

Before leaving the window he thought he could see the line at the corner of her mouth relax and a confident glint appear in her brown eyes.

Tragg drank his coffee alone at one of the small tables. From a distance he looked like a well-preserved fifty-year-old. His powerful shoulders indicated that he still had enough strength to pit himself against an opponent considerably younger than himself. He still had a full head of blond hair without a trace of baldness. He was unusually tall for his generation, over six foot two, and his movements were

20

smooth and harmonious. At close quarters it was above all his sensitive hands and his long, slender fingers which caught the eye. If he ever removed his glasses, practically no one could stare him down. His blue eyes were bright and intelligent but at the same time neutral and impenetrable, showing neither warmth nor coolness. Most people who saw him thus, naked without his glasses, treated him with respect in future without being clear about why.

Before Tragg left the table to return to his seat in the stand, he took out his wallet and ran his fingers over the back of the tote voucher. There was the microfilm, under the tape. Without more ado he separated the voucher from the notes and put it into one of the deepest pockets of his wallet. In two hours' time he could go home. The races would have finished by then.

# ❧ III ❧

"Welcome to the Republic! I hope the reception commit-tee behaved decently."

Marx emerged from the shadows around the car, which was parked in one of the side streets off Friedrichstrasse, a stone's throw from the crossing point in Berlin christened by the Americans 'Checkpoint Charlie.'

Marx had his cap in his hand and was smiling that peculiar smile which Tragg could never make up his mind about—was it cunning, or just embarrassment?

"Meticulously and courteously, and with the strain which has always characterized the uniformed servants of the working people; and hence not completely successfully," said Tragg, pulling out a whole carton of Camel cigarettes from the overcoat he was carrying over his arm.

"I used the old trick," he went on. "Changed two hundred marks more than I needed to. And yet there are those who maintain that the capitalists have no say in this country."

Marx accepted the cigarettes with something that sounded like a giggle, and moved quickly around the car to

23

open the front seat of the Wartburg. Over twenty years ago he had realized one of the Swede's odd habits was that, in contrast to all the prominent people in the capital of the Republic, he preferred to share the front seat with the driver in completely democratic fashion. Such an idea would never had occurred to Ulrich Langer.

They had half an hour's journey ahead of them. The thin covering of snow on the pavements was dirty, and when Tragg sniffed the air he could feel in his nostrils the soot which lay like a veil over this part of the city. He took it as a warning. It's just the same on the boats, he thought. Wash away all the capitalist trash and you're left with the acrid smell of lye. Like in a morgue.

"You have to be either pure at heart, or completely immune," he mumbled to himself.

"Most people can get used to anything," responded Marx, without turning his head.

They turned into Woxagenerstrasse, which still retained its cobbles from the thirties. Tragg sat there quietly. Here on this side of the border, he ought to feel safe. No B.N.D., no SÄPO. Here, if anywhere, he ought to feel at home. He did not. He would never be able to feel at home anywhere. The security which so many people carried on about and promised and strove after was not for him. Security is a mere illusion, and in his life every illusion was potentially fatal. In consequence he differed from most people on one basic point. Tragg did not regard security as something worth striving for. Without reflecting for one moment over the banality of the claim, he muttered to himself a German slogan from the Second World War: Life is no insurance company.

After Köpenick the street lighting became even worse. Every other lamp was out, and the distance between them was at least twice the normal one in Sweden. A row of miserable-looking apartment blocks jutted out into a muddy field, and Tragg noted that pink domestic lighting had become fashion-

24

able in the Republic. The pitiful, flickering lights looked scary in the increasingly gray February evening.

They were on their way to Müggelsee, the private estate on the edge of East Berlin were Ulrich Langer lived. Tragg wondered whether Langer still had his sailing dinghy. The last time they met he had been incredibly proud of this piece of property.

"Oh, yes," replied Marx. "It's fitted out with all the latest equipment. As if it were a luxury cruiser or at the very least a sea-going vessel. The doctor has taken to going for walks every day since he had that heart attack last autumn. He goes straight down to the moorings to make sure the tarpaulin hasn't blown off. There isn't a single boat on the whole of Mügglesee Lake that's better looked after than that one."

Tragg smiled. "None of us is getting any younger," he said.

"But we haven't lost our grip yet, eh?" claimed Marx with a broad grin. On this occasion it seemed more genuine than usual.


There were no obvious similarities between Greger Tragg and Ulrich Langer. The German showed no signs of after-effects following his heart attack, and he received Tragg in surprisingly energetic fashion. Since he was short in stature he gave a misleading impression of corpulence. His compact head was typically German and displayed characteristics most often found in Bavaria. Nevertheless, he displayed no signs of stubborn provincialism. His face was dominated by an unusually high forehead and dark eyes which were intelligent and alert, but equally often marked by emotion.

As always, Langer was dressed in an impeccable, almost exaggeratedly elegant suit. He wore a waistcoat, and the only sign of his prominent position in the Republic was the golden SED badge in his left lapel. It opened the door to benefits and

25

privileges without parallel even in the uppermost echelons on the other side of the Wall.

Tragg's tweed jacket and badly pressed trousers contrasted starkly with the elegance of the German, but then he came from a country where the director's suit had long since been banished to the bottom of the status scale together with the officer's uniform, which no Swede continues to wear outside working hours for fear of being mobbed.

The only peculiar aspect of Ulrich Langer's appearance was his hairstyle. With the passage of time his hairline had receded further and further above his forehead, but at the back it looked as though someone had stuck a saucepan on his head and without more ado clipped off all the thick, black hair that happened to stick out. The hairstyle was designed to hide a war wound, a partially misdirected lunge with a bayonet by a misguided Red Army soldier when Langer was taken prisoner on the Eastern Front only a few days after the attack on the Soviet Union. Thanks to this haircut, he looked from behind like a Jesuit monk—and if one wanted an accurate picture of Ulrich Langer's character, it is from behind he should be studied.

Tragg had always felt at home in Langer's apartment. It was furnished in restrained Scandinavian style with a lot of pine, and if it were not for the bust of Lenin placed prominently beneath a colored photograph of Erich Honecker, it could well have been an upper-class Finland-Swedish home in Åbo or Mariehamn. Sandwiches, vodka, and beer were waiting on the table. It was East German beer, and had not improved since Tragg's last visit.

Tragg had concealed the microfilms in the lining of his breast pocket, as insecure a hiding place as any other. On this occasion they contained documents summarizing discussions between the Swedish and Finnish defense chiefs concerning the threat of cruise missiles from the NATO side crossing Nordic territory, and Russian proposals on the subject. It was clear from the documents that there was a mutual desire to coordinate and concentrate defense measures in a triangle formed by Nynäshamn, Fårösund, and Hangö. Alex had included a few short reports on the exchange of views between representatives of the two countries. Quite informally, the Finns had undertaken to try and persuade the Russians to accept the proposed areas of the Baltic as a primary defense zone. From the Swedish side there was a willingness to ignore the complications that could follow from the fact that the island Gotska Sandön was located in the center of the triangle.

"Our neutrality begins on terra firma," the Swedish Defense Minister was reported to have said as he put his arm around the shoulders of his Finnish colleague.

"And ours starts at Hangö," replied the Finn, successfully wriggling out of the bear-like grip, and proposing a toast to a peaceful future for both of them.

Within a month, the exchange of views had led to the announcement of a so-called B-alternative, this time in the form of a rhombus whose corners included not only Fårösund and Hangö but also Landsort and Mariehamn.

Another document contained a paper produced by a special group of experts at the Swedish Foreign Ministry which tried to analyze the political and strategic situation that could be expected to arise if President Kekkonen were to leave this earthly existence and hence also his office, to join the exclusive and privileged group consisting entirely of respected ex-Presidents of Finland. The analysis contained so many alternatives that a first reading might suggest it was useless. On reflection, however, it gave a very clear picture of what cold be expected after the President's death.

"It'll be chaos," said Tragg. "But as you can well imagine, the people back home share not only the Russians' interest in the missiles but also the Finn's worries about the President's health. Both factors could disturb the neutral status quo we

27

think we have built up so carefully. At best people are counting on the two threats to balance each other out."

For the next half hour Langer inquired about Alex's physical and mental health, the excitement concerning the unmasking of the Swedish spies, Tragg's financial state and needs, and whether the emergency measures established earlier could still be regarded as satisfactory.

"The Soviet traitor," said Ulrich Langer, "had access to a limited amount of material which caused problems for our people in West Germany, but he knew nothing about our activities further north. Both the Swedish spy scandals just happened to break at the same time, and come to that, they should have been found out long ago. Alex doesn't need to worry about this talk of a third man. It's a provocation, not from us incidentally, and is designed to fend off a debate about whether the Swedish secret service is too biased towards the West. At long last your newspapers seem to have caught on to this incontrovertible fact."

Tragg laughed. "You mean the Communist paper *Norrs-kensflamman.*"

"The most obvious disadvantage of Swedish neutrality is that outside Scandinavia, it is only understood by one nation."

"Which one is that?"

"Russia, of course. When we talk about Mother Svea, the Russians get tears in their eyes and think they understand. Everybody else just thinks it's stupid. Which it is, of course. If you look at it like that."

They were both well aware they were talking for the benefit of the little sharp-eared boxes hidden somewhere in the room. It was nearly eleven o'clock, and Marx was due back with the car before twelve. They had done what was required of them and exchanged so much information that even a listener with tendencies to paranoid skepticism would have to be satisfied. That would do, then.

28

From the moment he arrived, under the supervision of a Frau Perchhammer, Greger Tragg had the sense to play the role expected of him. Langer received Tragg in a way which the Swede, at least, found surprisingly hearty. The excessively long handshake and the unexpected embrace were such a remarkable departure from their customary greetings established over thirty years that Gertrud would have noticed straight away. But Gertrud was dead. Langer had buried his blond, high-spirited wife over a year ago. After his heart attack and the ensuing convalescence at a home near the Czech border, the Party had allocated him Frau Perchhammer as his personal domestic assistant, but no doubt also his guard and informer. During his absence repairs had been carried out in the flat. It needed restoring, and there was also a convenient opportunity of fitting the tablet-sized microphones which nowadays security services the world over regard as essential for keeping track, not only of opponents, but also of their own people.

Frau Perchhammer was a well-indoctrinated woman in her sixties with a healthy and unmistakable mistrust of foreigners, especially if they came from capitalist countries. She met Tragg for the first time in her life and observed sullenly the emotional welcome between her doctor, who was normally so correct, and the untidy Swede. Five minutes later, when she left and drew attention to her departure by slamming the door unnecessarily hard, Tragg responded to his friend's smile with a nod. Tragg had understood, and Langer had counted on his understanding.

"Have you stopped smoking your cigars, then?" asked Greger Tragg.

"Doctor's orders. He has also told me to go for at least half an hour's walk before bedtime. How about a walk down to the lake? I've got my boat there."

The boat was beached on a strip of sand by the Müfflesee. Together with about thirty other boats it formed a petty bourgeois marina right in the middle of the socialist heart of the orthodox Republic. It was wrapped in a yellow plastic cover and backed well onto a wooden stand. During the ten minute walk to where the boat was beached, neither of them uttered a word. Tragg was sure they were alone there.

"I've been going down to this boat several evenings a week these last few months," explained Langer. "They think I'm in love with it as a sort of substitute for Gertrud."

They stared at each other. The cool breeze from the lake, the faint light from the distant streetlamps, the yellow plastic cover over the beached boat, wrapped up as carefully as a Christmas box in Santa Claus wrapping paper, the heavy silence so typical of February, hanging around both men, whose breath could barely manage to make itself visible in the air that was hardly down to freezing point—for a few moments everything was like a dream, with a threat like a black shadow behind the dead body of the boat.

"We've reached the end of the road," said Langer quietly. "Time has caught up with us. Sasha and Köstner are building up a new organization in the north. That's understandable as far as it goes. So is their intention of keeping us out of it. The only thing that is not quite clear is whether they are prepared to go along with it all."

"What are they thinking of doing with us? Putting us in quarantine?"

"That's possible. Something's going on, but I'm not quite sure what. The postal service within the section has been changed. They've put in a sieve. Nowadays there are various things they don't think concern me."

"How long have we got?"

"Half a year. Perhaps only three months."

"And then . . ."

"You're welcome to come and stay here. You know yourself what that involves. The first year you are regarded as an expert. Then you'll have a translating job, in the Scandinavian section. You'll become a has-been. A pension-

30

er, a burden. You'll get a two-room flat here in Berlin, and a pension big enough to live on. After a few years no one will care what time you turn up for work. You'll remain respected, but as time goes by you'll be squeezed out of things more and more. No one will want anything to do with you. Your financial situation will change. You and I might be able to meet every three months. No one will like it. You'll become a prisoner in your own past, a past which is no longer of interest to anyone but yourself. I'll also get a pension and a job as the boss of some museum in Magdeburg or Leipzig. I'll have lost my golden ace up in the north, and both of us will have become mere cast-offs. Every day you'll dream of being able to slip out through the Wall. Not to escape, but just to sit in a bar for a few hours, to hear a different kind of language, to be able to come out with the stupidest comments without running any risks. It will remain a dream. For you, the Wall will be more impassable than for anyone else. Often, all too often, you'll stand on the other side of the street in front of the barrier in Friedrichstrasse and try to see over into the West. From there you'll be able to see the Hilton's roof terrace, and sometimes a car with an S-plate will pass by after the occupants have had their passports glanced at. You'll have handed in your own long ago, and exchanged it for a Republic passport complete with a hammer and sickle."

Tragg said nothing, but nodded in agreement.

"When I was taken prisoner, I was nineteen," went on Langer. "Four years later I was among the first five hundred to return from Moscow. I had two years of intensive training and schooling behind me. You know how you look at life when you're young. I went all out and was convinced that I really could make a positive contribution in the name of justice and socialism. I soon learned that my background was against me. During the early years proletarian parents were a necessary precondition for a successful career. We others were tolerated, but remained suspicious bourgeois renegades even though I

31

could prove I took the plunge as early as 1941. We always got the hardest jobs. I was allocated Switzerland and Scandinavia, both of which areas displayed a dislike and, for a long time, a disdain for the Republic which was harder to take than the open hatred of West Germany. That's why they agreed to the arrangement with Alex and with you. You two were to be my greatest achievement: although nobody realized it at first, I had found an opening in Sweden. That was more than anyone had expected. Alex is the only person in the history of the socialist intelligence service whose identity has remained unknown to his master. He's an anomaly; a tumor, but a benign one, as Köstner usually says. But he is also one of our very top agents, and perhaps the one who has cost us more hard currency than any other."

"Is he going to be operated on now?"

"We'll only resort to the scalpel in an emergency. Alex is in no immediate danger as long as we can eliminate his one weak point."

Tragg stiffened. So there had been grounds for concern after all. It was not just his imagination. "You mean me," he said calmly. "And how had you planned to do that?"

"Don't say 'you.' Say 'Sasha and Köstner.' Within the next six months you'll be pulled out of Stockholm in an emergency. They'll give it the full treatment. Cars, airplanes, trawlers. There might even be a few extras to play the parts of pursuers. The whole operation will succeed, of course, and be conducted with dazzling brilliance. You'll be received like a hero by a relieved but simultaneously deeply worried Köstner. That very same day you'll have an audience with Sasha. He'll also say how pleased he is to have rescued you from a 10-year jail sentence in Sweden. At the same time he'll be very worried about Alex. He'll tell you it's a question of days, perhaps even hours before he too is exposed. With your help, though, it might just not be too late. They'll pump you dry of all you know. You can't refuse. That would be treachery. Like

32

so much else, penal institutions in the Republic are not of the same high standard as those in Sweden. You have no choice but to tell him everything."

"I'm beginning to realize that," said Tragg grimly.

Langer put his hand on Tragg's shoulder. He was half a head shorter than the Swede, and had to strain himself to look him in the eye. They could hear a whistling noise as the shrunken waves of the Mügglesee rattled over the frozen sand.

"Can you imagine me in charge of a museum? Why shouldn't I wind down and admit I'm beginning to grow old? The museum job is a respectable cultural post which doesn't require too much effort. Viewed objectively, it would be good for my heart. I would enjoy considerable status in Magdeburg, a half share in a semi-detached house with a garden to match. I could keep the car, and I expect Marx could go back home to Lehnitz. Since I'm a respected veteran with many years of much appreciated service to the state behind me, I'd be invited to all official functions; but apart from that I could mind my own business in the bigoted duckpond that is the cultural life of Magdeburg."

"You'd die of boredom."

"Exactly. I'd be dead within a few years. Every morning would be torture, and I'd drown in self-reproach for my own confounded passivity and inability to create a life of my own. Both you and I lack the basic skills necessary for developing into pensioners. I can't imagine you either, walking around and watering roses in a little Swedish town, perhaps a member of the local literary society and on the committee of the local cultural council."

"More likely taking early retirement on grounds of creeping alcoholism, and propping up the bar in the town's only inn."

"Whichever you like. But it is an indisputable fact that time is starting to run out for us. We have done our bit as harbingers of Peace. How's your socialistic conscience?"

33

"It's still there." Langer smiled.

"I'd expected no other answer. It's also a question of loyalty. Is there a limit to it? Being loyal usually means keeping quiet and accepting mistakes and the excesses of others. There's a difference between loyalty to a cause and loyalty to people who misuse the cause."

"What are you getting at?"

"A few weeks ago I was called before Köstner, who gave me a mission in which you play a key part. That conversation gave me an idea which could involve the final solution for us and our future. It could give us money, freedom of choice, and mobility. Naturally, it's not without its risks, but the risks are no greater than those we, or at least you, have taken every day for the past thirty years. My idea also has the advantage of allowing us to live on with our socialistic consciences intact. You can judge for yourself the complicated question of loyalty."


"Money is the most important weapon in our struggle with imperialism. The reason why so many revolutionaries fail is not a lack of support from the people, but insufficient financial backing. You need money to buy arms."

Colonel Lutz Köstner underlined his claim by beating his index finger rhythmically on the table edge. He had summoned Ulrich Langer, who was listening patiently as the slimly-built colonel delivered his high-pitched lecture. They disliked each other wholeheartedly, and although the colonel was responsible for the Nordschein Region and Langer his next-in-line, they avoided meeting as much as possible. The colonel preferred to mix with those above him in the hierarchy, and liked to keep his lesser colleagues at arm's length by communicating with them in writing. He had grown up in Moscow and been at the same school as Sasha, chief of all the harbingers of Peace and responsible for the

Republic's security forces within the Politburo. Both of them had been KGB officers during the war, and retained their Russian passports even when the Republic declared itself an independent state. Inside rumor had it that Sasha was at last beginning to grow tired of Köstner, but Langer put no credence in this. His experience told him the hard core of citizens of the DDR who had grown up in the Soviet Union always stuck together. In fact, they had changed nationality in name only and remained Russian, even if they spoke German and operated from offices in Berlin.

"Financial backing can be a problem," Köstner went on. "It's a question of priorities and availability of funds. The position is the same in our fraternal Socialist countries. When I was in Prague just before Christmas, I was invited to a very interesting discussion with some Algerian comrades which led to my offering them our services. They had hit upon an unconventional method which would scarcely have met with our approval, but they see things differently over there. They have a different way of life, different traditions."

Köstner took an envelope out of a desk drawer and handed it to Langer.

"Have a look at these papers," he said, sinking back into his chair and screwing up his eyes, the better to assess Langer's reaction.

The envelope contained a bundle of photocopies. Langer examined them calmly and methodically, without any exaggerated display of curiosity. The copies were of the most important section of a tender for advanced electronic equipment. It was addressed to the Ministry of Home Affairs and came from a Swedish firm. The covering letter, signed by the director of the firm, indicated that the bid was sealed and not to be opened before March 20.

Langer noted the deadline was still two and a half months away. One of the photocopies contained a summary of the costs, which amounted to forty-three million two hundred and twenty-six French francs. The page was signed by two Swedes and had marginal comments in Arabic which Langer was unable to make out.

"They seem genuine," he said. "The bad quality of the copies is no proof in itself, but it shouldn't be too difficult to establish whether they come from the same photocopier as other documents from that source."

"The material is authentic," said Köstner.

They exchanged brief glances. Langer became increasingly aware of the fact that tension had built up between them as the conversation went on, a tension which could not simply be explained by the mutual lack of respect characterizing their relationship. Langer sat in front of the desk, his eyebrows raised as if accompanying a polite question, and tried to conceal the ironic suspicion which began to take possession of him. Köstner leaned over the desk, cunning and skeptical, then suddenly and quite unexpectedly the distrust in his cold, Tartarish eyes gave way to a look of friendly understanding. He ordered coffee over the intercom, stood up and gestured in the direction of easy chairs in the corner of the room.

"It's good to have you back, Comrade Langer," he said kindly. "I have heard it said that a coffee with schnaps is good for the heart."

When the coffee had arrived and the door was closed once more, Köstner raised his glass with a friendly gesture, as if to propose a toast of reconciliation.

"It's a ticklish business, my old friend," he said in an offhand manner, sinking back into his armchair and stretching nonchalantly so that his feet ended up by hovering near the tabletop. "As you know, the Algerians have always been very generous when it comes to giving asylum to persecuted socialists from all over the world. Over the years they have acquired a well-informed understanding of all the revolutionary movements worth supporting. That includes Central

America, which has hitherto been the province of Cuba and the Soviet Union. Now the Algerians want to make a contribution outside their own continent. You can call it a test if you like, albeit on a much smaller scale than what the Cubans and Russians are used to. A group from Central America is going back home, and the Algerians have offered them support. That area is crawling with the CIA, and so the methods used in Africa are not appropriate. Amrs can be obtained in the U.S. There are depots run by Americans who are less than patriotic, but they want payment in cash, in dollars. The Algerians think it's only right that the Yanks themselves should provide the money."

Köstner relaxed in his chair. He looked very pleased with himself now. "A touch of genius, eh?" he grinned.

"I'm not sure I follow."

"It's all quite simple. Brilliant and totally without risk, even if we are unfortunately unable to copy their methods. Mainly for aesthetic reasons." He refilled their schnaps glasses. "*Prosit!* To our Algerian friends and the greed of the capitalist world!"

For the first time in many weeks, Langer longed for a cigar. Instead, he moistened his lips with the liquor and held it in his mouth for one delicious moment.

"If it's a question of earning money, the capitalists will agree to any conditions we care to make," continued the colonel, well pleased with himself. "The multinational companies lack any trace of decency and are prepared for anything as long as they can kick their competitors in the crotch. Times are hard just now and business is bad, even in the West. Everybody's looking for new markets. The French have had it all to themselves in Algeria so far, but the Algerians want to shake off their dependence on France and exploit the rivalry between the companies. If the Yanks can get a footing in North Africa they'll consider it a great success. This deal is the biggest the Algerians have ever announced in the

37

electronics field, and all the big multinationals have put in a bid. The Swedish firm is small, but is known for its high-quality products—and it's Swedish in name only. The board and the directors are Swedes, but the real power is with the multinationals. Both sides have good reason to welcome a deal with a firm based nominally in a neutral country."

"We've done business in similar fashion."

"But not on the same terms. The Arabs are well known as hard bargainers. They like to haggle and their wearing-down methods are even harder than our own. Besides, they're notoriously bad payers. It's not easy to sell to an Arab state, but it's a great feat to get paid for your goods, especially if the money comes on time. In this particular case the Algerians are prepared to offer the Swedish firm two especially favorable terms. They promise to complete all official negotiations within twenty-four hours, and they'll pay in cash—against commercial credit! Quite unique in this part of the world."

"And the conditions?"

"Just one."

Köstner took his time before completing his answer. Langer noticed a slight tremble in the colonel's right hand as he ostentatiously lit another cigarette.

"Sixteen per cent. Commission. On the gross amount. The seller will put it into an account in Switzerland."

"Sixteen!" Langer was genuinely surprised. "Is that really realistic?"

"Oh, yes! Work it out for yourself. Think of the time saved. The cash payment. A wide-open market earmarked for years to come. What's a few million to a multinational company with a yearly turnover as big as the gross national product of the whole Algerian state? And there's bound to be a generous cut for the hagglers themselves. Even Stockholm has no doubt heard that no Arab can do business without haggling and constantly introducing new demands."

Köstner had trouble in keeping a straight face. His

expression vacillated between delight and disgust. His eyes gleamed with the black sheen of treacherous thin ice. Langer began to grasp what had happened at the Prague meeting. The Arabs had surprised the colonel with a proposal he had seen through immediately: his first reaction must have been scorn and perhaps also fear. The threadbare cover story about money for arms shipments was so astonishingly naive that he must have had difficulty in maintaining the blank expression appropriate to a diplomat, and showing interest and understanding. Then, something must have happened to change his attitude and make him ready to cooperate. It was not an invitation to share in the bribes—Langer was certain Köstner would not entertain the idea of leaving the Eastern bloc for one moment. Corruption was a disease as yet spared to the Republic, at least in its most vulgar form. The number of East German accounts in Switzerland could be counted on the fingers of one hand, if indeed they existed at all. The Arabs must have persuaded the colonel to cooperate by producing some other convincing argument which pointed to advantages for himself without damaging the Republic.

"We need a middle man in Stockholm," Köstner went on. "Unfortunately, he has to be Swedish. Party contacts are excluded, and our choice is thus restricted. I've ploughed my way through Tragg's file: it makes impressive reading. He's done enough to earn his pension, and when the time comes he's welcome to come over to us. Can you vouch for him?"

Ulrich Langer hesitated before answering. He was growing increasingly aware that this was the chance he had been waiting for, that he had been preparing for without any obvious reason. His hesitation was both genuine and an act. While searching for the right words, he endeavored to ensure that his voice hit the correct tone pitched between loyal defense of a close colleague, and polite acquiescence in his superior's unusual but also irregular plans.

"Tragg is honest. Honest and loyal."

Köstner roared with laughter. "You sometimes express yourself in the oddest way, my dear fellow!"

"I've been working with Tragg for over thirty years," said Langer. "He sticks to the rules, and as long as nobody breaks them I think I can vouch for him."

"Tragg was arrested by the British police in Hamburg in 1946. You had signed a contract with him earlier that same year. They let him go after three days. No charge. There's nothing in the file to show whether that little incident was followed up."

"It was a private matter. He was cheated in some black market deal which ended up with a fight in a bar. Someone got hurt. He volunteered the information himself."

"Eight years ago he was arrested again by the British police. This time it was in Northern Ireland."

"He was released after a couple of hours. The British grew suspicious when he rented a room only a few hundred yards from the border, on the Irish side. The place was one of a chain of little guest houses dotted all over Eire. Tragg had booked the room at a tourist agency in Dublin, and the English were forced to give the Irish an official apology. We checked the story with an IRA contact who verified Tragg's version."

"Apart from that he seems clean. Do you think he's the right man to negotiate on behalf of the Algerians in Stockholm?"

"Yes," replied Langer without hesitation.

That was careless, and much too quick a reaction. A glint appeared in Köstner's eye, and Langer observed how he shifted his position in his armchair. The deceptive feeling of fellowship and solidarity was draining away. Langer's unqualified support for Greger Tragg had disturbed Köstner's vain and boastful superiority. The colonel had risen to where he was and stayed there thanks to the fact that he never relaxed

40

his instinctive distrust of everyone and everything. Langer had blundered. He took the only way available to him. "Tragg is a communist, a world revolutionary. It is that conviction much more than the rewards which has inspired all his activities. I know he has always dreamed of doing something for people in the underdeveloped and overexploited countries. If he's given this job he will do his level best to bring it to a successful conclusion."

It worked. Köstner fell into his own trap. But not without qualification. Somewhere in the back of his mind he noted that the relationship between Ulrich Langer and Greger Tragg had exceeded the limits appropriate to secret agents. He decided to keep that observation alive in his memory.

The instructions were already prepared, and were handed over to Langer. In future he was to report in person to Köstner. The transaction was not to go through the usual channels, and not even to be noted in his diary for the time being.

"It's a broker's job," said the colonel, "and our Algerian friends have asked for the highest degree of discretion, especially with regard to their American contacts. I don't need to tell you that failure would have extremely serious consequences for all concerned."

"What do we get out of it?" asked Langer quietly.

"Oil. A delegation is going to Algiers in April to discuss deliveries. They will be received most cordially if, in the meantime, we have managed to do this little job to everyone's satisfaction."


"It's a classic set-up," said Tragg cheerfully. "No one can be pinned down to anything. Everybody wins except those poor, browbeaten little devils known as the Algerian people. I can understand why they believe the earthly powers are in league with the genies. Should anything go wrong there's always Tragg in Stockholm to take the blame. Has anybody given a thought to alms for this disloyal swine?"

"Of course not! You're working for world revolution."

"That simplifies matters, of course. What's Köstner's cut?"

"Zero per cent. He'll become boss of the delegation in Algiers, irrespective of what the Foreign Ministry boys say. No one will dare to oppose somebody supported by the Algerians."

"A safe bet. And no personal investment. What about you?"

"The museum job in Magdeburg. We're finished, you and I. They are going to wake up a sleeper in Stockholm. Youngsters get on quickly nowadays, and Alex must be nearing retirement age. Do you know when?"

"Yes," replied Tragg. "I know when."

They saw eye to eye. No further clarification was necessary. Ulrich Langer started to loosen the rope fastening the tarpaulin to the boat. With Tragg's help he opened up a flap over the cockpit, held on to one of the props, and pushed himself up into the boat. A few minutes later Tragg was holding a weekend bag fitted with a lock of impressive dimensions. Tragg found it hard to suppress a smile. They always go over the top when a contact man plays at being a field agent, he thought. Langer produced a key, opened the bag and fished out a miniature black briefcase. That too was sealed.

"Here's all you need," said Langer. "Go through the material tomorrow and come to Friedrichstrasse Railway Station at six o'clock. Walk from there to Alexanderplatz, using the back streets. Marx will pick you up on the way, and I can promise you a dinner fit for a gourmet. Our boys at Checkpoint Charlie will ask no questions if you put this in your passport," he went on, handing over a visa covered in official stamps. "Are you afraid of the Americans?"

42

"No," said Tragg. "Besides, that's not the right place to move in and make an arrest."

Marx was waiting in the car outside Langer's house, and drove Tragg the half-hour's journey to Checkpoint Charlie. He passed through quickly and without incident. After changing taxies three times in the West and a quick visit to the subway station at Bahnhof Zoo, he went straight to his hotel, convinced that he was not being followed. He drank two whiskeys and a beer in the bar, with the little briefcase on the counter in front of him. The other customers were actors from the nearby theater, relaxing after the evening's performance. Not a single guest came in through the hotel entrance during the hour Tragg spent in the bar. When he went up to his room at about half past two, he ordered a call and breakfast for nine the next morning, then fell asleep immediately, without a thought for the future.

Breakfast was served on time. The waiter had even thought to provide a morning paper from the reception desk. By shortly after ten he had showered and changed. It was check-out time, and he had to wait a couple of extra minutes before the receptionist could change his ten-mark note into coins. It was two minutes past eleven when he started to dial the long number that would give him a line to Stockholm from the telephone booth at the corner of Joachimthaler-strasse and Kurfürstendamm. The phone at the other end rang only twice before someone answered.

"It's me," said Tragg.

"Good morning, Mr. Editor."

Piero Svanberg's voice was as loud and clear as if he were standing in the same booth.

# ❧ IV ❧

Armand de Riez drove a car as if a flashing light and wailing siren were permanently switched on. He threaded his way aggressively through the dense traffic in a series of slalom curves, dead stops, and angry surges. Tragg breathed a sigh of relief when they skidded into the narrow lane leading through the woods to the French restaurant at Wannsee, said by hostile and envious observers to be the real headquarters of the remaining French troops in West Berlin. None of the other road-users, with the possible exception of the local police, knew that the person responsible for the reckless driving was a high-ranking official in the French military intelligence service. The car was an ordinary Peugeot, and had no flashing light or siren. A plate at the back indicated to the initiated that the driver was above the laws others were obliged to observe.

It still happened occasionally that some new and overenthusiastic West Berlin traffic policeman took up the chase after Armand, and there had been times when he was caught and forced to a halt. The error was never repeated. As soon as he produced his identity card, the assumed success was transformed into humiliation. No one had the right to intervene, not even to question him, and the only course of action was to salute smartly and withdraw while apologizing profusely. Quite a few traffic police in West Berlin, normally sensible and reasonable men, had a secret ambition to be the person who, one fine day, pulled Armand de Riez out of a pile of wreckage that had once been a black Peugeot. Like so many ambitions, this one would never be achieved.

Armand de Riez was in his fifties, portly, black-haired, and stocky in that confidence-inspiring style always associated with the French, especially those from Brittany. His elegant, red-haired wife with the seductive name of Angela sat in the backseat and watched with amusement Tragg's awkward attempts to remain upright in the front. Like Armand, she worked for the French occupation forces and spent her days in the crumbling offices of the old Hermann Goering Barracks. Her maiden name was Nielsen, and her father came from Schleswig. At some point during the worst phase of the depression in the twenties, he had met Angela's French-speaking mother in Brussels. Since he spoke good French and was more Gallic than Aryan in spirit, viewed the world ironically and with a sense of humor, but most of all because he had a permanent job and good prospects of a successful career, her mother changed her nationality, in name at least, and moved to Berlin. When Adolf Hitler came to power, she protested against the new regime by refusing to speak German in the home. Angela became bilingual. At school she concentrated on English. Two summer holidays in Sweden were enough to enable her to get by in Swedish.

In the beginning of 1945, Hitler needed scapegoats to explain away the collapse of the German railway network. He had the Gestapo arrest a number of high-ranking executives who had managed to avoid becoming party members, and accused them of sabotaging the railways. The so-called sabotage was in fact a logical consequence of the Allies' systematic bombing of railway junctions and the equally ruthless attacks on trains and bridges by Russian partisans. No railway in the world could have performed better than the German one in those circumstances.

Angela would never forget the cold, gray morning in March when the Gestapo forced their way into the hitherto undamaged apartment and roused the terrified family from their beds. Her father was given three minutes to get dressed, and was dragged out of the apartment half-dressed, his shirt and jacket in a bundle under his arm. He had never possessed heroic qualities, and had tears in his eyes. He was not even allowed to kiss his wife and daughter goodbye. Soon afterwards he was found guilty and declared an enemy of the people. The method of execution was never revealed.

Only a few months after the end of the war, Angela was given a displaced person's passport. She ran literally straight into the arms of a British major at Luneburg, where she had fled to escape the Nazis and the bombs and to await the advancing Allies. She did not know what to do with her life. A message from Berlin said her mother had been killed in an American bombing raid.

The English major was quick-witted and without prejudice. He saw immediately that a farmer's son from Yorkshire only meets a woman like Angela once in a lifetime. Starvation rations and tattered clothes were inappropriate for a woman of Angela's outstanding beauty. The Englishman was won over at once by her flowing, auburn hair, the lively, intelligent look in her green eyes, and her shapely, slim body as well as her excellent and at times even witty English. He put his weight behind efforts to overcome the formalities. Angela's Nordic surname facilitated matters, and to be on the safe side and make sure of keeping her, the major gave her a job under his wing that very same day.

A few years later, the major's English wife decided it was time for her to investigate in person the persistent rumors about *la dolce vita* in the zone of occupation. Tactfully, she sent a telegram announcing that she was on her way with the two children to join her husband in waiting for that longed-for day when he would at last be sent home and demobilized. Angela had no choice but to leave.

She returned to Berlin more beautiful than ever, but in possession of skills and documents which opened doors into the French community there. They gave her a post immediately as an interpreter and translator. When she married Armand de Riez at the end of the sixties, she had long been accepted by the French as one of their own.

Angela de Riez had a strange weakness which Tragg had heard about, knowledge he shared in secret with Armand. In an old, ruined house near a rubbish dump, she tended a sizeable colony of wild cats; they had discovered a place where they were left alone and, as often as not, found a very necessary supplement to their diet. Armand and Angela had married late in life, and had no children. Her interest in the cats, which Angela never took to excess and managed to keep a secret from outsiders, was accepted by Armand as a substitute for the children he—but never she—had always wanted. He therefore let her do as she wished.

As a matter of routine, the Frenchman had compiled a thin personal file on Greger Tragg, in which it was noted that he was a close Swedish relative of Angela's, and that they had got to know each other during her summer holidays in Sweden. Armand himself had added Tragg's name to the list of Angela's acquaintances and contacts demanded by the security services before their marriage. No further action was ever taken. That would only have brought the services into disrepute.

Even Armand de Riez was under the illusion that Angela and Tragg were related in some distant fashion. In fact, they had been introduced by Ulrich Langer at the time when

Berliners could still move freely between the East and West sectors.

Tragg knew that at some point during the evening he would have an opportunity of being alone with Angela. Armand de Riez was a well-liked colleague and very much at home in the tight circle of high-ranking French officials and officers who lunched regularly at the lakeside restaurant. They were an isolated community in a city which regarded their presence as nothing more than symbolic. They had long since ceased to dissimulate for each other and pretend they were performing some meaningful task. Their resources were small, and they were sold short not only by the British and Americans, but eventually also by the Germans as they grew in self-confidence. Everyone distrusted them because of the way they flirted coquettishly with the Russians on the other side of the Wall. As a result, they devoted themselves mainly to the colonial way of life at which they were past masters. They conducted complicated love affairs, quarrelled in public, were reconciled just as often, gossiped about everything under the sun, but spent the most time indulging in the favorite hobby of all Frenchmen: partaking in the communal meal of the day.

Moreover, Armand considered it to be no more than normal Gallic politeness to leave Angela and Tragg alone for a while.

"Time for confession," said Angela coyly in Swedish, watching Armand retreat to the bar where he was welcomed by loud shouts of greeting.

"Have you missed me?"

"Of course, but not as much as you'd like to think, my dear cousin!"

Her Swedish was surprisingly good; her French "r" was not out of place but sounded like a cultivated southern accent.

"We'll have to do something about that. Even if it has to be mainly on the phone."

She burst out laughing, and managed to look like a mixture of an impudent minx from the working-class Wedding suburb, and a haughty grande dame from the Paris salons of yore. Their neighbors at the next table nodded in delight and huddled together to gossip about elegant Madame de Riez and her relative, the blond man with the clear blue eyes from that cold country in the far north.

"Thank God I've never been your lover," she said, merrily. "Love on the phone is not to my taste, but I suppose it might be something for you perverse Swedes."

Armand would be away at the bar for at least another half-hour, and she continued to prattle away. As always when she had an audience, she put on an act. She was nervous, more nervous than usual. She had trouble keeping her fingers still—maybe that was her way of compensating for the tension, or perhaps she was afraid. Tragg realized their relationship was not as straightforward as it used to be. He could not ignore the note of discord. He had noticed it six months ago when they last met, but it was only a hint then.

Suddenly, she turned to gaze coldly at the next table, where they had changed the subject and were now whispering about a stocky, elderly man who had sat down at one of the window tables with a slip of a girl who could have been his granddaughter. He ordered champagne.

"They call us Boche," she said contemptuously, "but they're far more petty than we are. If Armand is sent home to France, I'll seek a divorce."

That sounded honest, at least. Tragg let the silence linger awhile before raising serious matters.

"There are some things in which you and I have a mutual interest," he said. "Uncle wants you to start emptying the basket again."

The look of contempt still hovered on her lips, and he saw in her eyes how her hostility was redirected toward him.

"Does it contain any presents?" she asked sarcastically.

50

"Of course. Uncle says he's already been there."

"He's well-known as an old miser."

"That's an inherited characteristic you can never shake off. But I think you'll be pleased with what you find. You'll need a fair amount for expenses."

"What kind of expenses?"

"Telephone bills, mostly."

Tragg lit a cigarette and put the box of matches on the table between them.

"The telephone number in Stockholm," he said. "On the inside. It's a library. You're usually free on Monday afternoons."

"Yes," she said nonchalantly. "Shopping."

"The same day that you visit the cat farm?"

She did not even nod.

"Go there first, then call me at exactly 2:40 p.m. from a phone booth. Not from a restaurant or a bar, and not from the telephone company offices."

Angela looked offended.

"I'm not that wet behind the ears," she said bitterly.

"I'm sorry. I was only thinking about what's best for you."

He stretched out his hand, but she did not take it.

"Sometimes you might have to go back to see the cats again after talking to me. Buy a bit of extra cat food in reserve. If any other cat minder turns up while you're there, or somebody from the animal rights movement, or just an ordinary passerby, then the farm will have to be declared an infection risk. Send Uncle a telegram. He'll take care of it."

She began to show more interest and raised her head; he could see her throat pounding below her neckline, her eyes had lit up, and when she spoke the arrogant tone was back.

"You seem anxious," she said suspiciously. "If things are hotter than usual you'd better tell me. A girl like me has to think of her reputation."

"There's no need at all to worry," he said soothingly, and

51

remembered how he had used exactly the same words at the Solvalla racetrack only a fortnight earlier.

"Berlin would lose all its charm if my little red Angela were to come to any harm. That won't happen," he assured her.

"I'm not yours," she replied sarcastically, but reassured all the same. "I respect Uncle, and I'll dance to his tune on this occasion, just as I've always done. Without even hearing the music, as usual."

"I don't know it either."

"My dear Greger," she began, and he felt as if they really understood each other for the first time. "You are the most charming liar I've ever met."

When Armand came to fetch them for coffee and cognac at the bar, she fixed a black Gauloise in a six-inch silver holder and lit the cigarette. She put the matchbox in her handbag. They marched through the restaurant, and it seemed natural for her to attract everyone's admiration and envy. She smiled, head held high. Only Tragg, following a yard behind, noticed the pink flush that had spread around her neck.


West Berlin is a capitalist oasis in the communist desert or—looked at from the other side—a poisoned watering hole in a luxuriant savannah. In theory, there are four ways of getting in—or out. By air, car, rail, or boat.

The Germans used the claim that they had been denied a corridor to Danzig and East Prussia as a pretext to start the Second World War. They now have over thirty years' experience of corridors. Air corridors are not much wider than the jet stream from western planes that are constantly being ordered back into them by watchful MIG fighters. Most travelers to and from West Berlin prefer this mode of transportation, claiming it saves time. They avoid all the hassle at the border crossing points, and instead line up for hours at Tempelhof Airport. Others fly because they are afraid of the communists. The allied military airfields in West Berlin also churn out a constant stream of spies, military officials, and that peculiar type of specialist known by the CIA and Secret Service as subversive elements if they belong to the opposition, but which a neutral Swede like Greger Tragg would call infiltrators.

There are four road corridors to West Berlin, but two of them, the ones leading to Köstrin on the Polish border and Sassnitz on the Baltic coast, are not worthy of the name and are called transit routes instead. Route 96 to Sassnitz is completely integrated into the East German road network, and only differs from other roads in Mecklenburg in that here and there, a few blue and yellow posters with Swedish text appear among the series of drab, red banners in the villages and gravel-gray towns. The message is always the same: peace, the triumphant progress of socialism, and friendship with the Soviet Union. The two real road corridors to Hamburg and Southern Germany are filled every day with long, well-disciplined trails of West German vehicles which, for the only time in their lives, are driven in accordance with the speed limits designated by the authorities.

Rail traffic to Sassnitz, Hamburg, and Munich is busy. Passengers going north or east must leave West Berlin from the main line station at Bahnhof Zoo and reckon with at least half an hour's journey to nearby Ostbahnhof in the East. Checkpoints, stairways, and a lack of porters make this mode of transportation less than attractive for passengers with weak hearts or limited patience.

Boat traffic to West Berlin consists exclusively of barges chugging slowly along the Spree and over the lakes before joining the canal network. Going by barge was the first alternative rejected by Tragg when he started to think about getting home.

Armand and Angela de Riez had driven Tragg back to his

hotel in Meinickestrasse. When the night porter gave him his key, Tragg asked for his bill to be made up ready for the next morning. He did not claim a refund for the remaining two nights still booked in his name. Tragg had taken a package tour from Sweden, using the train and a ferry to Sassnitz. The Swedish police check the passports of all passengers from East Germany to Trelleborg, but there are several ways of disembarking from a ferry without troubling the police or customs, and that minor detail was not crucial to Tragg's decision not to take that route. The real problem was getting out of Trelleborg, since access roads are few and easy to watch. He therefore cancelled his return ticket at the Swedish travel agency on the Kurfürstendamm, a necessary precaution since the courier was bound to miss him and tell the Swedish consulate he had simply disappeared.

Tragg moved into a bed and breakfast place in Schlyterstrasse, somewhere he had stayed before. He had booked by telephone the previous day, and said they should not expect him until about midnight. He explained that his train was due in quite late. After checking out and having lunch in the hotel dining room, Tragg embarked on a 10-hour sightseeing tour of Berlin. He spent an hour studying the world-famous aquarium at the Zoo; displaying special interest in the crocodiles, caymans, and alligators. He came back three times to the little bridge that forms an observation post over the steaming prison where the reptiles are kept, always approaching from the same direction. He left his hand luggage at a little bar in Wedding he had first visited in the early fifties: the owner was still the same. He said he would return for it shortly before closing time. Next, he turned his attention to the West Berlin local transport, changing frequently from the municipal railway to the subway and back, sometimes several times at the same station. In between times, he took a few taxi rides or went for a stroll through the Tiergarten, which is deserted at that time of year. For over half an hour he was the only sightseer at the Victory Column, which looms like a vulgar and isolated relic in the middle of the Platz der Republik, reminding onlookers that even the Kaisers had their glorious dreams about Lebensraum. You can only get to the column through one of four hundred-yard-long pedestrian subways, one from each point of the compass. He had a Bratwurst and potato salad at the decrepit café in Mariendorff, then walked the mile and a half to the trotting course. There he got talking to a West German professional gambler from Hanover who had recently been to Charlottenlund in Copenhagen. When the races were over, the West German gave him a lift as far as Fehrberlinerplatz. When he rang the night bell at the guest house in Schlyterstrasse, he was quite certain he was not being followed. The manager was expecting him and gave him a brandy. He paid for two nights in advance, with a fifty-mark tip. Nobody mentioned filling in registration forms.

Tragg would almost have preferred being followed. In that case he would not have hesitated to take a flight to Hamburg to try to shake off his shadows there. One attractive possibility was to go on one of the high-speed smuggling boats that plied between Rostock and the Danish islands, but Sasha was in charge of that traffic and there was no need to risk having Ulrich Langer hauled up to answer awkward questions. Tragg therefore decided to go to Hamburg by bus. It was an undramatic solution, and probably also the last of the exits the West German police would think of closing when they got word from Stockholm to look out for him.

The next afternoon Tragg made a deal with one of the bus drivers taking pensioners from West Berlin to visit relatives in West Germany. The West Berlin Senate subsidizes these trips, and the buses are never full at that time of year. Tragg bought him Steinhäger and beer, assured him repeatedly he was not on the run from the East German police, that his passport and visa were in exemplary order, and received one of the vacant seats at the back of the bus. He explained he had

had a little disagreement with a butcher's family in Reinicken-dorff consisting of four brothers and a heavyweight father who all swore up and down that Tragg was guilty of breach of promise concerning the only daughter. "It's just not true," said Tragg. "You see, I'm already married." The bus driver was in sympathy, and two hundred-mark notes helped to convince him.

The East Germans found nothing wrong with his passport and visa the next day, and as usual, the West German police did nothing more than stick their heads in at the door and bid everyone welcome to the free world.

That same evening Tragg got as far as "Die alte Diehle," an inn three miles from Travemünde where many years previously Jean-Baptiste Bernadotte, later to become Karl XIV Johan, had negotiated with Swedish officers for the Swedish crown and was welcomed to his new homeland after having invested a million imperial dollars in its future. The restaurant was now of the very highest class, and its smoked eel was without parallel in the whole of Europe. The landlord had fitted out three rooms upstairs, decorated in pink, for occasional guests. They were dominated by magnificent double beds and enormous mirrors, as well as elegant nude paintings of high artistic quality. The bathrooms were tiled in black with pink baths, bidets, and washbasins which must have sent every ambitious bathroom fixtures executive into paroxysms of delight.

"First class," "Super," "Eine Bombe."

That night Greger Tragg was the only guest, and paid in advance as was the custom. He could not count on breakfast. The place was deserted next morning, and as agreed, Tragg dropped the key through the mail slot after locking the door. He caught a bus to Travemünde and took a taxi to the harbor. In the line of cars at the ferry terminal he came across a gloomy-looking man from Borås who had been to the casino and lost over eight thousand marks, although he still had his

Mercedes. The man saw the black side of everything, and Tragg had no difficulty in convincing him his car had broken down a few miles outside Travemünde, and that it would be several days before it could be repaired. Tragg got a lift as far as Hälsingborg, where they drove off the ferry without being stopped by the police. By way of thanks for the lift, Tragg paid for a tank of gas and lunch on the way. Their car was the last to embark in Helsingör, and the last to disembark in Hälsingborg. Tragg thought it was safe to assume they had not been followed.

It was only when Tragg got into his own car, which he had left for servicing at a garage in Limhamn near Malmö, that he began to feel worried. The journey home had gone much too easily. It was dangerous to play down Piero Svanberg's telephone warning, and the closer he got to Stockholm the more risky it became. He knew he could not foresee everything. Chance, he thought; no one can legislate for chance. But it is the mother of carelessness.

He had a trip of some four hundred miles to Södertälje, where he had booked a room under a false name at the Esso Motor Hotel. To start with, he took side roads across the Scanian plain and into Småland. The false license plates were at home in Stockholm, but they were useless now that the apartment had been searched. He tried to console himself with the fact that the weather was awful. It was snowing hard, and visibility was down to about ten yards in places. There was not much traffic about, and he did not see any police cars. They were probably on the main roads looking for stranded vehicles. When he stopped for gas he noticed that the snow and slush had obscured both license plates. By the time he reached Markaryd, he decided he would have to take the main E4 road if he was ever to get through.

Either they're looking for me, he thought, or they're counting on my coming back to Stockholm. They know I have to come back. Or do they? Who exactly was it that had taken an interest in him? The logical answer was the security forces of SÄPO, but it could also be the intelligence boys from IB. Cooperation between the two organizations was handled by one of SÄPO's sections, but he had heard that they sometimes made a mess of it. There were other possibilities, but he soon realized they were irrelevant. The German BND and the Swedish SÄPO were hand in glove, going back to long before the war. Sympathy for Germany had always been stronger in the police than elsewhere in Sweden.

They must have had pretty strong grounds for suspicion or they wouldn't have dared to search the house. SÄPO could scarcely do that without a court order. The IB, on the other hand, often used freelancers. But sometimes they offered tit for tat and ignored the rules, so it all boiled down to the same thing.

Compared with Alex he was a little fish. Alex must be their main objective. The scoop. The big prize. They knew of Alex's existence, but didn't know who he was. "If we eliminate his weakest link, he's not in danger," Langer had said. Alex's only link and hence his weakest one was Greger Tragg. SÄPO had got hold of one end of the link, and would be very careful about how they proceeded. He discounted Marika. She was merely an extension of Alex's arm.

So, they'd been through his apartment with a fine-toothed comb. That seemed illogical, given the risks involved, even given the fact that they'd waited until he'd gone away. If it was Alex they were after, should they not be very careful about disturbing Tragg? Perhaps they underestimated him and assumed he was still in blissful ignorance. He shouldn't take it for granted they suspected a connection between him and the faceless and nameless Alex. On the other hand, he was obviously on their list and they had waited until he'd gone away before making a move. How could they know he'd left the apartment? Had they just risked it on

58

seeing the car had gone? What mistake had he made? Why hadn't he realized they were watching him?

He took the E4 from Markaryd. There was no chance of following him in this weather, not even lying in wait for him at some junction. He decided he could go as far as Södertälje that night without risk, and that Södertälje and the Esso Motor Hotel were clear—but at the same time he was aware he had reached this conclusion simply because he had no choice.

Suddenly, he felt very tired. Not from driving. He did not mind bad weather and slippery roads. The exhaustion was not physical. It was only when he realized how testing and critical the next few months were going to be that he was overcome by weariness, distaste, and a recognition of how pointless it all was. For half an hour he drove without thinking at all, just headed on and on into the blanket of snow as if the dancing flakes were his only enemies. By the time he finally stopped for a last cup of coffee before the filling stations closed their bars for the night, and stood for a brief moment in the white silence, feeling the snowflakes caress his cheeks and turn slowly into wet, heavy drops, he had overcome his weakness. He had been through it all before. By ceasing to think, letting himself sink down into a black, bottomless abyss without hope, by simply waiting for the feeling to pass and for the black hole to melt away of its own accord, he was able to recover his strength and willpower.

Afterwards, he called it a cleansing process and even now, as he sat in the café with the hollow-eyed waitress trying to stare him out so she could at last get off to bed, even now he knew he would go on fighting to the very end. The odds could be better, but the stake was low compared to the prize. Moreover, he had already paid the first installment over thirty years earlier.

He had had a blackout. He was sometimes astonished to discover how badly he had thought things out and how careless he could be. Of course they had known about his trip because his telephone was tapped. He had arranged his Berlin travel by calling a travel agent from his apartment in Stockholm. As usual, he looked for the positive side of the situation. If he had not been careless enough to do that, he would not have known his phone was tapped. It did not necessarily mean they were on to him.

He used the rest of the way to Södertälje to work out the acute problems he would have to deal with straight away. He listed them one by one:

He had nowhere to live.

He would have to get rid of his car.

He had no telephone.

Without a place to live and a telephone he could not act for the Arabs.

Without a car he was as vulnerable as a hare in an open field.

What worried him least of all was his and Langer's suspicion that for some time now, Angela de Riez had been showing the contents of the basket at the cat farm to Armand before passing it on.

He did not give a single thought to the possibility that before long, he would be a millionaire.

# ❦ V ❦

The taxi skidded to a halt and ended up with one front wheel on the pavement. Fifty yards further down the one-way street two uniformed men standing under a blue and yellow sign bearing a coat of arms and the word POLICE in large, black letters broke off their conversation and turned to investigate. They were patrol men on their way to their car.

Piero Svanberg let go of the wheel and reached out his right arm in an imperious gesture which showed he would stand for no nonsense. He leaned back on the headrest and eyed the two figures in the back seat.

"Give!" he said calmly. "I won't ask twice."

"Now, wait a minute," burped one of the passengers, huddling into the farthest corner of the seat and holding the open wine bottle in front of his chin like a shield.

"This is a bloody democracy, for Chrissake!" The other man's slurred protest stopped short as he caught sight of the policemen through the windscreen. They were coming to find out what was going on.

"The fuzz!" hissed the man in the back seat, horrified. "Give him the bloody booze! Quick!"

61

His friend had difficulty in coordinating his movements and misjudged the distance to Piero Svanberg's hand. A stream of cheap, sweet wine dribbled down onto the floor before Svanberg could get hold of the bottle.

"The cork!" he demanded, staring with an ice-cold gaze straight at one of the drunks, who began to fumble about in his pockets and handed over a screw top with a gesture close to humility. Svanberg looked at the filthy fingers in disgust, and gingerly picked up the top. He had half screwed it on by the time one of the patrol men bent to look in through the window.

"Problems?" The policeman's voice was neutral and official.

"We've solved them now," Svanberg gave him his Sicilian smile as, with an ostentatious turn of the wrist, he finished screwing down the top.

"There's a smell of liquor," said the policeman in a hostile tone, breathing in deeply through his nose.

"Wine," said Svanberg. "From the liquor store."

He lifted up the bottle to display the familiar label, and that would have been that had not one of the passengers shuffled his feet and kicked the plastic carrier bag so that a clinking of bottles rang out loud and clear.

For the first time, the policeman turned to look at the pair of wretched dropouts in the back seat. He was young and had probably been drafted down to Stockholm from the far north; he did not like the big city. Perhaps he had grown up in a low-church family with a strict moral code. Such people turn surprisingly often to jobs where they can exert power and achieve revenge for their lost youth.

"Are they on welfare?" asked the policeman as harshly as his young voice allowed.

Svanberg nodded.

"There should be laws about these rides," went on the policeman in the outraged, nasal tone of voice characteristic of defenders of public morals. "It can't be right that taxpayers' money should be spent on liquor. A lawyer could probably make a fraud charge stick."

"Well," said Svanberg flippantly, "that may well be, but it's none of my business. I'm only a taxidriver . . ."

". . . and not a pig," he had been about to say. His irritation over the miserable drunks in the back seat had by now switched to the policeman, who was being more officious and pompous than the situation required. He was interrupted by the taxi radio.

"Car 1582," crackled the loudspeaker. "Come in, car 1582."

Svanberg switched on his microphone, and both policemen and passengers listened in the reverential way people do to radio calls.

"Car 1582. Go ahead. Over."

"You are to contact your father at home immediately. Over and out."

Really important messages usually need very few words. Svanberg's smile faded away.

"It could be my mother," he said in a serious voice.

Short messages can also be misinterpreted, especially if you do not know their real significance. The policeman's mother was still alive, but a few days ago he had received a letter complaining about pains in her leg. He had realized for the first time she was starting to get old. He therefore misinterpreted the radio message and Svanberg's brief comment.

"You'd better go and look into that," he said sympathetically. "You can use the station phone if you like."

He saluted and walked away without so much as a glance at the terrified pair in the back seat. A few moments later, the patrol car disappeared round a corner and into the traffic.

Svanberg switched off the taxi meter and turned to his

63

passengers. He was not surprised to see that one of them had tears in his eyes.

"Here's your damned bottle," he said fiercely. "It's your birthday today. If you're not out of this car within fifteen seconds I'll hand you over to the fuzz. You can pass on your credit coupons to somebody else."

They stumbled out through both doors, having difficulty in keeping their feet. One of them was holding the half-empty bottle by the neck, the other clung tightly onto the carrier bag.

"Bloody taxi drivers," were the last words Svanberg heard through the open window, but they contained a trace of approval and warmth.

Piero Svanberg switched off his "Taxi" sign as he drove into the courtyard of the Central Station and stopped just short of the zebra crossing. Tragg crossed over the street from the Terminus Hotel in a crowd of pedestrians. He was wearing his gray parka and a red woollen hat pulled down over his ears. Dozens of commuters on their way home were dressed in exactly the same way. Tragg went straight up to the taxi and got into the front seat. Svanberg was not held up at the lights for more than a minute before nosing out into Vasagatan.

"Where to?" he asked.

"Södertälje. You've finished work for the day."

Svanberg nodded. Then smiled.

"Welcome back," he said. "You're looking well."


There was no doubt that Greger Tragg's apartment had been gone through with a fine-tooth comb. The visitors were well-trained and had been careful to cover up all traces of their presence, but not even professionals can turn over an apartment without leaving telltale signs. There were no footprints on the hall carpet, but nor was there quite enough dust. The bathroom door had been closed and the cabinet

64

opened. The grid over the kitchen fan had been unscrewed. The screws were worn, but they lacked that yellowish, rancid sheen that can only be caused by innumerable breakfasts of fried bacon. The almost invisible pin left on the bedspread was lying on the floor. The books on the shelves were less dusty than they had been. Inexcusable carelessness, presumably sheer oversight, was the fact that one of the letters was postmarked the day after the newspaper under which it had been placed. Piero Svanberg thought this showed the exact date of the visit.

"Wednesday," he said. "Everything was clean and tidy when I came on Thursday morning."

"Did anyone see you?"

"Only if there was someone with binoculars in one of the houses opposite. I came in the back way. The elevator was empty, so was the hallway. But when I left, the Dane had left his door ajar, like he does when he's expecting the cat."

"The Dane," said Tragg. "We must find out a bit more about him. What did you do then?"

"Went on working."

"They only needed to make a note of your license plates."

"I don't think so," said Svanberg with a grin. "You're not the only one with a spare set of plates. The taxi plates were in the garage where I changed them for the spares. And I'm quite sure I wasn't followed."

"Let's have a late lunch," said Tragg. "We've a lot to talk about, and I'd like to offer you a little job."


The licensed restaurant at the motel, like all other Swedish restaurants, was deserted between three and four. The only waiter on duty had left them in peace after serving the main course, and had turned his attention to a crossword and cigarette in the kitchen. Every ten minutes or so he peered in through the swing door to the dining room. Tragg

65

had ordered a bottle of wine, and explained that they were in no rush.

"It's safer for you if you don't know all the background," said Tragg. "I'm not going to ask you to do anything which is seriously illegal. You can go on driving your taxi, even if we let the meter run without passengers now and then. That can go on expenses."

"Seven hundred a shift. Half to the driver."

"That can't be helped."

"Solvalla?"

"Business as usual."

"What do you want me to do?"

"Be at my disposal," grinned Tragg. "Run errands, be a messenger boy, but above all, keep watch."

"That doesn't sound all that strenuous."

"Don't be too sure. It will take up a lot of your time these next few months. You'll get ten thousand now and another forty when it's all over. I'll look after all your expenses."

"Can you afford it?"

"Yes," said Tragg. "What's more, you'll be worth it."

They raised their glasses and beamed at each other like a father and son who have just sorted out a family affair. They had achieved that rare level of understanding which makes too many explanations unnecessary, even off-putting. Tragg knew full well that all human relationships are fragile, and he knew how to handle young Piero Svanberg in a way which merely strengthened their bond. It was in fact a question of handling him rather than a genuine pact between equals. Tragg was using the young bookmaker and he knew it, but he had no intention of harming him. Svanberg would get his money, and if anything went wrong his punishment would be light.

"I need somewhere to live," said Tragg, "and a telephone that isn't tapped."

A broad grin crept over Svanberg's face. He leaned forward eagerly and his dark eyes shone proudly.

"I knew it," he said. "Caught on immediately. It's logical, isn't it?"

It's always a matter of intelligence, thought Tragg. I mustn't underestimate his brain or his will to act. He's growing up.

Tragg nodded.

"I know a two-room place in Sumpan," Svanberg went on. "On the square. Two guys I know were running a blackjack school there, but the police came down on them. That was about six weeks ago. They got fined five hundred each. That's all. They weren't playing for cash. Just chips. All the furniture's still there. The fuzz confiscated the table. The lads would like the apartment back, but they're lying low until autumn. They're small fry, like me. Trying to make a living. The fact is they were asking about the place, and I checked up the day before yesterday. Vacant possession. They want three month's rent in advance. Six grand. Can we make that?"

Tragg noticed the problem had already become theirs rather than just his own.

"Are they nosy?"

"We're all in the gambling business. We're pals at Solvalla. They're the ones who are benefitting. I can say it's for a chick."

"No," said Tragg, "don't say that. Tell them it's for a customer of yours who wants a pad when he comes to Stockholm. Somebody who's thinking of getting in on the racing game and wants to be left in peace."

"There's a garage in the basement."

"I can't use the car. That's got to disappear, or be put in mothballs."

"Easy. If you're not too worried about the price I can get rid of it for you tomorrow, license plates, log book, and all. The licensing computer will record it as a zero."

"Blackjack's a quiet game. How did the police get on to them?"

"One of the bettors spoke out of turn in a bar. They wouldn't let him in because he was drunk. The next week the fuzz turned up."

"Phone tapped?"

"I can't believe that. They're small fry, not the Mafia." Svanberg thought for a moment. "I might be able to check. A client of mine has some sort of job with the telephone people. He owes me over five thousand now."

"Put the screws on him. I'll give you a list of telephone numbers. Scrub the debt if he does the job properly. Tell him you're in a position to check what he says."

"You're throwing money around."

"True," said Tragg, "but if you want something done you've got to pay for it. Anything can be bought. Apart from friendship. But that assumes you share the goods while you have them."

He opened the little black briefcase Ulrich Langer had given him in Berlin, and counted out sixteen thousand-kronor notes. As he did so, Svanberg diverted his gaze in embarrassment. Tragg thought nostalgically of his own youth. He had been just as loyal, blindly loyal as they say, indifferent to money, reluctant to take it if it seemed to be casting doubt on his loyalty. Part of this youthful blind faith is a determination to ask no questions, to show no curiosity. That was why Piero Svanberg was embarrassed. He had decided to stick to Greger Tragg through thick and thin, and that kind of loyalty means never asking questions.

Svanberg put the money in his wallet after checking it carefully.

"Sixteen," he said. "When do you want to move in?"

"As soon as possible."

"Give me twenty-four hours."

"Let's say five o'clock on Sunday. A.M."

That was agreed.

Suddenly they were no longer alone. Two men with something unmistakably foreign about their clothes, speech, and gestures had come in from the hall. They went up to the bar counter, innocent motel guests, wanting a drink. The waiter, who doubled as barman in the afternoon, was still busy with his crossword in the kitchen. After a minute or two one of the new arrivals grew impatient and slammed the counter with the flat of his hand.

"Amigo! Amigo!" he yelled, urgently, but not as loudly as he might have done, out of consideration for the two diners at the window table.

No one seemed to take any notice. The next time Tragg looked in that direction, he saw that one of the two men had gone round behind the bar and was pointing to the bottles as if to select one. The next moment, they were on their way out at high speed. Svanberg had looked round to see what Tragg was looking at, and they both caught a glimpse of a bulky whiskey bottle one of the foreigners was trying in vain to conceal by holding it alongside his thigh. They were only a few paces short of the exit when a head waiter dressed in black came in from the kitchen. He sized up the situation, glanced over at Tragg as if for confirmation, and rushed back into the kitchen.

A minute or so later Tragg and Svanberg watched through the window as the Spaniards were stopped when they tried to drive away from the parking lot. They failed to understand why the restaurant should suspect them of anything wrong. Instead of ending in an ignominious retreat, the incident was building up to a major affair that could not be settled on the spot.

When Tragg heard the police sirens, he put a few notes on the table and said, "Look after the bill, will you? One witness is enough for a little do like this."

On this occasion, chance had been too long-winded. No one asked about Tragg during the twenty minutes he remained locked up in the gents.

69

# ❧ VI ❧

It is of course possible to maintain that a series of coincidences decided the course of events the next month. Some of them turned out to be highly successful, while others were to have disastrous and even catastrophic consequences for several people.

It was pure chance that the apartment in Sundbyberg was only a stone's throw from the library whose telephone number Angela de Riez had been given. She rang at precisely 2:40 P.M. the first Monday after Tragg's return: the conversation lasted fifteen seconds and gave the all-clear for the next stage. It was also a lucky coincidence that one of Piero Svanberg's clients happened to be a top man at the telephone company with access to the list of tapped phones in Stockholm and district. On the other hand, the fact that this man was in debt with his bookmaker, and could see no alternative to checking the list of twenty numbers provided by Tragg, was self-inflicted. It was also a coincidence that Tore Wattinius' secretary had an attack of migraine that same Monday afternoon Tragg made his first local call from the public phone booth at the library. Wattinius should really have been in

71

London but had been forced to postpone the trip, and for once he answered the phone himself that afternoon; he was the managing director of Intereloc, Inc., which had advanced plans for gaining a foothold in the North African market.

Afterwards, Tragg had good cause to remember with unusual clarity the week he spent in isolation, voluntary but absolute, in the two-roomed apartment on the square in Sundbyberg. Svanberg had turned out to be a masterly organizer. In the thirty-six hours at his disposal he had not only fixed the apartment and sold the car for an acceptable sum, but had also managed to ensure Tragg would want for nothing during the time he lay low in the apartment. The fridge and freezer were crammed full. Four bottles of whiskey and four cases of beer were enough for even a considerable drinker. The color TV was linked to the central antenna, and Svanberg had even remembered Tragg's taste for classical music, providing some of the Brandenburg Concertos and two Mozart symphonies for the stereo. The only thing missing was books, and Tragg often wondered if he should risk a trip across the square, down the subway, and up the other side of the railway line where the library was situated. He resisted the temptation since that would have involved filling in forms and showing some means of identification.

Svanberg had collected Tragg from Södertälje early on Sunday morning. The town was sound asleep, a blizzard was raging, and only the first shift of snowplows was out in the streets. Proudly, he showed Tragg around the newly cleaned apartment, unveiled the stocks of food and drink, and insisted the cost should be deducted from the money he had received for the Volvo. Since there was a race meeting at Solvalla that same afternoon, he stayed for breakfast. He had only two tasks to carry out in the coming week. The list of telephone numbers was to be handed over to the telephone company contact, and collected the following Sunday, duly marked. Svanberg also had to reserve two tickets for the Finland ferry leaving one Tuesday in the beginning of March. Two single cabins. Under no circumstances was he to hang around Tragg's old apartment, nor his new one, and he was not to call or get into any other kind of contact except in a dire emergency.

Svanberg accepted his new instructions without question. The only thing that confused him was the business of delivering the second ferry ticket.

They agreed Svanberg would come back to the apartment the following Sunday, after the Solvalla race meeting.

Even if many coincidences wrecked the carefully laid plans and produced unexpected surprises, some of them negative, it cannot be denied that Tragg had acted sensibly and with foresight. He had chosen to lie low for several reasons. His main concern was to insure that his telephone was not being tapped. He would not be able to negotiate with Intereloc without a telephone. He was also keen to insure whoever had searched his old apartment was in doubt as to whether he had come back to Stockholm, or was still abroad. They knew of course that he had not used his return ticket from Berlin, but they could only guess where he was now. The most logical assumption was that he had been prevailed upon to prolong his stay in Berlin by a week or so. If they remained passive for that long, the time gained would be considerable. Apart from anything else he would be able to make his trip to Finland without awkward difficulties. His decision to go there had been spontaneous and unnecessary, but it was too late to go back on his promise. In any case, the situation demanded a meeting with Marika in order to clarify things.

At best it would be another week or more before he had the bloodhounds after him, signalling the beginning of the cat-and-mouse game even they must realize he intended to play.

Negotiations with Intereloc ought to be completed within a month. In the immediate future he had no intention of putting himself in a position which forced him out into town and gave the watchdogs a chance to spot him. So far they had been content to keep an eye on his old apartment. Svanberg was convinced no one had seen or followed him, but Tragg was not so sure. The open door to the Dane's apartment in the middle of the afternoon was a worrying sign. It only needed a mirror in the hall for a watch to be kept on anyone entering or leaving the neighboring apartment. Tragg knew from his experiences last autumn that Clothilde was a night animal: it would never occur to her to go out in broad daylight.

Tragg had mastered the art of being alone long ago. For him, isolation was a state with positive advantages. Although he might seem inactive, he spent the week studying the situation systematically, and working out all the possible future circumstances. Up to now he had not given the future a thought. He had accepted Langer's suggestion, not on the spur of the moment nor from lack of interest, but because then as now it seemed to be the only solution to what would otherwise be inevitable failure. Now he had time to examine things in detail.

He recognized without a trace of concern that SÄPO—or IB—knew about his contacts with East Berlin. Their suspicions had been confirmed by his latest trip there. They must have been even more sure when he failed to return to his old apartment. Langer had been right when he claimed the Soviet defector knew nothing about activities in Scandinavia, so the Swedish security services must have had their suspicions about Tragg for some time, and introduced the Dane as his watchdog. He had been right about his suspicions six months ago, when the Dane had moved in with the cat as his only companion; Tragg had sensed something was wrong. Nevertheless, he had fallen into the trap. That did not matter much any more, but he ought to have realized before going to Berlin that he was now running the risk of being watched.

It also followed they knew about his routine visits to the Solvalla racetrack, and had put a shadow among the race-goers. Whoever that was had not yet succeeded in finding Tragg's drop-off point. He was forced to work on that assumption. The alternative was the game was up.

They could also have been very cunning and kept watch over him all winter, without him knowing. He found it difficult, very difficult, to believe this was the case. Perhaps they thought it was unnecessary to follow him to Berlin. The big catch would be made in Stockholm. That is where Alex was, and that is where his weakest link would lead them to their prize. Everyone seemed to be aware of Alex's existence now. Langer's warning could only mean that East Berlin was aware of the fact that SÄPO knew.

Tragg had suspected for some time that the East German MfS had a man planted in SÄPO. Was that why Köstner had picked him out for the Algerian job? In that case there was only one explanation. Köstner was counting on SÄPO arresting Tragg, and had no intention of organizing a dramatic rescue. Köstner must be certain that Tragg would remain at liberty until negotiations with the Arabs and Intereloc were finished. SÄPO would then be ready to act, and once Tragg was arrested, Köstner could set about securing his move to the Algerian embassy without hindrance. He was quite right in reckoning on Tragg refusing to betray Alex. Since the Swedish government will not agree to any exchange of spies (and in any case there was hardly a suitable candidate in the Republic to negotiate about) Köstner could in future devote himself to the joys of diplomatic life without the risks that a pensioned-off Tragg in East Berlin would involve. He could also be sure the Swedes would turn a blind eye on the bribes securing an improvement in the Swedish trade balance of over forty million kronor. Of course, Alex would still be a worry, but Tragg thought Köstner had calculated correctly even here.

Alex would renew contact within a year. He was all too dependent on the money.

It is often maintained that anyone working for the intelligence service cannot rely on any kind of loyalty from his superiors, but most always expect to be sacrificed for the cause; it is assumed further that this applies particularly to agents who are not nationals of the country they work for. On the other hand, it is also claimed that no intelligence service had the right to leave its employees in the lurch as that would have an adverse effect on recruitment, and that an agent has the same right to security as any other citizen. As is so often the case, such assertions are both true and false.

Prisons all over the world have their share of people sentenced for real or alleged espionage, but their employers do not lift a finger to help them either before or after their release. It is more difficult to assess how many dead agents have been sacrificed in cold blood, or even intentionally exposed by their masters. Dead men cannot talk. Even so, it is said that the life of an agent is no more dangerous than that of a fighter pilot in peacetime, or a man who has chosen to work in an asbestos factory.

As far as security is concerned, most countries exchange on the quiet people who have got into difficulties and landed in jail. Nearly all of them belong to the category described by the press as "top spies." Occasionally, spies are repatriated in quite remarkable circumstances that are kept secret or hushed up in order to spare the security service involved from the scorn heaped upon them by the press of their own country, which takes such delight in belittling an organization that cannot answer back. In almost all of these cases, there is good reason to suppose the person released imposes a much greater risk on his rescuers than his opponents could ever imagine.

A remarkable trade in human beings has been going on in the two Germanies ever since the fifties. Once a month, a bus load of prisoners is released and sent over to the capitalist world. In return, trucks travel eastward packed with advanced technical or medical goods, not infrequently materials that have been embargoed. Only a small percentage of the bus passengers are western agents. The rest are people who have previously failed in their attempts to flee over the Wall into the West.

The job of an agent differs in many ways from most others. He has no trade union and cannot take part in wage negotiations. Absolute obedience to his employer and complete silence about his working conditions are prerequisites, not only if he is to keep his job but also if he is to avoid punishment. He has no fixed working hours and is generally underpaid. Only rarely does he have an opportunity to fix his own price.

Alex was an exception to this rule, and he was unique in another respect as well. An agent is most often unsure about the identity of his real master. In Alex's case, it was just the opposite. Alex knew who he was selling his information to, but the purchaser had never been able to establish who he was.

All experience suggests that loyalty is something very temporary, and that betrayal is a much more normal quality among humans. Children fail their parents, a man deceives his wife, or vice versa. In such cases the two parties concerned draw a line below which betrayal is acceptable without the relationship suffering. This line usually gets higher as the years go by. The strongest of all emotions—habit—and a certain dependence on one's opposite number mean that increasingly serious betrayals can be tolerated without fear of reprisal.

These general rules, usually grouped under the heading of tolerance and paradoxically given high moral value, do not apply to agents. For them, the merest suspicion of treachery can be fatal. The intelligence services demand absolute loyalty from their employees, but on the other hand they are unusually broadminded when it comes to other human weaknesses condemned as inexcusable by society at large. Sexual perversions, criminal behavior, dependence on alcohol or drugs—all such matters are regarded as the individual's private affair. An agent, whose level of intelligence is always above the average, can allow himself any weakness except one: his loyalty to his master must be unswerving. He may not entertain the slightest hesitation on that score.

All the same, there is probably more treachery in this profession than in any other. The temptations are manifold, but above all else it is the uncertainty of the man in the field about his own role which undermines his self-confidence and resilience. He is trained and skilled in the art of avoiding danger, but all the same he knows he will occasionally have to open a door without knowing if anyone is on the other side. There must never be anyone there. If there is the game is up and he has failed in his calculations. These continual risks must never be allowed to become routine. The door must never be opened in the same way twice. The moment chosen for action must never follow a pattern. Living under such constant tension becomes a habit, it is true, but like all bad habits it gradually wears down the organs that must be in good working order if a breakdown is to be avoided.

Tragg took treachery for granted. Köstner had underestimated Langer's intelligence and his knowledge of what goes on in the upper echelons of the Republic. It was just a case of putting two and two together. Köstner should have realized that when a high-level appointment is made in the Republic—and in all probability the same applies to posts abroad—the details are always common knowledge in certain circles before they become official. Only the candidates themselves never get to hear the gossip. They are summoned to a minister out of the blue, and under a pledge of silence are informed that their names are being put forward in connection with a particular post. The minister is always vague and never names the other candidates. It is considered good man management to keep the candidates on tenterhooks for a while, so that they get the impression that the quality of their work between then and the time the final decision is made will be crucial for their chances. Köstner was after the ambassadorial post in Algiers, and was doubtless prepared to sacrifice Greger Tragg to that end.

While it was quite clear Köstner was plotting treachery, the problem of Angela de Riez was both more complicated and less significant. There was a possibility that Armand had unmasked her and set her up as a double agent. It was also possible that Langer had arranged a mutual exchange of information with the Frenchman and was using Angela de Riez as a go-between. He had seemed unconcerned when Tragg pointed out the changes he had noticed in her. Perhaps Langer was keeping Angela in reserve for a situation like the one which had now arisen. Tragg was not the only one who could claim foresight as a personal characteristic. Angela's task was to pass Langer's messages on to Tragg. Even if the French succeeded in cracking the code and catching on to what was happening, they would never interfere. The most they would do would be to gloat maliciously when it was all over—Arabs, Communists, and Americans being taken for a ride by a Swede with some French assistance. It would be a classic story and help the food to go down at lunches and dinners for years to come. Angela de Riez could no longer be trusted, but she was not a threat.

Tragg was aware that Langer had not put all his cards on the table. This did not worry him. He would even have considered it unwise to do so. Just as he assumed Piero Svanberg would trust him implicitly without wanting to know Tragg's real intentions, and for that very reason could be relied upon to do his job efficiently, Tragg felt he too was better able to act coldly and effectively if he submitted to Langer's guidance for the time being. In war, it is important to distinguish between tactics and strategy. Tragg's job was tactical. It demanded action, courage, and cunning. At the same time he was well aware that a battle can never be won from behind the desk: the decisive action is always in the field. When the crunch came, Langer was completely dependent on Tragg's honesty as the money would be paid to him and not to the German.

Relations between Alex and Greger Tragg had developed over the years into something resembling those between master and servant, as seen through Alex's eyes, at least.

Tragg had built up the image of a harbinger of peace on ideological grounds. Even as a young man he had seen through the criminal greed of the capitalist world and had never fallen for the freedom myth. Not least in his own country, widely regarded as democratic, he had discovered early on how those in power oppressed their fellow citizens in a variety of ways. He was born and bred in the slums, and lost his parents at an early age. As a young man he beat his head black and blue against the outrages and privileges of the ruling classes, which they preserved by slanting the law and imposing disgraceful restrictions on the intake of students to institutions of higher education. He soon became a communist and built a reputation as an intelligent member of the youth section with a bent for organization and writing. The uplifting advances of the Red Army in the closing stages of the war helped to convince him that he should devote himself in future to the cause of world revolution. At the end of the forties he was sent on his first training course as an agent to a school in a village between Rostock and Stralsund. At about the same time, he left the party. Even then he admitted to himself that paranoid traits in his character, urging him on to tension and action, played a significant part in his decision. As time went by he was forced to admit, at first unwillingly but later with bitterness, that there was no difference between

80

the hypocritical despotism in the supposedly Free World in the West, and the repugnant bullying, the absurd distribution of power, and the class differences in the nominally classless society of the Eastern states. The first crack in his hitherto firm conviction was a monstrous portrait of Stalin suspended from red-painted barrage balloons at a youth festival in Warsaw, at the height of the personality cult. It was to be followed by other, deeper wounds. Even so, he never contemplated for a moment abandoning or betraying the tasks he had taken upon himself. Just as one can go on living for a lost cause, one can remain true to a faded vision.

When Tragg first met Alex in the early fifties, the latter had already embarked upon the career which was to lead him to the top of Swedish society. They met by chance. One evening Tragg was persuaded by a friend in a bar to go to a meeting arranged by the Swedish-Iranian Friendship society. It was held in an attic room in the Old Town and proved to be an excuse for about half a dozen students to meet. While swilling down the wine, they had an opportunity to show off their intelligence and knowledge. One of them was later to become a bishop, another a drunken proofreader on a daily newspaper, a third Sweden's first woman president of a court of appeal, a fourth a career diplomat. Tragg felt out of place from the start in this pretentious and malicious bunch of students. He withdrew after a while, and left together with a tall, elegant man who had contributed occasional ironic comments to the rambling debate.

"I'm getting too old for this kind of game," he said with a smile as they went out into the street. "It's acceptable as therapy for an inferiority complex, but that's not something I suffer from."

He was arrogant and condescending, but at the same time charming in a mysterious way. They went to a bar, and had got to know each other within an hour. In fact, they could easily have made a pact that very first evening.

81

Tragg's new friend and, as it turned out, his first valuable contact, was at least his equal in every way when it came to the techniques of espionage. He was extremely careful, and the next time they met he produced a long list of terms to govern any cooperation between them. Tragg accepted without reservation. The most important condition was that the man should always remain anonymous to everyone except Tragg. He called himself Alex.

At first, Berlin accepted the anonymity of their new source of information. His reports were interesting but not yet high-grade. The material he produced would have been available to quite a wide range of Swedish government officals, but there was no need to risk scaring off such a contact. In fact, Alex's future significance could scarcely be overestimated.

After a year Langer wanted to know more. Alex's price began to rise rapidly. At first, he had asked for a few hundred kronor. When he started to demand a thousand kronor for every report, Berlin balked, requiring personal details and full identification. Western currency was—and to some extent still is—a rare luxury for the Republic and the other socialist states. At that time the exchange rate was one Westmark for four Ostmarks, and the Swedish krona was one of Europe's hardest currencies. Alex's demands seemed incredible. If they were met, his yearly salary would exceed the nominal sum paid to a Politbureau member.

Alex's response was all one might have expected of him. He gave Tragg copies of Top Secret documents, minutes kept by the Standing Committee on Foreign Affairs of discussions laying the basis for future Swedish government policy on a divided Germany. The only snag was that they were incomplete. The normally calm and reasonable members of the committee had disagreed violently, and this part of the proceedings was carefully recorded. Unfortunately, the pages referring to the Committee's final decision—formally unanimous—were missing. Alex announced his readiness to supply the missing documents on three conditions. He wanted guarantees from Berlin that they would not seek to identify him, either now or later. He made it clear that he was not prepared to work with any contact man other than Greger Tragg. And finally, he demanded all future payments in advance.

Berlin accepted Alex's ultimatum—albeit with great reluctance. They probably assumed there would be any number of future occasions when they could persuade Tragg how necessary it was to reveal Alex's identity. That was a misjudgement.

One of the reasons for Tragg's stubborn refusal to expose Alex was irrational. Their cooperation had rapidly developed into a mutually unpleasant relationship, comprising both contempt for each other and a certainty that neither would ever again have as good an opportunity for achieving his ends. They were dependent upon each other, and accepted that they had been drawn by fate into a state of symbiosis.

They were completely different. Alex felt himself to be above all ideological considerations. He was genuinely contemptuous of postwar man and his shortsighted dreams of a vegetating, effortless existence. He was scornful of all kinds of collectivism. Democracy or dictatorship, socialism or capitalism, national freedom or international solidarity, faith and honor—he was completely indifferent to all of them. The only important thing was himself. His basic premise was that he was blessed with intelligence exceeding anyone else's. He recognized he would die one of these days, and hence he had decided while still a teenager to fill his life with content benefiting only himself and pandering to his desire for domination. He sought power but scorned political parties, which he regarded as bastions of mediocrity. The power he wanted to exert would have to satisfy himself above all others, by underlining his influence on events. He knew right at the beginning of his career that it would carry him high up the social ladder, but that was still not enough. If he had been content with a position as one of the state's highest servants, he would have regarded it as self-betrayal. That was the only kind of treachery he considered himself capable of.

Alex's way of binding Greger Tragg to himself and protecting his own anonymity was ruthless and calculating. Alex recognized early on that he would have to take a wife for social reasons. Her name was Marika. He found her in left-wing circles in Uppsala. She was a Jewess, rootless and insecure, still shaken by the massacre of her relatives in Germany and Austria and desperate in her search for security, which she imagined could only be achieved by marrying a husband whose position would make it possible to escape the next round of pogroms. She was an easy prey. They married quickly and in great privacy. Within six months she was ready to follow Alex in everything.

Once he had used her several times to pass on material to Greger Tragg, she was completely under his control. He only needed to give her an offhand account of the legal punishment for treason one evening to bring her into line.

"The courts might perhaps take your youth and beauty into consideration," he said ironically. "You might get away with five years. I would certainly get life, no matter what."

Tragg never knew for sure whether Alex had pushed Marika into becoming his mistress. In the beginning their relationship was too nervous and their meetings too short and sporadic for him to confront her with the question. Later, he dared not raise the matter as he was afraid of the answer. Even later, it did not matter any more.

Tragg admitted to himself that he had acted irrationally in refusing to reveal Alex's identity. He also knew he would not hesitate to do so for one second if anything ever happened to Marika. Once she had become Alex's messenger, the two men very rarely met. They both had a hold on each other, and they both knew it. That was why neither of them wanted to be reminded of the bond between them, despite the fact that one of them saw himself as master, without the other accepting his role as dog.

Piero Svanberg rang the doorbell at exactly seven o'clock on Sunday evening. The telephone company manager had carried out his task as requested. When Tragg went through the list he discovered that only one number had been underlined in red. That was the one to his old apartment, outside which Clothilde was now parading her Persian beauty. All the other numbers—apart from one—had been taken from the confidential Red Book. Like his own new number, they belonged to subscribers who preferred not to display their names in the telephone directory.

"We're going to have a lot to do," said Tragg. "I suggest you go home now and get some sleep. Come back tomorrow night at six, but make sure you're not being followed."

# ❧ VII ❧

Tragg stepped out of the elevator that had brought him up from the garage to the reception area at the Sheraton Hotel in Stockholm, and realized immediately that the fresh-skinned man in the gray suit leaning on the porter's desk must be Tore Wattinius. In his youth he might well have been a middleweight boxer. Their eyes met briefly and, questions answered, they both smiled mechanically. The subsequent handshake merely confirmed what they already knew.

"We've got a couple of nice, quiet conference rooms six floors up," said Wattinius once he had introduced himself, and he ushered Tragg toward the elevator which was still standing open.

Neither of them uttered a word on the way up. The elevator stopped on every floor, unloading Poles, Englishmen, or Swedes from the provinces; they all stood huddled together in the confined space, staring straight ahead, with expressions of curiosity, embarrassment, or determination. Tragg and Wattinius were the only ones left by the time they reached the sixth floor. The meeting in the lobby and the journey in the elevator had taken less than a minute. Tragg was satisfied.

Wattinius led the way along one of those hotel corridors that seem to go on for ever. They turned corner after corner and finally came to a door looking exactly like all the other two hundred and seventy-five doors in the hotel. Perhaps it was a mistake on Wattinius' part to go first. Perhaps it was a sign of uncertainty and reluctance. If it was a conscious attempt to give an impression of decisiveness and drive from the very start, it was a doubtful move. Tragg followed a few paces behind and was soon able to sum up the man in front of him. He was walking quite fast, a little too fast for someone supposed to be showing the way. Wattinius strode out with the springy gait of a man accustomed to playing two regular rounds of golf a week, and mowing his own lawns. Only the little bald spot on his crown betrayed the fact that he was approaching his fifties. When they came to the door, he was noticeably short of breath.

Before entering the room, Tragg noted the emergency exit was less than twenty yards away. Presumably it led only to a fire escape, but it doubled his chances of getting away if anything should happen to necessitate a rapid retreat.

The larger room contained a long table and some thirty or so chairs, and was furnished in surprisingly spartan fashion. There was a battery of soft drinks on the table, and in front of some of the chairs were notebooks and pencils. A coffee machine with plastic cups occupied one corner, and beside it were a scribbling pad and some felt pens.

Intereloc was obviously trying to give an impression of puritan efficiency. Most modern American-controlled firms seem to think that that gives them a moral right to justify the millions they make. At the same time it stresses how unaffected and dedicated its officers are. If Tragg had been an Arab rather than a Scandinavian, he would probably have turned and left almost before entering the room. An Arab would have regarded these premises as an insult and refused to discuss a deal involving forty million in such an environment.

But Tragg was a Swede, and felt he had already scored a small success. Intereloc's experience of international commerce was obviously limited.

The small room was dominated by a group of dull-looking easy chairs and a sofa. There was also a TV set and two telephones, each surmounted by a plastic bubble. Tragg took it for granted there were microphones hidden somewhere among these spartan furnishings. It made no difference to him, and he assumed they were under the table.

Two men got up from the long table like overgrown schoolboys, and stepped politely forward. They each greeted him in that forced, formal way that only Scandinavians can achieve, looked him straight in the eye, and muttered their names. There followed an awkward silence.

"Shall we begin?" Tragg did not expect an answer but sat down behind one of the notebooks and placed his black briefcase on the table in front of him.

"My name is Greger Tragg and I've been asked by good friends in Algiers to make contact with you."

He waited for the others to sit down facing him. Then he took several plastic folders out of his briefcase.

"Unfortunately, I don't have a card, but I trust you gentlemen will accept my references," he went on in friendly fashion.

"Of course!" said the youngest of the men quickly. His smile was unforced. He, Lars Bunter, Intereloc, Inc., second section, director, was in the heavyweight class, but did not appear overweight.

Tragg noticed an almost unnoticeable stammer which reinforced the boyish impression.

"My contacts with Algeria go back to the time before the war of liberation," explained Tragg with a straight face. "They were intimate even then, and have continued on that basis ever since. My friends have now obtained positions of great influence in the state."

He observed the three men. Wattinius was watching him coolly and austerely, but he looked somewhat weary and Tragg was still not sure whether his veiled gaze was genuine or an act. He was more sure about Lars Bunter, whose lively, curious expression indicated that he was ready to consider any proposal. The third man had introduced himself as Fredrik Johnson, sales manager. He was listening avuncularly and nodding jovially, but his hands motionless in his lap reminded Tragg of a poker player.

"The greatest possible influence." Tragg emphasized his point. "This kind of negotiation demands extreme secrecy," he warned them. "The slightest leak could ruin the whole thing."

No one spoke. Lars Bunter lit a cigarette, the first man to start smoking.

"I think I can convince you that my proposals are genuine," said Tragg, handing Wattinius a photocopy. It was a copy of the letter accompanying the tender for forty million kronor. "I take it that is your signature."

Wattinius took the photocopy and stared hard at it. A slight flush began to spread over his throat. "I can't deny that," he said. He looked slightly worried, as if reluctant to accept the proof.

Tragg took out more documents. "I think you'll find the key parts of your tender are among these papers."

"Damn right they are," exclaimed Bunter, convinced.

In a couple of seconds he had established that the photocopies were identical with the ones in his own safe. He paused over the pages containing the financial details. His watchful eyes, indeed his whole body indicated he was all set for a fight. This kind of thing was right up his street.

There was one other document, a scrap of paper torn off a cheap note-pad and containing a dozen scribbled words.

"Your rivals," said Tragg. "Germans, Americans, Englishmen, Japanese, the French of course, and a lone Spaniard."

Johnson felt obliged to get up, walk around the table and, peering over Wattinius' shoulder, attempt to decipher the scribbled names.

"They're all there," said Bunter with a sigh.

"This will be the biggest investment of its kind ever made in Algeria," Tragg went on. "Whoever wins the contract can count on further orders over the six years of the plan. It will be a kind of monopoly, since all these international enterprises have different systems."

They listened eagerly.

"If I didn't think we could reach an agreement, then of course I wouldn't be sitting here now. As far as the money's concerned, you are about in the middle."

"We pitched our bid very low." Wattinius turned to Bunter for support.

"It's our policy to work on a fixed price basis. In the long run it's the only way of doing business." Bunter did not sound convincing and Tragg ignored the remark, looking down the table with a smile.

"Officially, these tenders won't be opened for another five weeks," said Tragg. "The whole thing will be supervised by people from the Chamber of Trade."

Tragg left it at that. It was now up to the Intereloc directors to decide if they were prepared to break the law of the land and enter into a contract involving corruption.

"How did they manage to reseal the envelope?" asked Johnson.

"I've no idea," lied Tragg. "Does it matter?"

"Of course not." Bunter sounded irritated.

"You need special skills for that kind of trick, old man," persisted Johnson. "Someone you're acting for must be an expert."

He was the first one to use an intimate term of address.

"My masters and the purchasers are one and the same," said Tragg.

Johnson nodded. "The purchasers, yes."

Wattinius broke the silence by clearing his throat.

"We are businessmen, not moralists," he said. "We are open to all reasonable proposals and I see no reason to probe into the actions of a prospective customer as long as they don't work to our disadvantage."

Fredrik Johnson shrugged his shoulders and clasped his hands once more. "Did you take part in the war?" he asked.

"In a way," replied Tragg. "There are many ways of fighting a war."

Johnson nodded again. "That's very true," he said.

The subsequent silence was broken by Lars Bunter. He was interested in the bottom line, and forty million was equal to a fifth of Intereloc's annual turnover.

"You mentioned our price," he said.

"Under certain conditions that need not be an insuperable obstacle."

"What conditions?"

To his surprise, Tragg noticed that his right leg had started to shake. He pushed his chair back carefully and crossed his legs so as to rest his right one against the table. It helped.

"I can offer you advantages and benefits that are unique in the Algerian market," he said. "For instance, I can guarantee that discussions on the contract will be completed within twenty-four hours. There need be no haggling over the price."

"We proposed commercial credit as the method of payment in our bid," said Bunter.

"That is acceptable. As far as I know, commercial credit of that order has never been given in Algiers before. It's up to you whether or not you score a first."

It was the duty of Tore Wattinius, in his capacity as managing director, to put the crucial question.

"You still haven't told us the conditions."

"Sixteen per cent," replied Tragg. His voice sounded a little weaker than intended, but no one seemed to notice.

Wattinius stared at him with a mixture of anger and confusion. He got up and walked towards the door, three, four, five strides. Then he stopped and turned. it was too soon. It was a bad move, melodramatic. Tragg put his right leg down. It had stopped shaking.

"Sixteen per cent," echoed Wattinius, stretching out his arms. "I can never allow the firm to accept a loss of that magnitude."

Tragg observed him calmly. He had no intention of saying anything. Wattinius avoided his gaze and turned instead to Lars Bunter. Both shook their heads. Even so, Tragg knew they had swallowed the bait.

Bunter cleared his throat, and the slight stutter was very much there as he asked, "Is that your last word?"

"I have my instructions," replied Tragg.

"Then you must come and have dinner with me," said Bunter cheerfully. "Have you any objections to the hotel restaurant?"

Tragg could not think of a single good reason for refusing. He took his leave of Tore Wattinius and Fredrik Johnson. The bargaining could commence.

# ❧ VIII ❧

Piero Svanberg thought he was beginning to catch on. He had been waiting in his taxi in the Sheraton Hotel garage when Tragg came down with new instructions.

"Go and change the license plates, then come back. You have an hour and a half to fill in. Sit in the bar and wait. When you see me leave the dining room, go get the car and pick me up at the exit."

"Will it be a quick getaway?"

"We don't want any flying starts. Cool, calm, and collected, as befits a Stockholm taxi."

Tragg went back up in the elevator. He had not been followed.

Svanberg was not lacking in normal human curiosity. There had been plenty of time to think this last week, and he realized Tragg was involved in something big. That appealed to him. Greger Tragg was not a small-timer like himself. The ten thousand he had already received and the forty thousand he had been promised were proof enough of that. Big jobs are always dangerous, and Tragg's meticulous care since coming back had confirmed that people were out to stop him.

Probably the law. Svanberg was used to breaking the law and had no great respect for its representatives. Although they went around in jeans and skiing jackets nowadays, and sometimes had beards, he never had any difficulty in seeing through their disguises.

It was not drugs. Svanberg was quite sure about that. Tragg was not the type. He was too unassuming. Drug pushers, whores, and their pimps live in the same world as bookmakers and casino proprietors, and the really big boys have a finger in all three pies. Svanberg had never come across a significant figure in this context who was not greedy and constantly on the hunt after big money in order to buy himself the luxuries of this world. That was what they were all after. Smart houses and cars, bars and in places, broads, jewels, luxury suites in Bangkok or Miami Beach, a month in Las Vegas or Travemünde. Their constant dream, day and night, was to acquire everything expensive and intended for the exclusive few, the established rich. The most successful of them had started to build up financial empires or real estate chains. But they always remained what they had always been: drug pushers, pimps, and gamblers.

Tragg was just the reverse. He lived modestly and quietly. Maybe he did keep society at arm's length while still living in it, like Svanberg himself, but he did it consciously and not just for money. He had principles, but he kept them to himself. One evening, during that period Svanberg called his university days, they had got on to politics. They had seen the TV news and some well-known Swedes had been interviewed.

"They're all bought," Tragg had said.

"All of them?"

"The whole bunch."

"Who's bought them?"

"Themselves," Tragg had replied. He did not sound as if he were joking. "That's what's so special about it. They've used the law. The social system. Ideology. The whole setup is

96

based on buying and selling. The most valuable thing one can sell is oneself."

"Nobody wants to buy me."

"Don't be too sure of that. You're much too ambitious to slip through the net."

Svanberg did not feel he had been bought by Tragg. He would have done his bidding for nothing at all, or at least, for a much smaller payment. It was Tragg himself who had set the price. It was high, and he intended to give value for money. The future would tell if it had been worth the risk. So far it had mostly been fun.

The simplest but the most surprising part of what Tragg had asked him to do had given him a key to what he was trying to puzzle out. Svanberg followed his instructions to the letter when he handed over the Finland ticket to the girl at the Tote (the betting shop) counter at Solvalla racetrack. Girl? Lady was the word that came immediately to mind, even if it felt unusual coming from him. One does not normally think of the staff at the windows as people, but rather as part of the machine they are employed to look after. This lady had made a big impression on him. There was class written all over her, as one might expect of a friend of Greger Tragg's.

Svanberg waited until the sixth race had started before going up the back stairs leading to the owners' room. There was a door there used by the boys who put up the results lists, and by other officials. The door was usually unlocked for convenience, and in fact it was standing open, just as Tragg had said. No one paid any attention to him: the place was almost empty and those that were there were busy watching the race on TV. He passed his twenty-kronor slip over the counter and she took it without even looking at him, counting out his winnings indifferently. Meanwhile, he took the envelope with the ticket out of his pocket and leaned it against the window.

"The boat goes on Tuesday," he said, switching on his Sicilian smile.

She was frightened even so. He saw it first in her eyes. It was a sudden onset of fear, like a stab in the chest. For a split second the world stood still. He could see how she clenched her fists so hard that her veins threatened to burst behind her blanched knuckles. She recovered rapidly and put away the envelope so naturally and definitively that for a moment he wondered if it had ever been there. She did not say a word, but as he was still there she went on looking at him. Fear gave way to surprise. Eventually she smiled and shook her head in reproach. He bowed slightly, and it seemed the natural thing to do.

"Have a nice trip," he said, and left the same way as he had come in. As he reached the bottom of the stairs, he could hear the crescendo of sound indicating that the horses were swinging round into the final straight.

Of course, there was nothing strange about Tragg having a woman. Nevertheless, Svanberg had been caught off his guard. He had never thought of him in that way before. Svanberg's own girls were more casual. Some had been keener on going out with him than he with them. They had soon lost interest. As yet, women were an expendable commodity in his world. Most of the ones he went with worked at casinos. He sometimes took the odd one home.

There are lots of theories about gamblers. One is that their sexual appetite is below average. That is a doubtful premise. On the other hand, their ability to fit into normal family life or enter into a steady relationship is limited. Gambling, whether it be roulette, cards, or horse racing, is at its height on weekends, and nearly always takes place in the evenings or at night. A professional gambler does almost as much traveling as a member of parliament, and the only evening one can be certain of finding him at home is Christmas Eve. A gambler's responsibility for incidental expenses must always be kept to a minimum, since his stake must always come first. Before food and clothes, before pleasure, and in an emergency even before the rent. The only direct advantage of this form of existence is that a gambler rarely has tax problems.

The number of women who can feel at home in a relationship with a man who has chosen that kind of life is severely restricted. They are much sought after, and treated with great respect. The woman is usually responsible for the rent, buying food, paying phone and electricity bills, and looking after all the other costs. She is at work when the man is catching up on sleep during the day, and when she gets home he has usually left already. There is generally a definite agreement between them that neither will make demands on the other. Income is clearly divided, and the woman never finances any gambling. Her reward is a share in those intoxicating days when a killing has been made—a lucky streak, or a bet that has paid out in at least five figures. Gifts, holidays, everything is possible when that happens. Both partners in such relationships tend to be unusually faithful.

The lady at the Tote counter was not only Greger Tragg's woman. She was also his accomplice. Svanberg was sure of that. She also knew more about Tragg's plans than Svanberg, but he did not consider himself slighted. Tragg had said it was better not to know too much, and that he would not be asked to do anything seriously illegal. So far he had not needed to step outside the law, no more than usual, that is.

Svanberg was almost sure that Tragg was selling secrets, or was about to do so, and that he had started negotiating with the purchaser. That would explain why his apartment had been searched and his telephone tapped. Svanberg had read about industrial espionage in a men's magazine; how firms were prepared to pay practically anything to get hold of their rivals' secrets. Tragg was a technical journalist and knew about such things. That was how he had got on to something big, and now he had found a buyer. Svanberg did not intend to raise the matter with Tragg, but he aimed to do all he could to fulfill his side of the bargain. The only thing he did not really understand was how the woman at Solvalla fit in.


The roulette croupier at the Sheraton Hotel greeted Piero Svanberg with a nod. This was where the casinos picked up their clients. Small-time gamblers were left alone, but keen-looking foreigners with fat wallets were usually approached as the evening wore on and asked discreetly if they were interested in a more serious game played according to international rules. The Sheraton croupier worked two nights a week at a backstreet casino in Arbetaregatan, and sometimes escorted potential clients there. He was recognized as one of the best croupiers in Stockholm.

Svanberg bought a few chips out of politeness. He still had half an hour to kill. It was early yet, and things had not gotten into full swing. They soon found themelves alone at the table.

"Are you out slumming?" asked the croupier with a grin.

"A change is as good as a rest."

"Quite right. The food down in the Sheriff room is not too bad as long as you avoid the special."

"I'd thought of having a drink."

"Expensive. But the bar pianist is pretty good. Straight from Harlem."

"What about skirts?"

"Forget it. There's a bald guy in a black suit sitting in the reception entrance. House fuzz. Since they tightened up the law you can't even send a postcard to the chick opposite. Pick-ups are out."

"A drink, then. Jazz. I like jazz."

"Sit near the piano. There are a few bar stools there. The music's first-class and the broad seems hungry. She's been all on her ownsome for nearly a fortnight now."

100

"You mean. . . ."

"A sure thing. If you don't mind 'em black."

"I'm a bit of a mulatto myself."

The croupier grinned.

"Switch on that spaghetti charm of yours. Then you're all set up. If you can manage to sit that long."

"You have to play 'em before you strike."

"Too true."

Svanberg had staked his chips on the same triple number every time. He noticed the croupier was doing his best to help, and he appreciated the gesture. He had not managed it yet. "You seem to know a lot about this place."

"Part of the furniture, as you know. Been here nearly three years now."

"What if a guy needed a bit of inside information about somebody here?"

"Staff or customer?"

"Customer."

"Within reason, yes."

"There'd be bread in it, of course."

"I didn't know you were in that line of business."

"I'm not. I'm just an errand boy." Svanberg smiled.

"As usual."

This time the ball fell into the right hole. Svanberg let his stake ride. Right again. A new arrival looking like a provincial businessman had covered all the last dozen numbers. He sighed.

"Fluke."

The croupier exchanged Svanberg's chips for bigger ones.

"You can cash in at reception," he said with a wink. "That should be enough for a drink or two."

They were on the same wavelength.

Svanberg was content. You could never tell what Tragg might want to know about the place where he had started negotiating. It sometimes paid to look ahead.

. . .

The bald security man was drinking Coca-Cola. The pianist had not arrived yet, and Piero Svanberg was the only one near the piano. He had a good view of the room from there, and took a look around; the lighting was dimmed, but good enough for observing people. The imitation leather furniture, deep sofas and armchairs, was arranged singly and in groups behind long, shiny black tables. The wall-to-wall carpet was half an inch thick and seemed to suck up the subdued buzz of noise. In the middle of the room was an electric open fire whose silent, artificial flames were held back by wrought iron and plastic glass. Everything was simulated, a mixture of European and American decor, but not without a touch of artistic quality. It was an "in" atmosphere designed to put off anyone who felt he did not belong. All who came in, men or women, behaved in exactly the same way. They descended the steps down from the lobby with an air of offhand indifference, and it was clear they expected to meet only people of their own kind in this bar.

Svanberg was served by a discreet, uniformed waitress who first addressed him as "sir" but then chatted familiarly in Swedish. It was and hour and twenty-five minutes since he had seen Tragg in the garage.

The pianist was darker than he had expected. She moved with self-confident, practiced elegance. Before adjusting her long, stylish, printed gown and sitting down at the piano, she curtseyed modestly to the audience.

Svanberg gave her a wink. She noticed his dazzling Italian smile, and her big brown eyes lit up with curiosity. When she placed her long, sensitive fingers on the keyboard and began to pick out a tune, he nodded encouragement and listened attentively. She was an excellent pianist with warmth and brilliance, and her confident technique never went over the top into bravura.

Svanberg was the only one to applaud her first number.

102

She acknowledged his enthusiasm and said something to him in English.

"I like music," said Svanberg.

She responded with a flood of words he did not understand.

"I don't speak English," he said, blushing.

She pouted and looked at him with her big, damp eyes. Then she moved her lips and eyebrows in an expression which seemed to indicate that did not matter.

"I like you," she said, leaning over toward him.

He was nonplussed, and she saw that. She was touched. Perhaps she found that attractive.

A man appeared at Svanberg's shoulder and began to address her in a brash American accent. Svanberg could not understand what she said, but he noticed her stiffen. The American's voice sounded superior and condescending. She seemed to resist him at first, but when he raised his voice, becoming arrogant and argumentative, she gave in with an impersonal professional smile and a brief nod. She shrugged and winked knowingly at Svanberg as she started playing again.

Svanberg had not been studying the bar guests with any great enthusiasm, but the American's brusque behavior annoyed him at the same time as the interruption rescued him from awkward embarrassment and brought him back down to earth. He was sitting here in the bar because he had a job to do. He needed to be on his guard. If he had understood Tragg rightly, there could soon be ugly developments. He could not allow the girl at the piano to cloud his judgment.

The American had gone back to his table. He had been sitting in the same place when Svanberg came in, exchanging an occasional word with an elderly man opposite who looked like a traveling salesman. They were obviously together, despite the plinth of flowers separating them.

Alarm bells rang, and it dawned on Svanberg that the American might well be a police officer. He was tall, fit, and his eyes were never still behind his steel-gray glasses. He radiated cool calm and calculating brutality. Only his clothing jarred. The suit was too expensive for a policeman. It was the kind of five-hundred-dollar style managing directors and drug pushers usually buy when they visit London or Zurich.

The pianist was just finishing the medley of American standards she had been ordered to play when Tragg entered the bar. He was preceded by a young giant Svanberg had never seen before. The elderly man at the American's table rose to his feet and waved. Tragg and his companion paused; Svanberg could see that Tragg was refusing an invitation to join the group, and taking his leave instead. Svanberg had expected the traveling salesman to introduce the American to Tragg, but Tragg seemed to be intent only on making it clear that he had no intention of staying. The conversation ended with Tragg leaving the bar.

"I must go," said Svanberg, leaning over the piano. "I come back. I must go."

She was surprised and disappointed.

"Tonight?"

"No." He was searching for words in English. "Tomorrow. I come tomorrow."

He paused, wondering how he could convince her. Then he crossed his fingers and held them up in the air with an entreating gesture. He looked very serious, but she smiled back at him and started to giggle. She was old enough to know young men sometimes need a night in order to realize that an opportunity rarely repeats itself.

Svanberg rounded the piano in time to see the American rush out of the bar. He was wearing his overcoat, which he must have had behind his chair. His companions had turned to stare out through the glass doors at the lobby, where they and Svanberg could see Tragg disappearing through the swinging doors. Fifteen seconds later, the doorman in the admiral's uniform was saluting the American, who went the same way that Tragg had gone shortly before.

· · ·

The taxi came to a halt at the hotel exit to the rear of the building, and Tragg climbed unhurriedly into the back seat. Svanberg had changed his jacket and put on his official cap. They turned smoothly in the direction of Tegelbacken, and without asking, Svanberg moved into the Kungsholman lane.

"We've got company," he said.

"Yes," said Tragg. "He nearly fell over me when I stopped for a moment in the Tysta Mari passage."

They cruised past the city hall at normal speed, and proceeded toward Norr Mälarstrand. There was not much traffic about, but a little further along they were held up by a red light. When they came to Fridhemsplan, Svanberg took the Södermalm lane, still without asking. As they crossed the Västerbron bridge, he took another look in the mirror.

"The company's still with us," he said. "A Toyota."

"Let's find out who's being curious," said Tragg.

They stopped at another red light near Hornsplan, and the Toyota had no choice but to close up behind them. The street lighting is unusually strong just there, and Svanberg was sure he could make out the man in the steel-gray glasses in the passenger seat.

"It's the American." He was sure of it.

"What American?"

"Shall I explain now, or shake him off first?"

"We've got the whole night for telling fairytales."

Nothing is as difficult to keep track of as a taxi with a driver who knows his city. It is almost impossible to follow an experienced taxi driver even if you are right on his tail, and a hopeless task if you do not want him to know he is being followed. Svanberg had never needed to show off his knowledge of the backstreets and one-way systems in Älvsjö. No sooner had they reached the traffic circle just before the exhibition center than the shadow was in doubt as to whether he was heading for Stureby, Örby or Hökarängen. They gave

105

up and went back to the city center. There was no question of not being able to match their quarry for speed; they had simply lost them when Svanberg doubled back on his tracks.

Tragg stayed in the taxi while Svanberg called in at the garage in Hallonbergen to change license plates. They ordered another cab over the radio, then had a couple of whiskeys in the apartment on the square while Svanberg reported. Tragg listened attentively all the while, and showed his approval in several ways. He said nothing about what had happened to him at the Sheraton Hotel, but Svanberg assumed from his relaxed attitude that everything was going according to plan.

"Things could have been worse," said Tragg. "This American is obviously a kind of policeman, and it's good to know he's there. He's no danger at the moment."

"Shall I have him checked up?"

Tragg hesitated. "Can you trust the croupier?"

"He delivers, and he's eager to hang on to his job. Both jobs—the one at the Sheraton and the other in Arbetare-gatan."

"Can he keep his mouth shut?"

"He earns at least a grand per week in tips. Net. Nobody in his field can afford a reputation for being unreliable."

"Find out what the American's called and who pays his bills. It would also be interesting to know if he's in touch with the Swedish police."

"Excellent. That's just the kind of task Johnny's expecting me to give him."

Svanberg stayed in Tragg's flat that night, since his services were needed early the next day. He too was pleased with the way things had gone. The only thing he hadn't reported was his conversation with the dark-skinned pianist. He fell asleep with her image imprinted on his retina. The next night he would be back in the Sheraton bar. He had his orders.

# ❧ IX ❧

The March sun was shining brightly, and the biggest news item from Stockholm was that the average temperature over the past twenty-four hours had climbed above zero for the first time this year. The evening papers leaned over backwards to suggest that spring was on the way. They had been informed of a crocus blooming in Årsta (in fact it had been forced indoors before being planted outdoors surreptitiously by the owner). Several bunches of aconites had been brought to the editorial offices by eager schoolgirls: they were genuine as that particular flower will not grow at indoor temperatures. A birdwatcher in Järfälla insisted he had heard the first thrush singing, but photographers sent to investigate could only report that the bird had been overcome by inexplicable shyness and refused to appear for pictures.

Not a single news item from Stockholm was reported abroad. The wire service boys huddled round their beer glasses and felt as if they had been deported. Alongside Outer Mongolia, Sweden became the most obscure place on earth. Although the thaw had set in, it was as if the country had entered a new ice age.

107

Just as in Ulan Bator, this image (or absence of an image) was an illusion. Life in Stockholm went on just as hectically as usual, and many citizens would go to bed that night with consciences just as bad as they had ever been. What the snow hides comes to light in the thaw, and even if the first attack of spring was beaten back, the snow would soon melt away, revealing all the rotten decay in its full hideousness.

Although they certainly knew about it, most news correspondents ignored the reception given by the Soviet Embassy in Stockholm that evening, in memory of the day the starving workers of Petrograd had taken up arms sixty years previously. More than five hundred people, most of them with invitations but some gatecrashers, would attend the party. Some of the guests were really important. Top of the list was the Foreign Minister and the Defense Minister, the latter a well-known communist-eater. The Lord Chamberlain and the Chief of Staff, together with the heads of all the armed forces, would be there. Our big neighbor in the East cannot bear to be ignored. Among all the commercial giants, leading politicians, industrial leaders, editors-in-chief, and prominent or merely thirsty members of the local Communist Party was also the man whom only a few knew by his cover-name of Alex, although there were many who wanted to meet him. He was very high on the guest list produced by the embassy secretary.

No editor saw anything newsworthy in the fact that the ferry to Helsinki left from the Stadsgården quay on time. The number of passengers was surprisingly low, that is true, but not abnormally so for the time of year. The ice had started to drift on the Finnish side, but was considered perfectly safe for the reinforced ferriers. The icebreakers Ymer and Atle were up in the Åland Straits.

The Stockholm gossip reporters had taken the evening off, claiming nothing of interest was going on. They never covered embassy parties on principle, not even Russian ones.

It did not occur to anyone covering entertainment to go to the Sheraton Hotel bar and hear a piano virtuoso from Harlem conjuring forth melodies with an ease and accomplishment well worth a picture and a line or two among their notes on local personalities. Still less would they have paid any attention to a twenty-five-year-old Swede with a dazzling Italian smile and black, curly hair. Most of the evening he sat faithfully by the piano behind a glass. For one more month he would be just another member of the anonymous gray masses. Come April, he would be reassessed and his face would feature on the first page of most newspapers.

A keen crime reporter should perhaps have tried to get an interview with Bengt List, the head of SÄPO's security section, who had hitherto consistently refused to answer questions. Such a reporter would have found him at the Soviet Embassy party, to which he had gone with grave misgivings. List never went to such parties as a rule, although he was always invited because of his leading position in the police force; but he had no desire to go home and carry on the row he had had with his wife that morning. Over the last few months she had developed into a rabid women's lib supporter. For the same reason, he would find himself taking a drink in the Sheraton bar, where he was destined to stay much longer than he had planned. List was a musical person who thought good music facilitated good thinking. The most acute problem he had to solve was whether or not to start divorce proceedings.

On the other hand it would have been quite unreasonable to expect any Stockholmer, journalist or not, to know about the intimate gathering over coffee attended by four gentlemen in Algiers. They were discussing a message they had received that afternoon; it had originated from a public telephone booth outside the cloakroom at the public library in Sundbyberg. In written form and translated into German, it had lain hidden behind a loose plank in a shed in West Berlin. The place was swarming with wild cats, and it was collected at about the same time as a young French decoding expert fed the text somewhat reluctantly into his machine. He was assisted by an expert in the Swedish language who had been called in on short notice.

The message was carried without incident on the municipal railway through the Wall, for which Walter Ulbricht will be remembered in history. A few dozen sharp-eyed policemen had watched impassively as a simply dressed old woman with trembling hands and a West German passport announced her intention of visiting relatives in East Berlin. The message had been decoded there once again and eventually appeared in readable form on Ulrich Langer's desk at home. He held on to it overnight since it contained nothing requiring immediate action. His first task next morning was to hand it over in person to Lutz Köstner.

At about the same time, the Swedish expert and the young Frenchman went to see the latter's boss and told him that either the code was insoluble, which went against all previous experience, or that the message was not in code at all; in either case, it was incomprehensible.

Lutz Köstner had no such problems but reacted positively by sending immediate instructions to an East Berlin firm, ordering them to telex an export organization in Algiers. The message now looked the same as thousands of other telexes between businessmen the world over, and concerned the pricing of goods for sale.

In its original form the message had said: *Both geegees alert. Don't get the odds.*

After lively discussions the four gentlemen in Algiers agreed to reduce their demand by twenty-five per cent. They saw this as a conciliatory gesture and thought it would confirm their readiness to keep on talking. In order to cover all options, they also decided that the most junior among them should be provided with a passport and valid exit visa so that, if circumstances required, he could fly immediately to Copenhagen and from there take a train to Stockholm. The passport was produced the same day and could never be proved false since it was obtained originally in accordance with the law and contained all the correct stamps and signatures. Only the bearer's name was changed beyond recognition.

Tragg was aware that he was sitting on a gunpowder barrel. As long as he himself was not blown up, he could only feel sorry for the victims. Statistically, they were just as inevitable as the predicted number of annual traffic deaths. Even in a profession where death must be taken into account as an unavoidable factor, proximity to the victim is bound to take its toll.

Tragg never received most of the information he needed in order to predict what was going to happen next. Planning and lines of communication were deficient in many respects. Instead, he was forced to work on the basis of hypotheses, especially when it came to the intentions and actions of the opposition. The problem was his opponents could be regarded as both friend and enemy, and in the face of all logic they were prepared to enter into unholy alliances.

Most people live the whole of their adult lives in the roles they have fashioned for themselves, generally a chameleon-like role for the outside world, a static one for the family circle, and a diffuse, secret role exclusively for themselves. An agent cannot afford a profile of his own, but if he wants to avoid discovery has to tolerate his own deficiencies and try to put up with the dull image of himself as seen by others. In public he plays his roles as consciously as an actor, and always keeps his audience at arm's length. Tragg was an effective negotiator in his contacts with Intereloc, an idol and undisputed leader for Piero Svanberg, a shadow to the Swedish police, a useful dossier to Lutz Köstner, and a tool for the gentlemen in Algiers.

Tragg was on board the Finland ferry, which had got about as far as Hangö. For the first time in ages he was not

111

alone in bed, but shared it with a woman. That evening she ought to have been accompanying her husband to the reception at the Soviet Embassy in Stockholm. She had decided to be completely honest during the trip, and expected Tragg to be just as intimate and uninhibited in return. This was another role Tragg was quite capable of playing, without discord and without raising doubts about his loyalty.

# ❧ X ❧

Fifty years ago he would have worn his uniform and represented his country in appropriate style. The Russians, to whose embassy in Stockholm he was on his way, have nothing against uniforms. On the contrary. They like medals, too. Their great men and women are proud of their medals. Was not Leonid Brezhnev made a Hero of the Soviet Union three times? Or was it four?

He tried a comparison. Hero of Sweden. Hero of the Kingdom of Sweden. Order of the North Star. Order of Vasa. No. It did not work. The first time he had been offered a Swedish medal, he had refused. On principle, as he put it. The Social Democratic government of the day approved of such gestures, and he was sure it had helped him to gain a promotion. The offer had never been repeated, but in fact he did not mind being without medals. He would have had to wear them on his uniform; they would look ridiculous on a dinner jacket—and simply stupid on a dark suit.

The taxi should be here any moment. He took a last look at himself in the hall mirror. He was tall, elegant, and still full of energy. He looked like the man he was: important, influential, one of the few with real power, a pillar of society. He was happy with what he saw, but at the same time anger smoldered within him. She should have been here as well, his wife, standing at his side, admiring him, supporting him. She had refused. She had refused to bow to his will, and he could not or dared not force her to submit.

"My life is at stake as well," she had said. "Not just yours. We must find out what he knows."

He had produced several reasonable arguments. They could not afford to be seen together. Perhaps Tragg was being followed by the police. She was exposing them both to unnecessary risks. If the situation was as serious as they suspected, there was only one thing to do: break off the relationship.

She had listened to him, but would not change her mind. He had eventually grown furious, and yelled, "It's an order! Do as I say!"

To his surprise, she had stood up and stared at him in a way denoting both resolve and courage. Her eyes had a look suggesting pity, and more instinctively than consciously he realized he could push her no further. She had shaken her head and walked away. She turned in the doorway.

"You have no authority to give me counter orders. It's me he's summoned, not you."

They had avoided each other all evening, and the matter had not been raised again. The next morning she left before he got up.

The taxi driver saluted as he opened the car door. His passenger was familiar from TV and the newspapers: not loved, but respected. Everybody accorded him the significance he strived for. In the rear mirror, he looked just like his pictures. Strong, arrogant, and possessing the superior self-confidence and reliability which led the leader-writers to describe him as a pillar of Swedish society, a fearless, imperturbably consistent wielder of power whose strictness

114

and resolution would be an invaluable asset in the times of severe crisis that lay ahead.

Nothing could be more off the mark. The man in the back seat was frightened and desperate. All the way to the embassy he sat there repeating to himself the same name, over and over again: Tragg, Tragg, Tragg. . . .

He cursed him. He was being inconsistent and illogical. The risk of exposure could no longer be ignored. They ought to cooperate, meet, put aside all feelings of personal dislike and set about reinforcing the invisible barricade around them which no one must be allowed to penetrate. But hate feeds on other emotions. Alex was in the grip of his own pride. He had conquered everyone, everybody but this one man. Things had now gone so far that he regarded Greger Tragg as an enemy rather than an ally.


The embassy gates were wide open. Anybody could get in. No one asked to see the invitations, although most people apart from official Swedish guests had them with them. Who had not heard about the suspicious nature of the Russians?

Alex did not know who was really in charge at the Stockholm embassy. It could hardly be the ambassador himself, an old veteran of the Revolution who had been prominent in the early days but managed to survive even so. It could be one of the cloakroom attendants, the chief counsellor, or the man behind the bar. The real power could lie anywhere. Perhaps the man wielding it was not even at the party, but preferred to chat to the array of government and diplomatic chauffeurs guarding their limousines in the courtyard: on these occasions they all loved to gossip and exchange stories about their superiors. The man with the power was sometimes in uniform, a military attaché perhaps; or he might be a third secretary. Whatever his role, he was number one at the embassy, feared by all but unknown to most of the staff.

Like a good democrat, Sweden's Foreign Minister was standing in the line parading before the Ambassador, who shook hands enthusiastically with each guest. He spoke to all of them, the same incomprehensible Russian phrase, and pointed them in the direction of the cold buffet on a thirty-yard-long table in the middle of the room. When the Ambassador had his attention drawn to the Swedish VIP, he immediately ordered his First Counsellor to take over. Ignoring everybody else, he raced over to the minister, the interpreter trotting behind him, in order to rescue his important guest from the awkward situation he had landed in, against all Russian protocol. The mere thought that the man in glasses over there was the counterpart of his own Andrei Gromyko put him in a state of shock.

The minister allowed himself to be plucked out of the line with dignity, but could not help noticing a certain consternation on the part of his host. There was something behind him which seemed to be causing embarrassment. The minister turned and caught sight of the man known to a few as Alex four places back. With the boyishness for which he was renowned, he flung up his right arm in greeting and shouted:

"Hello, old man! Are you here as well?"

The Ambassador had no choice but to relieve Alex of the indignity of waiting on line. Together with the interpreter, he led Alex and the minister into the side room reserved exclusively for statesmen. Here, a gourmet buffet had been arranged which contrasted strongly with the food mountain out in the main hall. It was dominated by a large tub of Russian caviar; artistically prepared game and stuffed fish were draped with the feathers and skins given them by Nature as protection until the cook killed them.

Bengt List regretted going to the reception, and wondered if there were any rules about how long one ought to stay in order to be polite. He was already on his second vodka and

116

had withdrawn behind one of the pillars supporting the ceiling of the ceremonial hall. The place looked like a 1930s gym with walls of Karelian birch dominated by a huge crystal chandelier, reminding all present of the Soviet Union's imperial heritage. It was swarming with people, far too many, and it was practically impossible to move. He had refrained from sampling the cold buffet, where the guests were crowding round in the undisciplined way one expects on the Åland ferry on a Saturday night. He never failed to be amazed by the appetite people always have when the food is free.

Karin, his wife, would have enjoyed this, he thought with a pang of conscience. Occasionally she would forget about women's liberation and instead liked to play the desirable wife of an important man. Her constant complaint was that he never took her along to the various functions to which he had been invited. He had never been able to make her understand why. Only a few of the guests here knew who he was, and still fewer were aware of his real position. They could be divided into two categories: the first avoided him, and the second pretended not to know him. Karin would have forced him to push and shove his way around, and afterwards admonished him for not having introduced her to a single interesting and important person. He knew what she was really looking for: another man. Not as a lover, or for dallying, but for good. For some strange reason she was convinced it was at receptions and suchlike official functions that she would be able to embark upon a new conquest. He knew she would never accept a husband from outside the Establishment. Another necessary condition was that his successor not be a policeman.

"Looking for somebody?" said an ironic voice behind him, in a Gothenburg accent.

He turned and recognized immediately the man who had addressed him: the editor of a Communist newspaper, schemer, influential in the party, good connections with militant organizations throughout Europe, international secretary for several years and always traveling around, probably being trained, suspicious.

List had helped to draw up his dossier himself.

"I thought the Swedish Communist Party had severed relations with the mother organization," he said in the same tone.

"Let's say," came the editor's sarcastic reply, "that our relations are no worse than yours."

List looked for a way to escape. He was twenty-five yards from the entrance, and reckoned it would take him at least five minutes to get that far without causing a commotion. The nearest obstacle was a giggling Englishwoman leaning on a stiff-backed officer clad in the operatic uniform Her Majesty's guards officers are required to wear on ceremonial occasions.

"Is it true there's a leak in SÄPO?" persisted the journalist, staring at him coldly from behind his thick spectacles. "Or even higher up?"

"If I knew that I'd have plugged it by now," said List, and immediately bit his tongue. He should have ignored the question.

"So, you are denying rumors that there's another traitor in the same class as Colonel Wennerström?"

List suddenly realized the man was extremely drunk. The glazed look behind the thick glasses became more threatening. This man was not just trying to provoke him, he hoped to spark off a scandal. What headlines it would make! *SÄPO Boss Strikes Well-Known Communist Newspaperman at Russian Embassy.*

He received help from an unexpected quarter. A young woman forced her way purposefully through the crowd and put her arm around the journalist's shoulder. He had approached List threateningly, and seemed about to spit into the policeman's face.

"Gunnar," she said reproachfully, "remember what we agreed."

118

As so often happens with drunks, he changed his attitude in a flash. His hatred turned into scorn, his anger into malice. He took a step backwards and pointed at List in disdain.

"Sister," he said solemnly, "allow me to introduce one of the biggest assholes in the country, the head pig himself, spy boss extraordinary. He's the man who draws up the blacklist."

The woman turned to List, her gaze appealing as much as cautiously watchful.

"Forget it," she said. "He's had too much."

List nodded. No one had noticed anything amiss. The buzz of conversation smothered them in a blanket of noise. He bowed slightly and slipped past the Englishwoman's left shoulder in an unguarded moment. As he thought, it took him five minutes to get to the cloakroom. He was just in time to catch a touching farewell ceremony. The Ambassador, looking not unlike a dancing bear, hovered around and dispensed Russian goodwill as the schoolboyish Swedish Foreign Minister was helped on with his fur coat and hat. The two statesmen then walked to the door together, pausing for just one more embrace and a final energetic handshake.

List was not surprised to see who left with the Foreign Minister. In order to maintain good relations with the Superpower, it is important for the Kingdom of Sweden to live up to the demands of protocol upheld so slavishly by representatives of the worker and peasant state. Sweden is forced to weigh in with its strongest wills and cleverest brains when dealing with the Russians. List thought the Foreign Minister had made a wise choice of companion for this evening's visit. The minister himself had attained his present post thanks to a strange illness not unlike the *Ten Little Indians* which had swept through his party. One after the other, the party leader and other capable men had faded away, and he was almost the only one left. His strong suit was his gift for formality, in speech, manner, and behavior.

119

If a small country like Sweden is to survive and remain free, she must constantly reaffirm her integrity. It is essential to have the respect of the Russians, as List well knew. Narva and Poltava were place names all Russian schoolchildren were taught to remember with horror and pride. That is how it had been in his own schooldays as well. He was more doubtful about the criteria used by Swedish history teachers nowadays.

In a way, Russian espionage activities in Stockholm were a sign that the Swedes had been successful in their efforts to maintain their country's independence. The leaders in Moscow took Sweden seriously, and neither underestimated nor ignored the little country which had existed since time immemorial. Russian and Swedish history has much in common and their mutual respect is deep-rooted, in contrast to the attitudes struck by the frequently ill-mannered and infantile powers in the West.

List knew that the Russians had bought, or at least joined forces with a man high up in the Swedish Establishment who was supplying them with sensitive and dangerous information. It was his job to find that person, and over the last month he had begun to feel more optimistic about his task. It was by no means certain that there was a direct link between Stockholm and Moscow. It could just as easily go via Prague, Warsaw, or Berlin. When the moment of truth came, the Swedish authorities would be relieved if the Russians had in fact preferred a circular route through one of their European allies. Their mutual respect could be retained, and the Swedish position would be significantly strengthened.

Bengt List intended to forget about work that evening. He had to sort out his marital problems and come to a decision.

He left the embassy and felt the warm, spring breeze caressing his cheeks; it was much too early to go home. He started walking aimlessly towards the city center.

•  •  •

120

"I'd like to go and sit in the bar," she whispered, stroking his hair. "With you. It's too cramped in here. At our age we need more room than this for lovemaking."

He rolled over onto his side, pressing his back against the wall of the berth so as to give her more room.

"Wasn't it good?"

"Oh, yes," she said quickly. "But if I lie like this much longer my arm will go to sleep. And sleep is what I want least of all just now."

He drew her toward him and kissed her. She curled up like a little girl, and they lay there for a while, warm and satisfied, till they were forced to stretch their limbs again and she hit her elbow on the cabin wall.

"We're not twenty any longer," she said, sticking her finger into his side. "The first time we went to bed together you were so thin I could see your hip bones."

"Is that what you remember?"

"Yes," she laughed. "When I got home I compared your hips with his."

"What a bizarre idea. And?"

"His were better. That is, you couldn't see his hip bones."

"He always was a man of substance."

"Yes," she said with a shudder.

"Most aristocrats are degenerate," he went on imprudently. "It's not until they're in their fifties that their defects become obvious."

"Yes," she said, and he noticed how her voice had drained away.

"Please," she whispered, "not yet. Now now."

He understood what she meant and tried to make up by kissing her nose and mouth. "If you lie quite still, I'll try and get out of this bunk without serious injury."

He jumped down, to the floor, lit two cigarettes and gave her one. She gazed at him with her nut-brown eyes, curiously and a little annoyingly. He felt once again how quickly she could switch between dejection and high spirits.

121

"You're a voyeur," he said.

"Not at all," she said. "It's only you I like looking at."

He leaned forward to stroke her cheek, letting his hand continue over her throat and down on to her breasts. They were still those of a young woman. She closed her eyes as he squeezed her nipple between forefinger and thumb, but opened them again when he tapped her on the stomach.

"All right," she said. "I'm coming. A voyage without a visit to the bar is like a seaside holiday without a dip in the sea."

He helped her out of the bunk. Neither of them had tried to pretend they were younger and more vigorous than they were. When he pulled her toward him and embraced her, she submitted, but only long enough for him to revel in the smell of her.

"No," she said. "Not now. Later though. Tonight. If you promise not to let me down."

They had come separately to the ferry. Piero Svanberg had dropped Tragg at Kornhamnstorg, and he had approached Stadsgården Quay via Slussen. Only eight passengers had boarded after Tragg. Four were in wheelchairs. The other four were pushing them.

As they left the quay, Tragg went to look for his cabin. He could see from the cabin numbers that they were next door to each other. There was an adjoining door, locked; he could hear her moving around on the other side.

They sat well apart in the cafeteria, and he watched her in conversation with her neighbors. His own were a retired couple from Solna who made the trip regularly once a month. She was a stout lady who had worked for thirty years at a laundry in Näckrosen and announced she had never had it so good now that she had retired. She couldn't stop talking, but to Tragg's relief she was also fond of her food and returned

122

repeatedly to the cold buffet, where she spent a long time selecting her next course. Her husband was a willowy, taciturn seventy-year-old, and every time she went to fill her plate he ordered another schnaps.

"I used to work on the railway," he announced after his third.

Tragg spent an hour after dinner wandering around the ship, bumping occasionally into passengers making the trip for the first time and determined to investigate every nook and cranny from stern to prow. He felt increasingly sure he had nothing to fear on board. She had been sitting in a deck chair the whole time, reading. She looked up as he passed her for the third time: he nodded and smiled back, without pausing. Five minutes later she opened the adjoining door and looked him up and down.

"How practical," she said.

"You can't open it from this side."

"The shipping line has gone up in my estimation. If you think you can burst in and force your attentions on me, forget it."

"I wouldn't dream of trying."

"We'll see about that," she said as she approached him. "I must touch you. God, but how I've longed to touch you!"

They did just that. They made love like grown adults, with the least possible fuss and on their guard against the unbridled lust that threatened to overcome and consume their desire. They wanted each other and it showed, until at last they gave way and abandoned themselves to physical satisfaction.

He had to wait for quite some time while she made herself presentable. When she came into the bar, elegant and newly made-up, a spring in her gait, she seemed to him a timeless woman: young and yet mature, the Marika of old and

123

also of today. He was close to weakening. Her moments of happiness had been few, and never uninhibited—not when she was with him, at least. She knew he would have to break the spell, that the past hour had been merely a temporary respite. They were both bound up inextricably with their past, and with the tasks they had taken upon themselves so long ago. In a fit of youthful innocence and perhaps even frivolity, they had delivered themselves into the hands of a ruthless and cooly calculating organization of political gamblers without being able to foresee the future. As time went by they had realized they would never be able to extricate themselves without degrading themselves or being degraded by others. He knew that was how things were, or at least, had been until now. She stood before him and gazed at him with eyes that both pleaded for mercy and inspired him with love and irresponsibility; he was on the point of giving way to temptation and telling her everything.

"Wait," she said, sitting down beside him. "Let's sit for ten minutes without saying a single word. Just keep quiet together. Like a contented married couple who have already said all there is to say."

Her lips were trembling, but she still smiled at him. He fetched some drinks from the bar and lit a couple of cigarettes. She closed her eyes and let herself be lulled by the swell of the sea. They had one side of the ship to themselves. An orchestra was playing quiet dance music, but only a few couples were on the floor; most of them were about their own age, waiting for the evening's show. A woman laughed shortly on the other side, her voice piercing the air like the cry of a hungry seagull, voracious and insatiable.

"Will they be waiting for us when we get back to Stockholm?"

She sounded contemptuous, as if she felt it was nothing to do with her, not now at least.

He shook his head.

124

"Not this time."

"But they know?"

"They know nothing. But they suspect. They'll know more in a month's time."

"What does that mean? I want to know the truth."

"They have no hard facts to go on, only assumptions. Ulrich says things are heating up here in Sweden." He paused for a moment. "Somebody has searched my apartment."

She stared at him, and there was fear in her eyes, but she held it in check. He knew that from now on she would be assessing everything he did or said: exaggeratedly nonchalant, comforting, too suave, genuine. The trust between them had given way to watchfulness. He sighed. Despite everything, it was better that way.

"Was that why you sent the boy?"

"Yes."

"How much does he know?"

"Nothing. He didn't even ask why."

She thought for a moment. "Did they find anything in your apartment?"

"Only a couple of car license plates. The equipment is in a safe place."

"Safe." She grimaced. "There are no safe places. Not for them."

"Maybe not. But they'll have to have a gigantic stroke of luck if they're going to stumble onto this particular hiding place."

"Are they following you?"

"Not any more. I've changed my address."

She stared at him in disbelief, then turned around quickly. It was a natural reaction, but there was nothing to see apart from dancing pensioners and a few bored youths who were miserable because they had chosen the wrong company.

"They don't know where I'm living. They're not even sure I've come back to Stockholm."

"How do you know?"

He paused for a fraction of a second, but saw straight away she had noticed. There was only one way out. He must be honest with her, or at least appear to be honest. He decided to tell the truth, but not the whole truth.

"I didn't know the apartment was under observation until I went to Berlin."

"How did you get a new apartment in a matter of days?"

He smiled as if he thought the question was irrelevant.

"Solvalla. You know that estate agent intent on losing all he owns?"

She nodded thoughtfully. It was reasonable and required no further explanation.

"There is a risk that they might pick me up again," he continued studiously. "I must make sure it's too late if they do. For them, that is."

She emptied her glass and he went for a refill. She needed time to sort out the implications of what he had said, to realize that her situation, and theirs, had changed completely. When he came back, it had sunk in.

"They can only get at Alex through us, is that right?" she asked in a matter-of-fact tone.

"The weak link."

"What?"

"That's what Köstner calls us."

"I didn't know he knew about us."

"He doesn't. But he knows about me."

They sat there in silence, as they had done when she first came to the bar. The warmth between them was still there, but the heat had gone. Their bond was now fear of discovery. When they looked at each other, they each knew what the other was thinking—that they had to escape, they had to retain their freedom, however limited it was, they had to survive. But not together.

For a while he had toyed with the idea of taking her with

126

him. That was unrealistic and impracticable. You can change your life, your appearance, and your personality but only if you are alone. If you rub out your old name and assume a new identity, you must also destroy everything that contributed to that old existence. A man and a woman fleeing together take with them a common past, their memories and their roots. They are a constant danger to each other and prevent the new person from emerging. It will only work if they become strangers to each other.

"I'm the only danger to you both," said Tragg. "Destroy the cameras and everything else that looks suspicious. Then they'll never be able to find conclusive evidence."

"What about you?"

"I'll have to disappear. Forever."

There were tears in her eyes, and he realized she would not be able to choke them back immediately. She bent over her handbag as if looking for a handkerchief, but hesitated. To his surprise, she started to laugh. Her shoulders were shaking, and she had to put her hand over her mouth. At first he thought she was hysterical. Then he saw it was an outbreak of gallows humor, a way out of the pain and tension and a recognition of present realities.

"Take this," she said. "A farewell present."

She had hidden the envelope with the microfilm in her handkerchief. He put it in his wallet. Of course. Why should Alex have stopped delivering? He gradually realized they would have to break a routine that had grown up over thirty years. What would there be left for her and Alex? A vacuum, perhaps. But as far as he was concerned, he felt relief for the first time.

"He wants to be paid," she chuckled.

"He'll have to wait this time."

"He'll take it out of me."

She wasn't laughing anymore. When she came into the bar she had looked gay and youthful, and her body had that freshness about it which satisfied lovemaking leaves behind like an echo. Despite her makeup and the warm lighting, despite the drinks, he could see that her face had turned pale and the corners of her mouth had contracted, making her look her age. They had come down to earth, chained to it by their unbreakable commitments. She knew she was condemned to play out her role for the rest of her life.

"What's he like?"

She sat up and her face tightened. For the first time, he could feel a chasm between them.

"I live with him," she said drily. "I'm his errand girl, his housekeeper, and occasionally when he's had too much to drink, his mistress. It's only when we're dining with the King, at the Nobel Prize reception or on some other official occasion that he treats me as his wife. He hardly ever brings home visitors, and we have no friends."

"Has he changed?"

She looked hard at him.

"Yes," she said. "He thinks he governs the country. On his own. At the same time his scorn goes deeper than ever. Perhaps his self-disgust as well. He's always been able to build up and knock down at the same time, but it's only lately he's begun to hate."

"What does he hate?"

"You," she said calmly. "You are the only one he can't manipulate. You don't jump when he pulls the strings."

"He's needed me just as I've needed him."

"You are equals, that's why he hates you. He can't give you orders. You pay him. You're the only one who knows who he really is."

"I'm only a go-between."

"Not for him. You are the whole lot. The Superpower, communism, the Insurance Company. As you've never given him away, you are all the people you represent. Your power is greater than his. That's how he sees it, and that's why he hates you."

"When you get home you can tell him I've disappeared out of his life. Forever. If he likes, Alex can go down in history as a faceless phantom, the unexposed master spy whose very existence will be squabbled over by sociologists without their being able to prove a thing."

"That's precisely why he's going to hate you even more. You are discarding him, throwing him into the dustbin, treating him like trash. You are putting him on a par with all those people he has been trampling all over without a trace of hesitation or conscience. You are going to break up your relationship when he's the only one with a divine right to treachery."

"There's only one alternative: we get found out."

She looked at him with a mixture of irony and condescension.

"You've never understood him. Not properly. I know him because I live with him, but he doesn't count me. He may well prefer to be found out rather than have the whole world know how great he is. He's quite capable of treating exposure with a roar of laughter."

They stayed in the bar and watched one of those popular performers whose job is to make people think they are happy. They went on drinking. When they went back to their cabins after dancing for a while and trying to convince each other that nothing had changed, Tragg bought a bottle of champagne. Before they undressed, she asked him for his new telephone number. Alex would probably want confirmation of what she told him. If Alex thought it was worth the risk, that is. If that happened, it would be their first meeting in nearly two years.

The next morning Tragg hoped that a meeting with Alex would go as smoothly as that hour spent in her cabin. They had made love again, not without tenderness but without violent outbursts of passion. Suddenly, they did not have much more to say to each other, as if they had already said

129

farewell and were now going through the motions out of politeness.

He slept in his own cabin. The berths really were much too uncomfortable for two. He even closed the connecting door.

Since taking Greger Tragg to the ferry in Gamla Stan early that morning, Piero Svanberg had enjoyed a pleasant and eventful day. He was on the morning shift, and after a few short fares had found someone who wanted to go to Norrköping seventy miles away. Long trips of that nature are every taxi driver's dream, and the price agreed with his customer was very attractive. He was able to enjoy the sunny spring morning undisturbed as the foreigner in the back seat did not utter a word. On returning to Stockholm he had driven straight back to the garage, cashed in, and left the cab. He then got changed and decided to make the most of the day.

He was pleased with the outcome of his chat with the croupier at the Sheraton Hotel, who was on duty from 2 p.m. onwards and thought he could probably obtain the required information by that same evening. At about eight o'clock, he claimed the bar stool nearest the piano, and five minutes later he was confident he had found himself a bed for the night. The pianist from Harlem had given him an unequivocal welcome, and when she asked how long he expected to stay this time, he told her that was up to her.

"In that case, we can leave together."

Two things prevented Svanberg's evening from being perfect. He could feel one of them hard against his chest under his jacket, and he almost regretted submitting to impulse during the afternoon. As usual, he had been worrying about Tragg's situation and the task he had taken on. Tragg had said he should be ready for the unexpected, and that he must be prepared to react quickly. It was obvious Tragg was

130

under threat. He had not said how or from whom, that was true, but the American who had followed them was a danger. Anyone could see he was a professional. Svanberg had met the type in casinos, and knew that most of them were armed. That is why he had gone to Sergels Torg and acquired an address in Skånegatan where, after giving the necessary passwords, he was soon able to buy a Walther for four thousand crowns. The pistol felt awkward, and he told himself over and over again he must remember to hide it before going to bed. Not even a pianist from Harlem would think it natural for him to run around with a loaded pistol.

The other irritation had suddenly appeared and sat down on the bar stool beside him. It was very odd of the man not to have picked an armchair down on the floor. Svanberg thought he recognized him. He was not a member of the Cabinet, but something like that or even higher. Such people do not sit on bar stools, not in Sweden at least. They avoid mixing with ordinary mortals. The nearest they get to being democratic is to take an occasional taxi ride.

Svanberg felt put down. He felt himself shrinking to the insignificant plebe he undoubtedly was in the other man's eyes. Not even the pistol in his inside pocket made up for his feeling of insecurity and inferiority. The man beside him treated him like a dim shadow in a windowpane. He did not even bother to say "good evening" as decent people usually do.

The pianist from Harlem was impressed. She chattered to the elegant, distinguished gentleman with the unnatural politeness ordinary folk seem to assume when talking to well-bred, educated people. They talked about music and Svanberg picked up names like Carmichael, Petersen, Krupka, and Dave Schönbach. When she started playing, he felt a twinge of jealousy as she strove to excel herself. It was soft music, melodic and rhythmical. Suddenly, in mid-tune, she changed tempo and the piano began to croon a more exciting and

131

seductive tune over thundering bass rhythms. She looked up at him and winked. Everything was all right again. It was as if she were saying: the job has to come first right now, but then it's our turn and we can be alone.

By the time she finished, there were four of them.

"Bengt List! I thought I saw you at the embassy," asserted the voice beside Svanberg.

The newcomer nodded.

"We left at about the same time. The Foreign Minister seemed in a good mood."

"He was happier when we left than when we arrvied. In spite of the presents. Their goodwill is sometimes overwhelming. It seems we'll never learn how to handle them properly."

The man known to a few as Alex gazed arrogantly at the security chief.

"It's in this country's interest to maintain good relations with our neighbors, and not to make them unduly suspicious."

He beckoned a waitress and paid her.

"It was a strange idea of mine, coming here. But it's nice to feel like an ordinary human being now and then. Do have a pleasant evening."

He bowed ever so slightly and strode out, oblivious to the looks that followed him from every quarter of the bar.

On the way home in his taxi, he wondered whether their meeting was a coincidence, or whether he should take List's pointed comments as a warning.

Back at home, the bed was still unmade and the pots unwashed; he decided the significance of List's presence in the bar was irrelevant. During the course of the evening he had finally made up his mind. The Russian Ambassador had helped him to do so.

"The Great Fatherland War brought with it immense suffering which the population of the Soviet Union have constantly at the forefront of their minds," he said pompously, his eyes misting over. The Swedish Foreign Minister had stiffened and glanced ominously at Alex. The vodka glasses in their hands seemed to double in weight. They both knew that statement and the one which was bound to follow were a part of the Soviet Russian diplomatic ritual that had been repeated thousands of times all over the world—so often that no one took it seriously any more.

"We Russians are a peace-loving people, just like you Swedes. Let us drink to peace!"

They drank the toast.

"But if we are forced to act, we shall not hesitate," went on the Ambassador. "We are well prepared, and anyone who thinks he can catch us unawares will find he has underestimated our foresight."

That was the moment when Alex decided he would have to kill Greger Tragg. There were far too many signs that the security police were beginning to catch up with their prey. They still had no idea who they were looking for. Tragg was the decoy, a timid jackal they knew was slinking along in the tracks of the lion, and who would sooner or later provide them with what they were after.

Alex would surprise them and strike while they were still holding off. Once Tragg was dead, the hunt was over and the prey would escape. There would be no living proof that Alex had ever existed. It was as if he were preparing a reincarnation: he would rise again, but in new form. He would materialize in about six months' time, make a new contact on his own initiative, and produce incontrovertible evidence to prove he was who he said he was. Meanwhile, he would also solve the only remaining problem: Marika.

He went to bed eventually, well pleased with himself. He would devote the next few days exclusively to eliminating the weak and increasingly dangerous link which bound him to the past. From now on, he would look only to the future. The last of his worries would be eliminated. Only Greger Tragg stood between him and the fulfillment of his own greatness.

• • •

Bengt List, the man who knew more about more Swedes than anyone else, did not quite know where he was that evening.

It had been a mistake to go to the Russian reception. Why he had chosen the Sheraton of all places for a drink was another thing he did not understand. On the way from the embassy, he had wandered aimlessly past both his own office and the police headquarters without giving a thought to his work. He had quite simply strolled into the first bar he came across, and now he was sitting on this bar stool and feeling at odds with himself. He had picked it because it was one of the few vacant seats in the place, and he was miles away when it dawned upon him who his neighbor was. He accepted that the latter had every reason to be surprised, and did not mind being snubbed. Policemen have to be careful when they are off duty, at least as careful as when they are working. They seem to carry with them a whiff of interrogation and arrest, and nobody wants to know them, not even those responsible for appointing them and paying their wages.

He could not go on like this. He would have to make up his mind what to do. He must sit down and think hard about seeking a divorce, how much it would cost him, and what the other consequences might be. He suddenly noticed he was hungry and thought what a fool he had been—a whole mountain of food sitting looking at him for almost an hour at the embassy, and nobody preventing him from taking as much as he wanted. There was no point at all in staying put.

While he was waiting to pay, he wondered whether he would find his own name in the next morning's surveillance report. He was in the odd position of having given an order which now meant that he himself was being watched. Some of his men were on duty in the hotel, and they were eager to

134

demonstrate how wide awake they were by noting both his time of arrival and departure.

The dark woman playing the piano was unusually attractive. Anyone could be forgiven for thinking that, even one of the country's top men. He banished the thought, and instead observed the young man sitting nearest to the pianist, following her every movement with a wide, happy smile. He could not help feeling a twinge of jealousy. It was a long time since he was that age, even before he got married and joined the police force.

As List rose to leave, he took another look at his neighbor and suddenly had the feeling he ought to know who he was. He banished that thought as well. He had gone out to think over his marital problems, and that was precisely what he was going to do. Everything else could wait until tomorrow.

Only when he was sitting over a cup of coffee—he had gone to the Riche restaurant where he knew he was not being watched—and realized that no one with his income could afford to start divorce proceedings and hence he must leave it up to his wife to take positive steps in the hope of reducing the alimony, only then did he remember who the young man in the Sheraton bar was.

A few weeks ago he had seen a blurred photo of him. It had been taken by some bungling Dane the force had no further use for. The young man with the Italianate face had been wearing a taxi driver's hat and was the person who would lead them to the journalist who in turn would point them in the direction of the traitor who was the eyes and ears of the Russians at the very top of the Swedish Establishment.

He considered briefly going back to the Sheraton Hotel, but thought better of it. The taxi driver would no doubt have left by now, and in any case, a list of all the interesting people who had visited the hotel would land on his desk the next morning. This was the last mistake Bengt List made that night, and possibly his biggest. Piero Svanberg was still sitting on his bar stool without a care in the world, and no one bothered to note his presence. There were much more interesting names to play with.

# ❧ XI ❧

The man from Algiers introduced himself as Ahmed Kassir. He was barely five feet tall, but erect and well-made. Like many short men, he tried to make up for his size by nonchalant behavior. At the moment, his arrogant face was radiating suspicion and contempt. His need to assert himself was considerable, and had he been born at the right time he would doubtless have been able to develop into a Dolfuss or an Alexander the Great; unfortunately, he lacked all sense of proportion. When he was given his first command in the war of liberation, he felt sure he could achieve a glorious victory all on his own and was responsible for a bloodbath by ordering his men to launch a brave but pointless attack on a French position that was far too well defended. From then on he was kept under strict control. He was punished for his stupidity but rewarded for his heroism (he had led from the front and was one of the few to escape unharmed), and since he was ready to learn, he soon developed into a perfect number two who never questioned an order. After the liberation, they tested him by giving him a number of jobs, each one shadier than the last, and there was never any question about his loyalty. He was feared by many in his own country since he was known as an extension of the arm of authority when authority preferred to remain invisible, and he was as much at home in secret terrorist circles in Paris, Rome, or Munich as he was in the company of his less secretive colleagues in Beirut or Ouda Ouda.

It was the first time he had been as far north as Stockholm. It was also the first time he had been offered the prospect of payment in anything but dinars. His share was one-tenth of the consultancy fee Intereloc was expected to pay in order to secure the required signatures on the gigantic contract which was due to be made public in Algiers in a few weeks' time.

"You think you can fool us," hissed M. Kassir. "You've made a deal with Wattinius. Two per cent for him, two per cent for you. We have proof."

"Negotiations are still not complete," replied Tragg, who was more impressed by the little man's operatic posturing than the incredible impudence of his claim, and he wondered what would happen if he asked Kassir to produce his proof.

"You're asking for twelve, and they're prepared to pay six," he went on impassively. There was no need to humiliate the Algerian by challenging him to support his claim. He would probably need hours, or even days, to get over the fact that he had been exposed as a liar.

"In my judgement we should be able to stretch them to eight per cent."

"Never!"

M. Kassir spat out the word.

"Do you think we would sell a whole market, a monopoly, for small change?"

"I can arrange for you to meet Wattinius and Bunter. Probably today."

The Arab stared at him in undisguised scorn.

"I'm sure you can," he said sarcastically. "And what would that prove? Only that you are in league."

138

M. Kassir thought at first the ensuing silence meant Tragg was lost for an answer. That was not so.

"In that case," replied Tragg at last, in the cooly neutral tone the Swedes adopt so effectively, "I have no alternative but to contact my employers and recommend that they either find a replacement for me, or they decline to offer their services. As you know, my firm has no financial interest in the affair."

That went home. M. Kassir produced a bottle of whiskey from his wardrobe and fetched two glasses from the washbasin. He poured out a third of a glass for Tragg, and gave himself a few symbolic drops that barely covered the bottom of the glass. So far he had remained standing in order to spit out his insults at Tragg, whom he had placed in the modest hotel room's only chair.

"Let's not be hasty," he said in a friendly tone, and gave Tragg a dazzling smile. "I have come here to sort things out, but nobody—not a single person apart from you and your driver—must know of my existence."

Tragg nodded. He felt he had won the first round. M. Kassir had misjudged things. His behavior was presumably intended to demonstrate who was in charge, and as a test of Tragg's nerves and reliability. That kind of thing might work in North Africa and the Mediterranean countries, but it was bad tactics north of the Alps. In a way, it was instructive. The Algerians were keen to bring off the deal. That meant there was room to maneuver.

Tragg had heard about M. Kassir's imminent arrival from Ulrich Langer, whose message displayed an unusually humorous streak in that he called the Arab an "emissary." The message was coded, and the French expert in Berlin at last had an opportunity to demonstrate the speed and efficiency of his machines. The revelation that Kassir had the rank of emissary led the local security people to decide they no longer dared

139

accept sole responsibility, and Paris was informed with a request for further instructions. These did not arrive for another week, and there was a further delay of some days before the French Embassy in Stockholm could release a man to look into the matter. At about the same time, M. Kassir was esconced in his sleeping car to Copenhagen on the first stage of his journey home.

The only thing Tragg could do on receiving Langer's message was to book the Algerian into another hotel in a different part of the city from that mentioned. He then went to meet the emissary at the Central Station.

It all went easily and quickly, according to the plan evolved by Tragg and Svanberg. M. Kassir was the only passenger on the morning train from Copenhagen answering the description of a short Arab. He marched proudly along from the platform to the station entrance, eyeing his new surroundings with appropriate curiosity, and joined the line for a taxi. It was obvious that the emissary had a keen interest in big, blond, and preferably buxom women. A mother of three from Johanneshov, just back from a well-earned holiday, was subjected to a long tirade, first in French and then in German, by the neatly dressed little man with gleaming eyes, and he paid her the kind of compliments she had spent her life dreaming about. Unfortunately, she could not understand a word. She was rescued by her husband and their three children who were waiting to greet her at the barrier. They were all struck dumb by M. Kassir's elegant and polite leave-taking:

"Madame! Monsieur!"

A netball star from the Alvik ladies' team who was about eighteen inches taller than M. Kassir thought at first he was inquiring about the way to the Central Hotel, but she understood enough German to catch the gist of his meaning and dismissed him with a single word:

"Jerk!"

M. Kassir was in a good mood as he joined the taxi line

140

and completely ignored the tall Swede in a parka standing behind him until he felt a pistol between his ribs, and without a word of protest or displaying the least sign of surprise allowed himself to be bundled into the back seat of a taxi while the driver took care of the luggage. It seemed as if that kind of thing happened to him every day.

Even before the taxi had left the entrance, Tragg showed him the "pistol." It was one of his pipes. While Svanberg made sure they were not followed, Tragg explained who he was and why he had felt obliged to resort to such drastic measures. He told him about the American working for Intereloc and their unwelcome habit of delving into his activities. M. Kassir asserted sourly that he approved, without showing any trace of admiration at their efficiency.

"You are certainly the first Arab to have been hijacked the moment he arrived in Stockholm," joked Tragg.

"We Arabs never allow ourselves to be taken prisoner," insisted M. Kassir haughtily.

During his short stay in Stockholm he frequently displayed his amazing ability to distort reality and ignore the facts, even if they were plain for all to see. His basic assumption was quite simply that he was always right, even when he contradicted himself. In such cases, he was right both ways.

Tragg was not fooled into thinking that all Algerians behaved like this, but he recognized the symptoms. Despite his self-confidence and tone of arrogant superiority, he was nothing more than a terrified errand boy sent on his way with the usual threat of reprisals if he failed, but rich rewards if he did his job well. To the gamblers in Algiers, he was a useful chess piece. They had given him his instructions, and they were thorough; but like all instructions they were full of contradictions and could be twisted to suit a variety of circumstances. Ahmed Kassir lacked the ability to distinguish between circumstances. Since he knew his superiors in Algiers were prepared to sacrifice him at any time, he lived in constant fear, and in later years compensated for this with barbiturates.

He had been told his race was far superior to the uncultured swine he would have to deal with up there near the Artic Circle. Even so, he was unsure about his own superiority when faced with these cool, unemotional northerners who always seemed to lack the imagination needed to understand the threats he uttered.

His orders were always to behave like a worthy representative of his country and his religion. He should be hard and gentle, cunning or diplomatic, and under no circumstances was he to mess things up by a crude lack of tact. The legitimate demands he made should be put forcefully and cleverly. He was authorized to dictate terms, and he should never betray his own pride. If the other side did not agree to their conditions, then he was to put a stop to it on the spot—with a shrug of the shoulders. This possibility was only theoretical, of course. Only in an extreme emergency—a sort of contradiction to end all contradictions—should he telephone Algiers for new instructions.

When he went to bed that night, his head neatly swathed in a white turban, the only thing M. Kassir remembered about his earlier conversation with Tragg was two figures. The first was six, quite out of the question. The other was eight. It was less than ten, the minimum he could accept. The semi-failure, as the minister put it.

He spent some time wondering whether the proposed emergency telephone call (which was certainly expected in Algiers) meant his masters were in fact prepared to go down another one or two per cent. What he feared most was that they would accept the lower figure but take it out of his own share.

Then he abandoned himself to dreams of tall, blond, phlegmatic Swedish girls. He promised himself that the next night he would be able to enjoy them in the flesh. He had no lack of self-confidence in this respect. Experience told him the opportunity would arise, and such occasions never caused him any problems whatsoever.

Greger Tragg and Lars Bunter had been negotiating for four days, mainly by telephone, and they both realized they had gone as far as they could go.

Bunter had flown to Brussels, where Intereloc's American parent company had its European office. He said he had come back with their final instructions, and Tragg had no reason to doubt him. The big multinational company had reached its final decision in accordance with the complicated procedures laid down by its own bureaucracy. There had to be a limit somewhere even to its flexibility. They had their own moral code and their own self-sufficient pride formulated in mathematical terms and a commercial catechism without scruples. The Algerian market was interesting, of course, like all markets, but it was not indispensable—not more so than any other market—and it really was not of crucial significance for little Intereloc. Moreover, the multinational company had a secure future, unlike the people who were trying to dictate the terms for Algeria. The weakness in their argument was the indisputable fact that their interest in further business would cool as soon as they had secured their future in a Swiss bank account.

When Bunter called Tragg to fix the crucial meeting, he sounded tense but also more decisive than he had been. Bunter had received his final orders, and had been told there was no point in discussing the matter any further.

A weakness in Lars Bunter's intellectual resources was the fact that he had been weaned on the spirit of discipline and organized decision-making required in order to get ahead in a multinational company. As a result, he never doubted Tragg's assurance that he was in constant contact with Algiers, and that he could now say with certainty he had exhausted his influence.

143

Tragg's assertion was false. Needless to say, he had never been in touch with Algiers, and in so far as M. Kassir could be considered to have the final say where the Arabs were concerned, Tragg had even held back information from him as to the state of play; his explanation was that Intereloc's directors had flown to consult with their top bosses in the U.S.A. in order to report on the situation and receive their final instructions.

M. Kassir expressed his approval of the action allegedly taken by Wattinius and Bunter. It was quite in accord with his own assessment of the importance of the deal.

"You don't get a new market opening up every day," he said with a statesmanlike gesture when Tragg informed him of what was happening.

"And on such generous terms," he added with a benevolent smile. "But time is short. I must have a decision by the weekend."

According to Piero Svanberg's reports, M. Kassir had then proceeded to fulfill his promise to himself, and entered into brief but intimate friendships with Swedish blondes.

"A different one every night. Each one fatter than the last," reported Svanberg. "He picks 'em up in the lobby."


Tragg had suggested the Grand Hotel in Sigtuna, some thirty miles north of Stockholm, as a venue. Bunter turned up in Intereloc's limousine, an impressive-looking American monster complete with uniformed driver. Tragg came by taxi, and it had taken him and Svanberg twice as long to cover the same distance. Tragg was impressed by Piero Svanberg's familiarity with sideroads in the province of Uppland.

The ice on Lake Mälaren had started to turn blue, but was still firm and reliable although the sun had managed to melt the snow on the flowerbeds in the terracelike garden outside the dining room window. Way out in the bay, a few isolated fishermen crouched over their holes in the ice. Spring was in the air, that spring Stockholmers stubbornly claim to feel despite the fact that night temperatures fall far below zero and the slush is still squishing under their tread.

"The winter holidays start on Saturday," said Bunter, gazing thoughtfully over the ice at the old Viking castle in Runsa. "I'd thought of taking the family skiing. For a few days at least."

Tragg nodded sympathetically. A kind of mutual trust had grown up between them in the course of this transaction. It was fragile and could collapse at any moment, but it was convenient just now since both of them knew the final decision no longer depended on them. They had played their cards well, and there was no longer room for maneuver. The unspoken question was: what was the value of the opponent's one remaining card? They must both be the same.

"I wouldn't plan to leave before Sunday," said Tragg. "Unless of course we have to abandon the whole thing here and now."

Bunter sighed. Then he pulled his powerful frame erect and gave Tragg a friendly if guarded smile.

"Well, here we go!" he said, hovering slightly over the "g" without actually lapsing into a stammer.

Tragg nodded. "What's your lowest bid?"

"The same as yours, I hope. If you accept eight per cent you can book an air ticket to Algiers next week."

"Eight."

Lars Bunter leaned forward over the table. "If we say seven, I can agree straight away. Then we're all finished."

Tragg shook his head with a smile, as if he did not take the suggestion seriously. "We've got past that stage."

Bunter stared at him goggle-eyed. Then he burst out laughing, surprisingly gently considering the size of his heavy frame.

"Damn me if we haven't made it," he said. "Your eight is solid, I suppose?"

"Ninety per cent solid," replied Tragg coolly.

"What the hell do you mean?"

For just a brief moment Lars Bunter's correct multinational front fell apart and he looked naked and frustrated. Then he took a grip on himself, but the intimacy between them had vanished.

"I need three days at most to convince my masters that it's eight per cent or nothing," said Tragg calmly.

"You're sure they'll agree, though?" asked Bunter in despair.

"Quite sure. I'll give you a call as soon as I have confirmation."

Bunter explained he would be at home all day Saturday and until noon on Sunday. Then he was going skiing, no matter what.

For his part, Tragg also expected to be leaving Stockholm on Sunday, even though he was no more than ninety per cent certain that M. Kassir and his friends would accept the agreement.


M. Ahmed Kassir's behavior was annoying to say the least. He displayed the same symptoms as a man suffering from severe colic. His face was screwed up into the most horrible grimaces, while his doll-like feet stamped the floor with Napoleonic force. Occasionally he grasped himself round the stomach with both arms, as if trying to push his guts back into place.

"No, no, no," he yelled.

Tragg did not move a muscle. He wondered when the little man would realize the comic effect his behavior was having, or at least get some idea of the absurdity of the whole situation. Tragg looked at his watch and saw there was another two minutes to go before the time he had foreseen he would have to allow for M. Kassir's convulsive performance. The dialogue was one-sided.

"You seem to think we are crazy."

He shook his head with worrying force.

"No, no, no! We are not crazy. You're trying to make fools of us."

He marched up to Tragg, who had been placed on the only chair as usual. The Arab stretched out his fist to within an inch of the Swede's face.

"We have no intention of accepting these colonial tricks," he said threateningly. "You tell Wattinius and Bunter and the rest of the imperialists that we could never agree to a deal that is nothing more than a humiliation for us."

When M. Kassir drew back a couple of paces in order to prepare for his next attack, Tragg saw his chance and jumped to his feet. Compared with the Algerian, he seemed taller than usual—a giant with blond hair and blue eyes, not breathing fire but glistening with the frosty chill that causes snow blindness in strong light.

"I thought you were my boss," said Tragg ruthlessly. "As far as I am concerned, I have completed my task. I will inform Intereloc you are unable to accept their offer."

M. Kassir froze. "Sit down," he said absentmindedly, but the next moment realized how perfunctory that must have sounded and corrected himself at once.

"My dear Monsieur Tragg. Please do sit down again."

Ahmed Kassir sat down on the bed and Tragg returned to his chair. He noticed how boyish the Arab's face looked when not distorted by unbridled emotions. It was easy to imagine what the forty-year-old Algerian must have looked like when, in the blindness and enthusiasm of youth, he had joined the liberation movement in order to fight the French. All revolutions start to go rotten the moment they succeed, thought Tragg. The decay gets a grip on people, and they don't want to be reminded of the time when they were fighting for all the ideals they have since abandoned in order to hold on to power. We are just the same, him and me. We were the same then and we're the same now. Neither of us is a traitor as there is nothing left to betray.

147

"Are you sure this is their last word?" asked M. Kassir, shaking his head in sorrow. "I can't believe it can be."

"If you don't accept their offer by nine o'clock on Sunday morning at the latest, they will assume the deal is off and leave Stockholm. Wattinius is going away on Friday in fact, and Bunter is leaving before lunch on Sunday at the latest. It's our winter sports week."

"Winter sports week! And we're talking about millions!"

There was an undertone of respectful amazement in the Arab's voice.

"It's a sort of holy celebration," explained Tragg. "It's inviolable for many families, especially those who are well off. It's like your Ramadan."

M. Kassir gave Tragg a poisonous look but choked back his vexation. The comparison was outrageous. What did this Swede know about the only true religion? He came from a country where they surround themselves with ritual but godless customs like a kind of religious substitute, the vain effort of the unbeliever to give his life a meaning. M. Kassir was a good Moslem who observed the five obligatory duties. He had made his second hadj and was generous to beggars, not only when somebody was watching.

He smiled, and suddenly felt invincible. From now on he would approach the situation with the superior manner that was his birthright, thanks to his race and religion.

"The tenders will be opened in Algiers next week," he said guardedly.

"Bunter will be there if you let me tell him agreement has been reached."

"Monsieur Tragg, you may ring me at nine o'clock on Sunday morning. You will hear our decision then."

The audience was concluded. When Tragg had taken leave formally and closed the door behind him, he wondered how many other roles M. Kassir would be forced to play during the next few days. Innumerable, he supposed. By the time he

148

gets out into the street, he will have changed already. "They want us to regard them as unpredictable," he muttered half to himself and got into the taxi. Svanberg looked up in surprise. He was not used to Tragg thinking aloud.

"I nearly fell into the trap," laughed Tragg. "When someone is skilled in the art of duplicity, we tend to forget there's no basic difference between people of various nations and religions. Russians and Americans, Swedes, Negroes, and Arabs. It makes no difference. We're all driven on by the same motives, we've just assumed different guises. Strip us naked and we're all the same."

Svanberg mumbled something unclear and blushed. He had reached the same conclusion these last few nights. Mind you, he would place black women, at least, a little higher than their paler sisters.


Tragg called at exactly nine o'clock on Sunday morning. The phone rang seven times before M. Kassir condescended to answer. In the flood of words and explanations that came pouring out of the telephone, there were even references to good relations between Algeria and Sweden.

The decision was positive. M. Kassir assumed his announcement would be passed on word for word to, as he put it, the honorable President Wattinius and Vice-President of Intereloc, Lars Bunter.

M. Kassir said he was also looking forward to his next meeting with Greger Tragg, and hoped it would be in Basel in six week's time. He spent several minutes telling Tragg how important it was for him to follow in detail the instructions he had received on what to do next. There were to be no self-indulgent escapades, he stressed strongly; the phrase was no doubt one that had stuck in his mind following one of the many nocturnal telephone conversations he had had with Algiers. Despite these warnings, he intended to inform Tragg's

149

superiors that he had carried out his instructions in a satisfactory manner.

M. Kassir ended by announcing his intention of leaving Stockholm, that miserable, dirty, gray, dull town, that very afternoon. It was his earnest hope he would never be compelled to return.

Bunter must have been sitting over the telephone, as he answered after the first ring.

"I'm afraid," said Tragg, "that you'll have to break off your skiing holiday in the middle of next week. Your presence is required in Algiers on Friday."

"No reservations this time?"

"None whatsoever. They've accepted your offer of eight per cent, and assume we will stick to the timetable and methods we have agreed."

"Of course."

They wished each other the best of luck, and agreed that Tragg should make contact again when Bunter had returned from Algiers.

"Five more minutes and I'll be on my way to Åre," laughed Bunter. "The family's waiting in the car already."

That was not quite true. Before he left home Lars Bunter first informed Tore Wattinius that everything had gone well. Then he had rather a long conversation with the American who had displayed such interest in what Tragg was up to. They dwelt for several moments on what the American had discovered about the young curly-haired Swede who paid regular visits to the Sheraton bar. The American was fairly sure he was Tragg's accomplice, even though he did not know his name.

While they were talking, Tragg called Svanberg at home. To be on the safe side, he used the public telephone in the square at Sundbyberg.

150

# ❧ XII ❧

The situation was awkward and Bengt List regretted having agreed to meet the man. He could have refused on purely formal grounds. Mr. Hawley at the embassy had been at pains to point out the business was not part of their normal routine.

"I know him personally," said the CIA man. "He used to work for us until he went over to the private sector. Incidentally, the organization had nothing against that: it's preferable in every way for the multinationals to use experienced security staff rather than turning to the open market. They can sometimes do us a favor, and you yourselves can sometimes benefit from our arrangement. But do as you think fit. It won't make any difference to our relationship, whatever you decide."

Now the American was occupying the chair in front of List and referring to their mutual friend Mr. Hawley. He had introduced himself as Mr. Jones, and that was presumably his real name. It is just as impossible for an American to use Jones as an alias as it would be for a Swedish agent abroad to hide behind the name of Andersson or Johansson. People of a

151

suspicious bent always prick up their ears on hearing an ordinary everyday surname. Its owner must always expect its genuineness to be doubted if he stands out in any way from his fellows.

Mr. Jones certainly did. He looked as though he had stepped straight out of an American gangster film. He had the tough appearance of an ex-baseball player, and was nowadays no doubt pretty good at squash. His sardonic smile suggested his interest in women was still very much alive, but fickle. List was also quite sure the American was carrying a pistol in a shoulder holster under his elegantly cut jacket, without a Swedish license. To top it off, he spoke in a Western drawl.

"I'm interested in two people," said Mr. Jones.

"Swedes?"

"Of course."

The American seemed surprised, and it underlined the awkwardness of List's position. It went against the grain to pass on information about Swedish citizens to a private security man, even if he had been recommended by the CIA, and worked for a well-known multinational company whose economic and political ambitions were well-known the world over.

List's job was to protect his country from illegal intelligence activities. It was going on all around him, all the time, usually under the umbrella of diplomatic immunity. Although Sweden was neutral, it was assumed that all spies were working for the East. The explanation was simple: information to the West was wide open. Politicians and businessmen maintained close relations with their colleagues to the West, especially the U.S. and England. Only a few of them were on the payroll of the CIA or the Secret Service. The rest were rewarded in more subtle and less obvious ways. Contracts were given an easy passage with regard to both exports and imports. Unwelcome competitors got into difficulties for no obvious reason. General agencies changed hands, and private transactions of a financial nature were frequently helped along, even if they were not strictly in accordance with Swedish law. Friendly politicians could count on votes and support when they ran for one of the many well-paid and tax-free directors' posts in the ever increasing flora of international organizations. Prominent Swedish military men were offered directorships, both at home and abroad. There is no record in Swedish criminal statistics of anyone being found guilty of indiscretions in their contacts with the two English speaking nations.

Relations with the French and Italians are less intimate, and the attitude towards Germany is more ambiguous. The Swedish security services have remained pro-German, although the friendship is restricted exclusively to the German authorities controlling the area west of the River Elbe; the Swedish people themselves continue to have a healthy skepticism regarding both German republics.

List found it difficult to imagine that any of the agents he was busy keeping an eye on would have time or inclination to bother about international commerce. He did not expect, therefore, that the names Mr. Jones was about to reveal would be of any great interest to him. This did not mean, however, that the names would not be on one of the many (officially nonexistent) lists to which he had access. He decided to play a waiting game and to make no comment even if the names happened to be familiar. Sweden's trade situation had deteriorated rapidly in recent years, and there were now many occasions when one turned a blind eye, especially if the outcome might be an improvement in the sensitive area of oil supplies.

"Well, Mr. Jones?" said List, expectantly.

"Sir," replied Jones. He had with him a black attaché case which he now placed on the table and unlocked with keys chained to his waistcoat. He took out a large official

153

envelope with the multinational company's logo printed on the front. The envelope contained photographs.

"Piero Svanberg," said Mr. Jones slowly.

List shook his head: the name meant nothing to him.

"Greger Tragg," continued the American, pronouncing it with some difficulty and quite unlike a Swede would have done.

List swallowed rapidly, cleared his throat, and gritted his teeth. Of all possible names, this was the least expected. For the last four weeks his men had been unable to find a trace of Tragg, despite the fact that the task had been assigned the highest priority. Both at home and abroad, hundreds of men and women were keeping a lookout for the tall Swede, but no one had seen the slightest sign of him. After a while, some people had put forward the theory that Tragg must have stayed behind on the other side of the Wall; List refused to accept it. It was not logical. Tragg was not just a postman, he was first and foremost the link to what might well turn out to be the most important spy ever to operate in Sweden. Tragg would only retire if that man left the country. But there was no indication of that happening. No really important Swede had resigned his post in recent months to go and enjoy a well-earned pension in some warmer climate.

"They don't ring any bells," said List in an effort to catch the American idiom. "But I'll get my people to run a check."

The American smiled his approval. Back in the States, of course, a security chief would have had access to the necessary information within minutes, but he knew about the problems connected with secret files in Sweden, and was fairly sure they did not even have the data on computers.

"These photographs might help you," he said in a friendly tone, handing over a dozen or so large pictures. Six were of Tragg, the rest of Svanberg.

"Thank you," said List, staring at Piero Svanberg's cheerful, boyish face smiling enraptured at a dark-skinned woman in a long evening dress. List recognized them immediately and could not help giving a little start.

"Recognize 'em?" asked Mr. Jones, who had noticed the slight change in List's expression.

"The woman," said List. "I recognize the woman, but I can't place her."

"She plays the piano at the Sheraton bar."

"Of course!"

List tried to whistle, but failed. It was intended to make up for the start shortly before.

"An attractive woman."

"For the last few days she has been the mistress of that man there."

"Really?"

It sounded like a sigh of envy, and it was genuine. Mr. Jones' face hardened. He had no time for mixing of the races.

"She's of no interest," he said coolly. "But the man, on the other hand . . ."

"Who is he?"

"His name is Piero Svanberg and he drives around in a taxi."

"Drives around?"

"His only client is the other man, Greger Tragg."

List studied the pictures, which were sharp and clear. Tragg must have been photographed in some conference room without being aware of the camera. One of the pictures was of a taxicab from behind. The taxi sign and registration numbers were clearly readable.

"Do you know where they live?" asked List.

"Afraid not. That's one of the things I'd like your help with."

"But what about this?" List held up the picture of the taxi.

"False plates," said the American in a drawling voice which suggested the question was not worth asking and the answer obvious.

"Have you tried following this Piero Svanberg?"

"He's spent the last few nights at the Sheraton Hotel."

"What about the other?"

"He appears to have left Stockholm for the time being."

List looked hard at Mr. Jones. So close, he thought, so damned close.

"You don't know where he's gone?"

"No. Perhaps to Algeria. But I'm sure he'll be back. In a month at the latest."

List felt as though he had just been rapped on the knuckles by Fate. Why in God's name should Tragg want to go to Algeria? How could the American be so sure Tragg would be back in Stockholm within a month?

"I'll do what I can," said List. "Come back tomorrow afternoon and we'll see what I've got for you."

Jones rose to his feet.

"It may well be," he said in his Western drawl, "that you and I have a mutual interest in these guys. They're going about things far too professionally for my liking. There's no real reason for them to be playing hide and seek because of the contacts they've made with my firm. Not yet, at least. Mr. Hawley suggested I get in touch with you, and I think you'll find it was a good idea."

List shook his guest's hand cordially. Mr. Jones had indicated he was ready to make a bargain, and List wanted to show he had accepted the invitation without revealing just how keen he really was.

After Jones had gone, List sat at his desk for over ten minutes, thinking about his next move. He occasionally picked up one of the pictures and studied it carefully. Then he pressed the intercom button. He had made up his mind. This might be his last chance. Or, he thought, his first and only chance.

. . .

156

Greger Tragg was not in Algeria. On the other hand, it was true he had left Stockholm: Svanberg had arranged a month's car rental with the aid of a false driving license. The apartment in Sundbyberg was locked up but not abandoned, and the telephone booth in the library was no longer receiving long distance calls. There had been no word from Alex.

It was the wrong time of year for vacationers, but just right for traveling salesmen. Tragg duly arrived at a series of hotel rooms he had booked in advance, but nowhere did it occur to anyone that he might be anything but what he seemed. The police scrutinized all hotel registers and registration forms, but not even they saw anything unusual in the regular appearance of one Hans Lundberg day after day. On the contrary. Headquarters put Hans Lundberg on one side together with the hundreds of other traveling salesmen who did their regular rounds in the way their kind has always done. Nevertheless, Hans Lundberg alias Greger Tragg did differ from his colleagues on one remarkable point: he was the only one to pay in cash rather than by credit card.

Four picture postcards with seaside views were sent from various parts of Sweden to East Berlin that month, but did not attract the attention of the post office staff despite the fact that they were all addressed to the same person and carried the same unimaginative message: "I'm thinking of you. Look after yourself!" They were unsigned.

The croupier at the Sheraton was nervous and distraught.

Piero Svanberg had got into the habit of playing the roulette tables for a while before moving over to his regular seat by the piano, but tonight he signalled to stay where he was. Something had happened.

There were more bettors than usual, although it had only just turned seven. The table was dominated by a Yugoslav who

157

usually patronized the Natanya Bar; it was conveniently situated for his girls who worked from small hotels in Klara. The Yugoslav had been winning, and had quite a pile of fifty-kronor chips in front of him. He treated everyone and everything around him with the supreme contempt that only a rootless immigrant can call on.

Success at the gambling tables always seemed to have the same stimulating effect on this kind of half-assimilated citizen. Their pride was without bounds. It was as if they were trying to say: "Look at me, you stupid Swedes! This is something you couldn't do!" It was only a few hundred kronor after all, about as much as one of the girls in the Yugoslav's stall could earn in a couple of hours.

"Five more throws, then we'll take a break," called the croupier.

The Yugoslav took the announcement gracefully. It gave him an excellent excuse to leave the table while well ahead. The others looked surprised.

The little silver ball rattled its way around the regulation five circuits before falling exhausted into number thirty-six. Svanberg had won, and the Yugoslav, who had covered the first dozen numbers, lost one of his fifty-kronor chips. The croupier had raked in the lost stakes, paying out quickly and with the ease of a real professional. Even before all the new bets were placed, the little ball of fate was on its predestined way counterclockwise around the rim.

"Double!"

The Yugoslav had had enough. The next three throws were purely routine, and the croupier placed his rake diagonally over the table before heading for the staff exit. Svanberg followed him, a few paces behind.

"He's been asking about you," said the croupier, closing the door of the empty staff dining room behind them.

"Who?"

"The Yank. The one you asked me to nose out."

"What did he want to know?"

"Your name. Where you worked. Who you were."

"You didn't tell him anything, of course."

The croupier hesitated. He dropped his head guiltily as he took out his wallet and produced a few dollar bills.

"He gave me these. You can have them if you like. It's fifty dollars."

Svanberg pushed his hand away. He looked surprised.

"What did you tell him?"

"I told him what you were called."

"Why?"

"Well, you see," began the croupier, finding it hard to look Svanberg in the eye. "I had no idea he might be interested in you, for chrissake. He was with the hotel fuzz and gave me the bread straightaway. Then he asked what you were called. I tried to wriggle out of it at first, but no way. I'd told the fuzz your name the day before, although he'd forgotten, but not so well that he wouldn't recognize it if he heard it again. It was the second night you went up with the skirt to her room. We hemmed and hawed a bit, then I came out with it. That little bastard Piero Svanberg, or something like that."

Svanberg nodded. Fair enough. "Did you tell him anything else?"

"Some hot air. Nothing solid. Said I'd seen you at Valla, that kind of thing. Bloody nosey, he was."

Svanberg marshalled his thoughts. Then he smiled and put his arm around the other man's shoulders. "Take it easy," he said. "It could have been worse."

"There's more," said the croupier, relieved. "He's been to the pigs."

"How do you know?"

"He got their address from reception, then ordered a taxi. Cost me a hundred, that did."

"Has he been anywhere else?"

159

"Not that I know of. You know he's mixed up with that Intereloc crowd."

Svanberg nodded.

"You've done O.K.," he said reassuringly. "Any more?"

"Know anybody by the name of Tragg? He asked about him too, but I'd never heard of him."

"He's got nothing to do with this," answered Svanberg. "Forget him!"

"No sooner said than done!"

They agreed the croupier should get a hundred kronor for expenses, and another three hundred for being more careful in future. When they left the dining room, the croupier opened the door for Piero Svanberg and let him go first. It was now established who was boss between them, once and for all.


Svanberg did not go straight back to the bar, but went to make a call first.

"Mother," he said, "if anybody asks about me, you know nothing, right? You've never even heard of me."

It took him another five minutes to convince her there was no cause for alarm.

There are hundreds of Svanbergs in the Stockholm directory, and the risk that they might cross-examine Miss Agda Svanberg of Enskede seemed minimal. When he returned to his seat by the piano, he was in a very good mood. He was looking forward to the next few weeks. He started work again tomorrow, both the taxi and Solvalla. Moreover, he had a feeling he was going to meet quite a few new people in the near future. They were welcome.

# ❧XIII❧

Greger Tragg was in the kitchen when the phone rang. He was startled. It sounded like a crude word yelled out on a beach, coarse and shrill. There it was again, and again, repeating itself at what seemed like shorter and shorter intervals.

At moments like this, a choice had to be made. He could refuse to answer, in which case he would be dogged by worry and uncertainty. If it were a wrong number, it would be better to know. It might be Piero Svanberg, although that seemed unlikely: Tragg had been with him only an hour ago. But it could also be someone trying to find out if he was at home.

He let it ring six times before answering, and realized his palms were oozing sweat. He waited for the coin to fall and contact to be made.

"Yes," he said.

"Alex."

He raised his eyebrows, uncertain whether he felt relieved or uncomfortable. "It's a small world."

"It's getting smaller."

"No thanks to you."

161

Thirty years ago, when they had worked out the code together, the phrases meant something. Tragg had forgotten what. The voice at the other end was melodic but impersonal, almost impatient. There was no sign of pleasure, although it was almost two years since they had last spoken to each other.

"Lars Ekerot has come back."

"Can he still see into the future?"

"He claims everything will dissolve in flames again."

"How did he get back?"

"Same way as usual. Along the Green Alley."

The receiver at the other end was replaced with a click. The message was simple and clear. The first part of the code was for identification purposes, and in the second part Alex had requested a meeting which Tragg had agreed to. The final phrases established the place, time, and date. These had been agreed long ago, once and for all, and neither of them had ever seen any reason to change the arrangement. Although much of Stockholm had been rebuilt beyond recognition after the Second World War, no clumsy city planner had dared to touch the meeting place. It displayed the same austere, well-balanced exterior as it had always done, ever since it was built after the great fire almost three hundred years earlier.

Superficially, Tragg might have seemed weary or indolent, but neither feeling was the reason he submitted to the risks which habit always entails. In any case, can something be called a habit when it only happens once or twice every ten years? As the years passed, the majestic setting for their rare meetings had become more and more natural. No one who knew him would be surprised to see Alex in these surroundings, and Tragg did not even need to disguise himself to pass for an ordinary Stockholmer out for a stroll. During the tourist season their brief meetings took place in the midst of visitors from the provinces and Germans pointing eagerly at every

162

little thing; they came to the Royal Palace in the hope of catching a glimpse of the Princess and her commoner mother.

Twice is not a habit, either. When Tragg clambered into Svanberg's taxi at the Central Station shortly after lunch one day in late March, he followed the same routine as when he came home from Berlin. But his reception was rather different. After a racing start they roared out into Vasagatan, running the glaring red light and, hounded by screeching horns, raced into Söderleden. They roared through the labyrinthine traffic on Södermalm without even slowing down, and only when Svanberg had ignored the one-way signs down Katarina Bangata and turned back towards the city center did he slow down and say, "Lost 'em."

"The police?"

Svanberg burst out laughing and tapped his right index finger on his temple. "Them and the CIA. The Yank's been given a hand by the fuzz."

"How do you know?"

"They started to follow me around a week ago. As if they knew you were around somewhere."

Tragg nodded. "I get the picture," he said icily. "Put the car in Katarina Garage."

They made their separate ways out to Rinkeby by subway from Slussen. Tragg had parked his rented car at a filling station, and Svanberg turned up only a few minutes after him. They drove northwards towards Norrtälje, and stopped for ten minutes at the tight curve just after the Väsby stud farm, before you get to the railway bridge. Only one car went past in the Rimbo direction while they were waiting. It was driven by a young woman with kids in the back seat.


"I spent the night there. You should have seen their faces when we went up together in the elevator. They looked as if they were rooted to the spot, all three of them—the hotel

163

fuzz, the Yank, and the plainclothes pig. It must have been a hell of a soft assignment. Free drinks. Warm and comfortable. Good music. I took no notice of them, and strange as it may sound I don't think they ever caught on to the fact that I knew. The plainclothes boys were on two-day shifts. Johnny, the croupier, always tipped me off when a new one came in. Policemen can be bloody stupid at times—the new one always made himself known discreetly to the hotel fuzz. It would never occur to anybody else to talk to him if they didn't have to, unless they were on the staff."

Svanberg ate like a horse. They had stopped at the Gyllene Hoven, the inn at Rimbo. It was deserted at that time of day, and the fat landlord with water on the knee did not like to leave the reception area, which could be seen from the kitchens but was out of earshot.

"Then she flew to Düsseldorf," sighed Svanberg. "She had a contract with a nightclub there. I might have gone with her if I'd been free; she seemed pretty keen in any case. I took her to Arlanda in the taxi, and it was on the way back from there I realized someone was tailing me. It wasn't the Yank, it was a Volvo—probably the fuzz. I did as you said and let them follow me while I worked out where I was going to live in the future. The flat in Sundbyberg was out, and I had no desire to look for another skirt."

"I can see that."

"It had to be my old lady. They knew who I was after all, and it didn't seem to matter any more if they found out where I lived. They were after you, not me, or they'd have picked me up ages ago. So I just followed the old routine and didn't even bother to look whether they were still chasing me around. They might have caught on to the fact that you were going to be away for a few weeks."

"Right."

"All the same, I realized we'd have to be ready for a quick getaway when you turned up. They've put three different cars on to me since yesterday. I've made sure they've had a few extra problems at traffic lights."

Svanberg laughed. It was obvious he was enjoying it all, and pleased with himself. He was still one step ahead of the police, and didn't intend to let them get any nearer.

Tragg looked thoughtful. This was hide-and-seek and cat-and-mouse rolled into one. He lit a cigarette and sat thinking. Svanberg did not dare break the silence until Tragg got up to order coffee and cognac.

"What do we do now?"

"Have you got your passport with you?"

Svanberg shook his head in surprise. "It's at home in Enskede."

"You'd better go get it."

"Are we going on vacation?"

"In a day or two. From now on, you can regard yourself as working full time for me. By full time I mean twenty-four hours a day. It'll be all over by next week and you'll be forty thousand kronor better off. But you'll have to make your own way back to Sweden. I'll pay your fare."


Piero Svanberg's round-the-clock duties began with a surprise which so overwhelmed him he felt he was fully conpensated for the loveless nights in store.

After buying provisions at the local grocer's in Rimbo, Tragg announced they were going to pay a visit to the stables where his trotting horse was trained.

"It might well be several years before I can come back to Sweden," he explained. "Somebody has to look after the mare. Can you manage to pay the monthly charges if I turn her over to you?"

"She'll pay for herself, I expect."

"Horses have their ups and downs like everybody else.

165

Apart from anything else, she has to have a good man in the buggy."

Svanberg protested.

"Can't I buy her instead?"

"You can't afford it," replied Tragg. "In any case, she hasn't cost me anything. The horse is yours; do what you like with her."

Tragg kept all the registration papers in a locked safe at the stables. The trainer witnessed Tragg's and Svanberg's signatures, and when Svanberg was then taken by one of the stable lads to view his new property he seemed to have grown in importance by at least an inch, and acted like a youngster with his first car. He'd taken a step up the ladder.

Meanwhile, Tragg emptied the safe. There were odds and ends of the kind amateur jockeys use: gloves, whip, and overalls. The puffy nylon trousers also contained a little box whose contents are rarely seen in trotting circles, although they are indispensable for a harbinger of peace. The biggest item was a microfilm developer. It was hardly bigger than the camera, which was concealed in an empty king-size cigarette packet. Tragg put everything into a plastic bag which, unknown to Svanberg, he dropped into a pond a few miles northwest of Knivsta, and watched as it sank to the bottom.

The technical evidence linked with Tragg's activities had thus disappeared, once and for all. With one exception. He kept the felt pen made in a Prague laboratory; when handled properly it could release a single bullet, guaranteed fatal up to three yards.

Tragg was struggling to overcome a feeling of indolence, or perhaps it was repugnance. Somehow or other, the conversation with Alex had got to him. It ought to have inspired him. The meeting would not seriously affect the schedule. The day after tomorrow he would meet Lars Bunter at three o'clock, and be given the address of the Swiss bank into which his consultancy fee would be paid. Bunter would

166

also give him the code number which, together with his Swedish passport, would guarantee payment of the fee in Switzerland. Tragg assumed the discussions would be stretched out to half an hour or so, with mutual congratulations and feelers from Bunter about future cooperation and the opening up of new markets. He would have to refuse an invitation to dinner later that evening, and even though Bunter's role meant he was bound to insist on some kind of celebration, Tragg knew his refusal would not be taken amiss. The business was concluded and contact established. Next time, Bunter would doubtless think, he will be easier to deal with.

Tragg had every reason to avoid appearing in public at some restaurant. Moreover, he had no time. His meeting with Alex was fixed for 8:20 p.m., which gave him about forty-eight hours to fill in. He intended to lie low in the apartment, and from tomorrow Piero Svanberg would be there with him.

He did not like relying on luck, but he had no choice. He had left Svanberg an hour ago, giving him the task of finding a car with the Green Card so essential for driving on the Continent. The car was to be parked in the garage under Tragg's current apartment, soon to be abandoned, and Svanberg had assured him he could manage it in a couple of hours except for the green insurance card.

"The only way things can go wrong is if they arrest me when I fetch my passport," he protested when Tragg spelled out the risks.

"That is out of the question. But you can expect two or even three shadows."

"The more the merrier."

Tragg shook his head.

"You're underestimating them."

"No, I'm not," Svanberg assured him. "But I grew up in Enskede. When I was a kid we didn't play football, we played cops and robbers. I was the best! The best robber in the district! Everybody said so. Then, when we were a bit older,

167

we used to roam about there with our girls. You can't imagine how many secret routes we used to know—through basements and gardens, over hedges and fences. Nothing has changed around there. Show me the fuzz that I can't shake off in two minutes! Mind you, I might have trouble if they've started to recruit dwarfs."

"I don't think we need to worry about that."

There were considerable weaknesses in Svanberg's reliance on his local knowledge, but Tragg refrained from pointing out that his young friend had grown quite a few inches in both height and girth since the days when he had been the champion robber. He would probably find that some gaps had become noticeably narrower over the years, but then, his pursuers would have the same problem. Consoled by that thought, Tragg said instead, "No phone calls!"

"No sir! No phone calls! But a car, a Green Card, a passport, and yours truly. The car will have a full tank. They can put searchlights on me if they like, but that won't make any difference. From now on, I'm the man without a shadow!"

Tragg laughed and gave him a friendly thump on the chest. "Go and make yourself invisible as soon as possible! I don't want to see you again until tomorrow night."


Rapid progress in the field of automatic worldwide dialing, especially in Europe, has been a big help to Swedish exports and has made a big difference to the exchange of information, man to man, not least for members of the intelligence services. You only have to dial a certain number from more or less any telephone you like, and within seconds you can be talking to Milan, London, Paris, or Berlin. Needless to say, there has been a corresponding increase in phone tapping, but it has become more difficult to pinpoint the phone from which the call was made. Despite the fact that it seemed to be against the rules, therefore, Tragg had been able to ring Angela de Riez without risk from a telephone booth in Svenljunga, and three days later to do it again from Fagersta. Langer's reply was very satisfactory, and the next day Tragg drove directly from Fagersta to Stockholm.

Even when decoded, the message would no doubt have caused a few problems for the French experts in Berlin. When Tragg converted the coded numbers into words, it ran:

*One hundred. UN members. Mate on the way. The lion will inform. 150/3 as courier. White card. 325. Jamaica.*

With the aid of *Fischer's World Calendar* for 1976, Tragg had no problem in interpreting the message.

*One hundred*: All clear.

*UN members* (Fischer, page 214, first line): Twenty-first of April.

*Mate on the way*: Someone from Algiers intends to supervise the payment of the money in Switzerland.

*The lion*: Lars Bunter.

*will inform*: will tell you the agreed payment day in

*150/3* (Fischer, page 150, third down): Basel.

*as courier*: and will book a hotel room.

*325* (Fischer, page 325): Going by train.

*Jamaica*: Ulrich Langer.

The message and the information from Langer was correct but incomplete. The Algerians had been content to confirm the arrangement and supply the technical details for transferring the consultancy fee to the four numbered accounts which the envoy would reveal on meeting at the Swiss bank. Tragg was therefore in the dark about the final agreement reached between Intereloc and the Algerian purchaser.

# ❧ XIV ❧

Mr. Jones was sitting on the leather sofa outside Tore Wattinius's office, fuming. He had already been given two cups of coffee by Wattinius's blond secretary, an elegant, well-dressed woman in her forties who behaved like a lady in waiting and smiled like a TV hostess, but—as he had discovered to his cost—she was completely immune to flirting. Jones's somewhat risqué view of the liberated Swedes had taken a hard knock during his stay in Stockholm. It was no better than at home; if anything, worse. And anyway, he was not in the mood.

Wattinius had called him early that morning and ordered him—that was the right word—to put in an appearance at the office, ten o'clock sharp. The call had been brief, almost discourteous, and totally lacking in the friendly tone Jones had come to appreciate so much at Intereloc. It was now twenty minutes past ten and Wattinius had not so much as opened his door to apologize for the delay.

Five minutes ago, the secretary had gone in to Wattinius with what looked like a telex message. She had emerged a minute later, closed the door behind her, and given him a long, cool look without saying a word. Jones suspected the telex must have something to do with him. For the last twenty-four hours or so he had been trying to suppress a feeling that he might have gone too far in his cooperation with SÄPO. The old CIA-man in him had been roused when he began to realize Tragg was more than a straightforward errand boy for a few corrupt Arabs. Hawley at the embassy had encouraged him to contact the Swedes, and it was too late when it dawned on him that their interests were no longer compatible. He should have realized that from the start. Only when a multinational company's profits go hand in hand with the security and interests of a country can they enter into voluntary cooperation. In all other circumstances, the firm's interests must come first, and no account can be taken of any partners, no matter who they are.

Jones stubbed out his cigarette when the secretary informed him that Wattinius was ready to receive him. He adjusted his clothing and walked stiffly to the door, his back erect in military fashion, as if about to attend his own court-martial. If he had turned round, he would have been disturbed by the secretary's sneering smile as she followed him with her gaze.

"Sit down, Jones," said Wattinius curtly, indicating a chair drawn up in front of the desk.

Wattinius was not alone; Bunter was with him. Bunter gave him a restrained nod from the short end of the desk, where he had installed himself as a witness.

"Your assignment in Stockholm is over," announced Wattinius in the same clipped tones as before. "You're leaving on the flight to New York in three hours' time. We have taken care of your luggage and bills."

Wattinius handed over an envelope containing travel documents, and picked up the telex he had received only five minutes ago.

"Here you have confirmation from the head office. You

will notice the code word guaranteeing its genuine nature, and be able to verify the high level from which it emanates. As you will see, the text itself is quite clear. Your new orders are that you are to obey the instructions I give you conscientiously and without delay."

The American took the paper and read it. He gritted his teeth and thrust forward his chin as he looked Wattinius straight in the eye.

"The message is genuine," he said stiffly. "I'd still like an explanation, though."

"You have exceeded your authority and in doing so have put at risk a piece of business which is of great importance for the firm. As long as you remain in Sweden, you must in no circumstances contact anyone at all. Fredrik Johnson will see you off."

"I still don't understand."

"Shortly after lunch yesterday I received a telephone call from one of the top men at police headquarters, who I happen to know is head of the Swedish security services," answered Wattinius coolly. "He wanted to express his satisfaction at the high degree of cooperation attained by our firm and his section, thanks largely to your efforts. He implied that the moment of truth was imminent, and was particularly keen to establish the time and place of the crucial meeting with the man representing the foreign interests. That was how he put it, in any case. He didn't even attempt to conceal the fact that this information was of vital importance for him, and he expected either you or me to give it to him."

"What did you tell him?"

"That neither time nor place were fixed as yet. I regret to say my reply meant that the latter part of our conversation was less hearty in tone than the beginning. He had wanted confirmation of a time he knew I must be aware of, but which I refused to tell him."

Jones was an American and hence not well versed in

Swedish conversational techniques. It sometimes happens in Sweden that all those partaking in a discussion sit silently for several minutes with no air of discomfort while they all ponder the significance of the last statement.

It was far too soon when Jones felt obliged to break the silence.

"Your contact man is working for the Communists," he muttered, half audibly.

It was not a plea in his defense, merely a statement of fact, most of all an attempt to quell the increasing irritation he felt at the behavior of the two silent, motionless Swedes.

Wattinius looked at Jones with the patient indulgence normally reserved for a child.

"How interesting," he said gently. "But hardly surprising. It's not very remarkable for the Algerians to choose as their representative someone of proven loyalty to the political camp they more or less belong to themselves. In this case, I consider them to have chosen just the right man. He has gained our confidence not least because we have realized he has the full confidence of our opposite numbers."

"He might be a traitor to your country."

"That's possible," said Wattinius curtly, "but not because of the deal we are in the process of concluding."

Silence prevailed, and Jones realized this part of the conversation was closed. Bunter was the first to speak.

"When did you arrange to contact List again?"

"Two o'clock."

"Today?"

The American nodded. A glance at the clock showed him there were three hours to go: his plane was due to leave at ten to two. Bunter also looked at his watch and found he had just over four hours before meeting Tragg. He gave Wattinius a meaningful look.

"If anything happens to our contact man, it is not only this contract that will be put at risk," asserted Wattinius icily.

174

"A whole market could be closed to us for years to come. That's bad business. I'm convinced you, too, have an interest in the successful outcome of our discussions, since they are bound to affect the interview awaiting you on your return to New York. For my part, I really do hope that little chat will not result in your being accused of having sabotaged our activities here in Stockholm. If we lose the order at this stage, there might be grounds for suspecting that someone is working for our competitors."

Wattinius and Bunter rose from their chairs. Wattinius strode round the table and shook Jones's hand in farewell. Bunter did the same. Jones turned round when he reached the door.

"Have a good trip," said Wattinius, and there was neither irony nor sarcasm in his voice, just normal Swedish politeness.

"Have a good trip," echoed Lars Bunter.

Jones did not know what to say in reply, but merely closed the door behind him. He was met immediately by Fredrik Johnson's hoarse but always enthusiastic traveling salesman's voice.

"If we hurry straight to the airport at Arlanda, we'll have time for lunch in the restaurant. It's much better than the plastic food they serve you on the plane."


Following his failure two days previously, Bengt List, head of B-section within SÄPO, had drawn five conclusions:

1. The taxi driver had known he would be followed. Nevertheless, the way in which two of his best shadows had been left nonplussed in the gardens of the housing estate in Enskede was humiliating. One of them had even been arrested by a patrol crew called in by an outraged pensioner who objected to his flower beds and glass frames being trampled by

the clumsy and highly suspicious-looking character wandering through his garden for the third time.

**2.** Greger Tragg and the taxi driver were lying low somewhere in Stockholm. Neither of them would venture out into the streets until they were summoned to Intereloc, and so List had scaled down the watch being kept.

**3.** Wattinius had not told the truth, or at least had not revealed all he knew. The search for Tragg would be switched to Intereloc's offices in Bromma. List had assigned four cars and twelve men to the area, and this time they must not fail.

**4.** Mr. Jones was due to call by two o'clock at the latest. The American had proved to be a professional who kept his word. List was convinced he would soon know when Tragg was due to visit Intereloc. Behind Jones was Mr. Hawley, in whose interest it was to maintain good relations with B-section and its head. Even so, List felt uneasy and stared spitefully at the telephone in front of him. The clock on the wall said one fifty-three.

**5.** There was no logical connection between Tragg's sudden interest in international commerce—which it was undoubtedly in the country's interest to encourage—and his illegal activities as the link with the man continually supplying a foreign power with the most secret of Swedish secrets. It is true that there was no firm evidence of the man's existence, but the vast number of pointers, produced after years of effort and argument by his own section of the security services in close cooperation with the departments of trade and industry, indicated beyond all doubt that there was a traitor, and that he was still operating as diligently as ever. Another indicator was the growing stream of hints from foreign contacts that there was an even bigger leak than the one plugged when Colonel Wennerström had been arrested. Jones had mentioned in passing he knew Tragg was working for the communists. He had presumably received that information from Mr. Hawley, who had thus found an elegant way of informing the Swedes the CIA knew more than SÄPO.

176

For some unknown reason, the fragile contact Sweden had with MfS, or Stasi as it was popularly known, suggested that in return for as yet unspecified favors, the East Germans might be prepared to release the name of a man who would be of great interest to the Swedish security services. List was not sure whether Stasi and the CIA were referring to the same person.

The telephone rang at two minutes past two, and List sighed with relief as he picked up the receiver. "List."

The hoarse voice at the other end of the line did not speak English, but Swedish, with a pronounced Uppland accent.

"This is Matsson at Arlanda. I thought you'd like to know the Yank has gone home."

"Which Yank?"

"Jones. The one in the car with us when we were following that taxi driver who got away."

"When did he leave?"

"Ten to two. I called as soon as I could. After I'd checked the passenger list on the two forty-five plane for Russia. You know I'm on my own out here."

"Yes, I know. Thank you."

List replaced the receiver with a sigh. Even if the plane left at ten to two, Jones must have gone through passport control at least half an hour earlier, which meant Matsson had been sitting on his information for nearly an hour before he had got round to calling. He drew a deep breath, then slammed his fist down on the desk so hard that the telephone receiver jumped off its stand with a terrified "pling."

"Damn it!"

That damned Wattinius had led him up the garden path. He thought hard for ten minutes. Jones's rapid return home could only mean one of two things. One was that Intereloc had concluded its business with Greger Tragg, and Jones had therefore completed his mission. That seemed unlikely. Why

177

had Jones left Sweden in such a rush? Normal courtesy demanded that he should call in person to say goodbye and thank List for his help. Jones had realized how important Tragg was to List. The other, more likely, alternative was that Intereloc had put a muzzle on Jones and whipped him out of the country as quickly as possible, as they suspected Jones's contact with List might well lead to Tragg's immediate arrest. This shady deal with the Arabs could fall through if Tragg was at last put where he belonged.

"Bums!" muttered List scornfully, looking up a telephone number which he dialed rapidly.

Mr. Hawley at the American Embassy took the call himself on the phone he used for outgoing calls when he wished to avoid the operator; only a few people knew the number. List introduced himself, then asked: "Have you heard anything from our mutual friend Mr. Jones?"

"Not since yesterday. He was supposed to call me this morning. To tell you the truth, we'd arranged to have lunch together in town, but he's stood me up. Has anything happened to him?"

"Not that I know of," replied List. "But I'd be grateful if you'd ask him to get in touch with me as soon as he turns up."

"Sure. Damned strange, this business. You can usually rely on Jones. Could be he's hit on something interesting. Things are heating up about now, aren't they?"

"That's right."

"Odd that he couldn't reach a telephone, all the same."

"That would be difficult if he's left Stockholm, though."

"Left Stockholm? Why?"

"Oh, we sometimes have to go on these little trips. There's no cause to worry."

"I hope not."

They promised to keep in touch. When List replaced the receiver he was sure neither Hawley nor anyone else at the embassy knew Jones had gone home to the States. Intereloc's muzzle on Jones had been even tighter than he had feared. That could only mean one thing. It must be now, today or tomorrow, that Intereloc aimed to clinch the deal with Greger Tragg.

Before List ordered coffee and sandwiches in his room and prepared to continue his vigil, he issued two orders.

The first was to make a dramatic increase in his men watching the airports at Arlanda, Bromma, Sturup, and Landvetter. The other was to put out a warrant for the arrest of Greger Tragg, with the qualification that he was only to be arrested if he tried to leave the country. Because of an oversight, or maybe because both orders were sent out at the same time, no other border posts were informed—neither frontier crossings nor ferry terminals.


Lars Bunter admitted to himself that he was finding it all exciting. The Algerian deal could be his big chance. Intereloc was forced to move out into the international market—in the old days, the Swedish forces and occasional contracts with their Scandinavian neighbors had kept his section fully occupied for many years, but those outlets had melted away as defense budgets, especially in Sweden, had been reduced drastically.

Intereloc was only a small unit within the multinational company, but its profits had been excellent for some time now. With regard to profitability, and taking into account capital investment and number of employees (barely a thousand people), Intereloc was in the top ten of the multinational's four hundred and fifty branches throughout the world. No one had expected Intereloc to hold on to that position this year and next, nor had anyone supposed the little Swedish firm would be able to break into the Arab market, the most difficult of all, on its own. If this deal succeeded—

179

and it looked as though the "if" could be scrubbed—then a large proportion of the credit would go to him. From now on, Lars Bunter was a name to be reckoned with at the highest level at the American headquarters. It was consistent policy for the firm to support only winners. That was the same in all the multinationals. When the Algerian deal was finally clinched, Bunter could count on promotion; perhaps he would be given a managing directorship in South America or somewhere in Asia, with good prospects of further advancement. He was determined not to let this opportunity slip through his fingers.

Neither Wattinius nor Bunter had previous experience of business outside Europe. When they were visiting their European headquarters in Brussels, they had sometimes listened with surprise and not a little skepticism to the many stories of bribes or, as they called it, commission or consultancy fees. They had both been brought up in the Swedish tradition of honest dealing; a few tricks and some subtle means of persuasion were allowed, but it was rare for anyone to overstep the mark into what Swedes call corruption. Having sent the tender to Algeria, they realized they could expect demands and conditions way beyond those normally received from Scandinavian generals or armory executives.

They had hoped for a positive response from Algiers, but had not expected it to come via a Swede. Tragg's demands had seemed monstrous, and it was only after a quick check with Brussels that they decided to go ahead with serious negotiations.

"Ministerial commission," the Brussels expert had commented laconically when he heard about the sixteen per cent. "That means you really have made contact. But be careful. You can make pretty hefty counter conditions for that kind of money."

From then on they had consulted Brussels less and less often. Wattinius was summoned to the head office in New

York, and returned more decisive and dignified than ever. His discussions with the top men in the company had made it clear that Intereloc's "little" deal with Algiers was being followed with great interest at the highest level, and was regarded as a crucial tactical assault quite in line with the aims of the company's strategy over many years. It had even been given a code name at the head offices: Sesame, the implication being that doors would be opened.

On returning home, Wattinius delegated direct responsibility for the affair to Lars Bunter, following the line all managing directors must take in order to survive. Although he would not escape unscathed if things were to go wrong, the consequences would be less disastrous for him than for his subordinate. If all went well, Bunter would receive most of the credit but a not insignificant part of the glory would rub off on Wattinius. He had nothing against that arrangement. Wattinius preferred to stay in Sweden where he had a nice home, a sailing boat, a holiday home and a secure future independent of world markets and the performance of the multinational company.

During the six weeks that had passed since Bunter first met Greger Tragg at the Sheraton, he had come to realize that his opposite number was a man worthy of respect and even admiration. Despite his dubious role, Tragg had always behaved reasonably and had managed to create an atmosphere of confidence and mutual understanding. Bunter could not accuse Tragg of lying. Indeed, once the level of the consultancy fee had been agreed, he had been increasingly surprised to find the discussions and agreements proceeding exactly as Tragg said they would. Negotiations in Algiers had been concluded so rapidly, for instance, that Bunter had difficulty in keeping up with the hectic pace. Tragg's demands for absolute secrecy and his mysterious way of going about things had added extra spice to the excitement of it all.

Bunter had taken the secrecy thing very seriously. As he

sat in his office waiting for Tragg, he felt pleased with the extra care he had taken on that score. Jones's overstepping the mark like that could have put them in an uncomfortable, not to say disastrous, situation. Bunter was sure that, given the information the Swedish police now had, they would not hesitate to arrest Tragg if only they could find him. That must not happen. At least, not until the deal was clinched and the consultancy fee transferred into the appropriate accounts.

This would be their last meeting, and Bunter had decided to invite Tragg to the little two-roomed office Intereloc rented in a city center office block some six miles from the main building. There were no signs to show who owned the rooms, which were used exclusively by Wattinius and Bunter when they wished to have more intimate discussions, and when discretion was particularly important.

# ❧ XV ❧

Greger Tragg came on foot. Commuter train and subway make an excellent combination for anyone who wishes to travel between two points, both unknown to his hunters, in mid-afternoon.

On this slushy day at the tail-end of winter, most Stockholmers were uniformly dressed in padded parkas with thick and colorful knitted hats, and some pulled right down to their eyebrows. Tragg's hat was in blue and yellow, the most popular color combination all year round. In such a masquerade, reminiscent of Carnival time, the only way of finding a wanted man is to post lookouts at all subway station entrances—and the underground labyrinth in Stockholm has changed the town's fourteen islands into a group of enormous Swiss cheeses.

You need whole regiments to mount an operation of that size, and even then it is unlikely the hunters will have more than a passing glimpse of their prey. The subway crush is often intolerable, the possible escape routes are limitless. That is why Tragg left Svanberg and the car at home in Sundbyberg; they would not be needed until later that evening.

183

It was almost two o'clock when Tragg settled down at one of the window tables in the little working class café opposite the enormous red brick office block in Malmskillnadsgatan. If the building opposite was under observation, it would be unthinkable not to place a man in the café. It only took Tragg a few minutes to convince himself that none of the building workers or gloomy figures drinking cheap beer served by a taciturn Finnish landlord could be members of the security forces. From behind his newspaper, he could conveniently keep an eye on traffic and passersby through the dirty window. Everything was normal.

At about half past two, one of Intereloc's delivery vans pulled up at the entrance to the office block, and Tragg was barely able to suppress a whistle of amazement when he saw Lars Bunter jump out of the cab with a cap pulled down over his eyes. It was so amateurish! Tragg felt he was watching a class hybrid, something between a deep-blue upper-crust gentleman from Saltsjöbaden and a deep-pink proletarian from Tensta. Hardly had Bunter gone through the door than he removed his cap and bright red woolen scarf with his free hand. With his other hand, he clung tightly to the insignia of his dignity—an attaché case.

Tragg wiped the smile from his face. Bunter's choice of transport must mean he was trying to conceal what he was up to and that he was afraid of being followed. Tragg knew an amateur like Bunter had no chance of fooling a professional, and intensified his watch on the street and the remaining few thirsty customers still trying to catch the attention of the morose Finnish landlord.

By shortly before three, Tragg was certain Bunter's incredible maneuver had actually succeeded. He paid his bill, walked rapidly across the street and into the office block. During the seven minutes he stood in a cubbyhole near the elevator, the only sign of life was one person leaving the building. She looked to neither left nor right but hastened out through the door just like any other of the thousands of part-timers intent on doing the shopping and getting the evening meal ready before the family came home. Tragg began to be convinced he could conclude his business with Lars Bunter without interruption and in an atmosphere of intimacy.

He was right. None of Bengt List's watchdogs reported seeing Lars Bunter leave the Intereloc building. It was beyond their comprehension to imagine the managing director of a Swedish firm dressing up in a cap and scarf and driving away in a delivery van to clinch a deal worth forty million kronor.

"We have taken every possible precaution to insure our business can be conducted in strict privacy," explained Bunter formally. "I have received confirmation today that the Swiss bank has received the credit note for the sum designated as the consultancy fee for this part of the contract. It is issued in Panama."

Tragg hesitated. "Would you mind explaining what you mean by 'this part of the contract'?"

Bunter looked up, his expression indicating faint surprise. "Needless to say, we can only pay commission on the amount that has been paid in."

"Naturally."

The penny began to drop. Intereloc had been unable to deliver all the material at once. Why had no one told him about that? How big or small was the first delivery? How much money was running through his and Ulrich Langer's fingers at this very moment?

"I haven't been given any precise figures," he said cautiously. "They told me in Algiers you would fill me in on that, since I need it for password and identification purposes when it comes to paying out."

Bunter nodded. "That's right."

185

He seemed satisfied with Tragg's explanation, and picked up one of the papers on the desk in front of him.

"The credit our bank has received amounts to twenty-one million three hundred and eighty-four thousand, five hundred and twelve kronor."

He handed over the piece of paper, his hand trembling slightly as if he were suppressing a stammer. It was a plain sheet with no letterhead, empty but for one single set of figures: 21,384,512.

"The eight per cent commission thus amounts to one million seven hundred and ten thousand, seven hundred and sixty kronor and ninety öre."

He handed over another sheet of paper containing the same figure as before, but someone had added a few extra figures at the side with an electric typewriter: 1,710,760.90.

Half. They had lost half.

"As you know, the rest of the contract will be fulfilled by three further deliveries starting in January next year. I'm sure we shall be able to keep to the delivery dates," said Bunter. "In the meantime, I can't see you or your friends getting into financial difficulties."

Despite the smile, there was a trace of envy in his voice. Tax-free funds. Unearned income. But risky. Bunter rose to his feet and pointed to a group of chairs in the corner of the room.

"Let's have a whiskey to celebrate the successful conclusion of our little deal," he suggested. "There's also a minor problem I think we ought to talk about."

They drank to each other's health, solemnly, as befits the Swedes.

"I trust the contact we have made will not be broken now that our little ship has been brought safely to port," said Bunter. "But let's leave thoughts about the future until the next payment in January. Just now, there's a small problem I must tell you about."

186

"What problem?" Tragg sipped his whiskey, apparently unconcerned, and seemed only moderately interested in whatever it was Bunter was having difficulty in coming round to. Bunter was embarrassed. Otherwise he would have seen through Tragg's offhand attitude and realized it was a sign of tension.

Bunter was searching for the right words. "There's been a leak."

They looked each other in the eye, coldly, but without animosity, amicably but without trust.

"A leak? Who?"

"You m-must understand," said Bunter with a marked stammer, "that this sort of deal can be risky for the seller. Practically no contract is signed in Europe with the Arabs without the supplier being approached by various people while discussions are taking place, all of them wanting consultancy fees. They all claim to have crucial influence on the outcome of the affair."

Tragg nodded. The Arabs were gamblers; they risked their hand and were convinced of their ability to get the better of Europeans and Americans whose business code they regarded quite rightly as hypocrisy and self-deception.

When news of some contract with the West filters down as far as the middle layers of Arab bureaucracy, it is routine for a few key figures to get together and send out some relative with a rudimentary knowledge of the language to the desperate seller, who is persuaded by cunning, threats, or even sheer persistence to offload the odd per cent or two. The initiated observer can gauge the relative importance of the visitor by the percentage demanded. One or two per cent indicates small fry, a small tip which might make payment come a little easier or insure the customs people will refrain from introducing unforeseen demands that are difficult to meet, taking advantage of the mass of vague or contradictory regulations upon which it bases its activities.

Eight per cent or more is an indication that people with real power are behind the moves. Anyone who knows how to deal with customs officers and bureaucrats does not need to pay a penny.

"During the last months I've been visited by two gentlemen who, quite independently, have each demanded their one per cent," said Bunter with a grin. "I sent them both packing. They were obviously not aware of the method of payment we have agreed on. Incidentally, one of them threatened reprisals before leaving."

"I shall inform Algiers," said Tragg.

"If you think it necessary. As far as I'm concerned, the matter is closed."

They were still talking around the main question. Bunter raised his whiskey glass once more and wished Tragg good health before emptying the glass and filling his lungs with air.

"Our experience of business with the Middle East and North Africa is limited," he said, quietly and thoughtfully. "Head office offered to help us avoid the worst pitfalls. A man who specializes in this type of question was sent over from the U.S.A. and put at our disposal. Unfortunately, as things turned out, he went too far in his inquiries, although it was some days before we became aware he had been in touch with the Swedish authorities in rather worrying circumstances."

"Which authority?"

"The p-police."

"We haven't done anything wrong yet," said Tragg calmly.

"No, of course not. Don't misunderstand me." Bunter was talking far too fast in order to avoid problems with his consonants, but what he had to say was of central importance.

"The situation is none of our doing here in Stockholm. We were led up the garden path and knew nothing about it, which is why we have tried to put things right. We want to do all we can to make it easier for you to fulfill your obligations to

188

your friends. We're businessmen, that's all. The business code varies from country to country, and a multinational company like ours has to adapt to whatever is normal in different parts of the world. If problems arise, we always follow the code of the purchasing country, so that nothing can stand in the way of good relations between ourselves and our customers."

"Who is this person who has, er, gone too far?"

"Jo-Jo . . . His name is Jones. He's left. He flew back to the U.S.A. from Arlanda airport an hour ago. Fredrik Johnson saw him off. All his contacts with the outside world were broken off early this morning."

"What did the police want to know?"

"When and where we were going to meet," answered Bunter with an embarrassed smile.

"Did they receive that information?"

"No." Bunter shook his head vigorously. "We told them that neither time nor place are fixed yet."

"Told?"

Bunter looked Tragg straight in the eye. "Yesterday, Wattinius received a telephone call from a police chief. He wondered when our next meeting was going to take place. The way the conversation went, it's likely he'll contact us again. That was when we realized Jones had been talking out of school."

"How much did Jones know?"

"Not a lot. Certainly not everything. Only Wattinius and I know the details of the agreement between you and me. Head office is in the picture, but at a level where no leaks are possible. Jones's job was to find out more about the people we were entering into a contract with, and to make sure we didn't fall into a trap."

"Did he succeed in his task?"

Bunter managed an awkward smile. "That depends how you look at it. With hindsight, it's obvious it was a mistake to accept Mr. Jones's services. But your friends in Algiers are still masked, even if we can guess who a couple of them are. The

189

only solid piece of information Jones has come up with is the name of your driver."

"Congratulations," said Tragg drily.

"I . . . ," went on Bunter hesitantly, "I'm pretty sure the police don't know your address in Stockholm. Jones has asked about it several times, but I've been able to say quite honestly that I've no idea. It was sufficient to point out that our agreement meant you would always take the initiative and be the one to make contact."

Tragg nodded. The situation had not changed fundamentally, this was just confirmation of what he already knew. But he might be able to exploit it.

"My person," said Tragg formally, "is now of extreme importance. Not just for me. If anything should happen to me, it's inevitable that quarrels would ensue between Intereloc and my employers."

"We are well aware of that."

"It's of great importance to you yourself and to your firm that I should be able to turn up in Switzerland," Tragg went on. "It's not just a question of money. My friends invited me to represent them in this affair in order to show their appreciation for my services in FNL's war of liberation. The only correct expression for our relationship is that we are . . . blood brothers."

"I appreciate that," agreed Bunter. "During the time we've known each other I've grown to realize how close your contacts are with your employers. Everything has gone as you said it would when we first met. We haven't really had a single real problem. Apart from this unfortunate business with Jones."

Bunter looked decidedly worried. The situation would have to be resolved somehow or other. Tragg and his friends must get their money. What happened afterwards was none of his business, and he was sure that, if necessary, the Arabs would find a replacement for Tragg when it came to discussing the next delivery in January.

"We must assume the police are tapping all telephone and telex contact with Algiers," said Tragg cautiously. "Is it part of your instructions to send a telex to Algiers giving the time and place for payment?"

Bunter looked up and nodded.

"That gives us the chance we need for me to do what I have to do."

"What do you mean?"

"You must give the police false information."

"A fake message?"

"Exactly. Fake. But credible. When has the bank been told to make the payment?"

"On request."

"That solves our problems. Tell them Zurich instead of Basel as the place, and give Thursday and Friday as alternative days for payment. Repeat the days of the week."

"How will the recipient know the message is fake?"

"By your repeating the days of the week. Moreover, I'll be in touch with them tonight via a link through another country. The correct information will get through all right."

"And that is?"

"Basel, two P.M. on Tuesday."

Bunter thought for a moment. The minister in Algiers had been adamant that the crucial telex must be correct and its contents one hundred per cent secret. 'Nobody, nobody at all except you and me must know what it says,' the minister had emphasized. "I'd prefer some other method," he said, hesitantly.

"What other method is there?" Tragg's voice was calm and he sounded as if he really did want to know what other way was possible. Bunter could not help smiling back as he observed Tragg's guileless expression. They had known each other for two months now, and everything had happened

191

exactly as this man had predicted. Not even now, with the Swedish police at his heels, did he display the slightest sign of unease. What would happen if the police arrested him and he started to talk? The newspapers would accuse Intereloc of being a company operating on the basis of bribery and corruption and, worst of all, one not averse to blatant tax evasion. The Bank of Sweden would demand an investigation. A scandal of gigantic proportions would evolve, and Bunter himself would be pilloried as the man responsible. The firm would abandon him and make him a scapegoat. His career would be at an end.

The hint of suspicion which had quite reasonably flitted through Bunter's mind moments ago gave way to thoughts about the consequences of the matter being made public. Once Tragg left Sweden, the immediate danger to himself and Intereloc would be over. If in addition Tragg managed to divert the money into the right accounts before being arrested, then Bunter's future was rosy, to say the least.

"There is no other way," he agreed. "We'll do as you suggest."

When Tragg closed the door of the elegant office behind him and returned to the hustle and bustle of Stockholm's slushy and dirty streets, Bunter clasped his hands as if in prayer. Five minutes later he set to work on the telex machine in the outer office. Half an hour later, the message was handed to a smartly dressed man at a ministry desk in Algiers. He read it in obvious delight, and passed it around to his friends that same evening. The next morning one of them began to prepare for his trip to Zurich in Switzerland. He was glad to have so much time to get ready, and that he would be able to spend the weekend at home.


On the train back home to Sundbyberg, Tragg sat fingering the pen specially made for him by a firm in

Czechoslovakia. Correctly handled, it was a murder weapon. If everything went according to plan, he hoped he would never have to use it. By sending the false telex to Algiers, Lars Bunter had unwittingly saved the life of Ahmed Kassir. Tragg and Langer had originally assumed they would have to kill the Arab in order to visit the bank undisturbed. They had examined every other alternative, but the necessity for absolute security was overriding. They had not anticipated an opportunity of obtaining the money without Algerian supervision.

Tragg had bluffed, and the bluff had worked. In fact, bluff was against his principles. Bluff is a poor weapon, and no one can foresee how it will turn out. It is different from an ordinary mistake in that if it is called, there is no alternative, not even retreat. A bluff successfully called means comprehensive defeat.

To have just lost—he worked it out in his head—eight hundred and fifty thousand kronor felt strange and hard to grasp. He knew a large proportion of the money he counted on getting would have to be spent on safety precautions before he could be sure his new existence was water-tight. With only half the sum at his disposal, he realized he would have to start worrying about expenses. Nevertheless, he decided to put off that problem until he and Langer had actually got their hands on the money which was still locked away.

Bunter had confirmed that SÄPO was after him. That fact did not change his predicament, it merely replaced his suspicions by certainty, a kind of double confirmation. He still judged his chances of getting away with it as good. Getting out of the country presented mainly technical problems, and he had an advantage over the police. They worked on the basis of routine and compulsory overtime, when they would much prefer to be at home in the warm, comfortable marriage bed or pursuing some other pleasures. They were underpaid, and often ill-informed about the particular task they were

193

required to perform. All the secrecy in the security services, the many chains of command, bureaucracy, rivalry between individual forces, all these things can be exploited by someone with nobody to care about but himself.

Twice so far his intuition had served him well. Or was it just straightforward good luck? Tragg disliked the concept of good and bad luck. They were more or less taboo words in his line of activity. Even so, he could not deny he had enjoyed good luck. He had guessed, and had guessed right. He had done so against a background of logical assumptions and knowledge of the darker areas of the human mind, but all the same. . . . If the Algerians had not arranged for Bunter to send a telex giving them time and place for the payment, Tragg would have been exposed.

Could he trust Lars Bunter?

Tragg shook his head as he left the train in Sundbyberg and joined the crowd milling down the all-too-narrow underpass in the direction of Landsvägen. He could not trust anyone. All people play too many roles at the same time, and sometimes these roles conflict with each other. The only things one can be fairly sure about are greed and fear. Both Bunter and the Algerians would play the game according to the rules, because they imagined that if they did not, they had too much to lose.

# ❧ XVI ❧

The windshield wipers scraped noisily against the glass. Sleet, typical April weather, a breakthrough for a belt of air from the Arctic. The sparse, yellow street lamps along Klara Strand seemed to shrink in the wind, gleaming coldly with an evil glint like the eyes of a young bear.

Tragg was driving. Five minutes ago, instead of heading for Essingeleden and the E4 highway, he had turned down towards Klaraberg. Svanberg wondered why.

"The Palace."

It was clear from Tragg's voice that he expected no further questions.

They were on their way at last. Several months of hide and seek would soon culminate in a Swiss bank, where Piero Svanberg would receive his forty thousand kronor for services rendered. But we're not there yet, Tragg had warned him. Imagine two hares out in an open field, freezing cold and chased by hounds. That's us, and we have to get over that field—without being seen.

Although he had listened carefully to Tragg's warning, Svanberg's mood was mainly one of carefree self-confidence and keen expectation. Not even the dreadful weather could spoil his boyish enthusiasm. He did not intend to return to Stockholm for a fortnight—he planned to take the shortest and quickest route from Switzerland to Düsseldorf. To be on the safe side, he had noted down the nightclub where she was playing in a newly acquired memo book he had inserted in his wallet. As he smiled through the side windows at the glimpses of Kungsholmen that flashed by, harrowed and bleak over the frozen bay, he checked to make sure he had his passport in the inside pocket of his sports jacket. At the same time, Tragg skilfully skidded the car around the hundred-and-eighty-degree turn into Kungsgaten. Svanberg was forced back into his seat, and when his fingers brushed against the heavy shoulder holster with the Walther pistol, he banished his daydreams.

Tragg went through his usual security routine. He drove all around the Old Town, waited for several minutes at Nytorget, stopped at all the traffic lights, and finally parked at Mynttorget, a few yards from Lejonbacken. The time was 8:17 P.M.

"I'll only be a quarter of an hour at most," said Tragg curtly. Svanberg watched him disappear up the steps leading to the Palace, and remained restlessly in the front seat. Was he supposed to just sit here, waiting?

After a few minutes, he got out and looked up and down the street. There was not much traffic on Norrbro, just a stone's throw in front of him, and in the middle of the bridge a bareheaded man was struggling bravely with the wind and the driving snow. Perhaps he was on his way to the Opera Bar, that watering hole for Stockholm melancholics waiting for spring to arrive. A police car turned gently in the direction of Skeppsbron. Behind him, a few of the Chancery lights were still blazing through the snow. Only the massive stone walls of the Palace seemed unconcerned and deliberately indifferent.

A squad of soldiers on guard duty, they looked like the home guard, in fact, marched past in strict formation: a puffed-up color sergeant in the lead, two forty-year-olds in single file behind him. All of them were wearing their fur coats. They disappeared up the same steps as Tragg had taken.

The place was now deserted, and Svanberg began to feel worried and insecure. He thought for a while. Tragg could hardly return by any other route than the steps leading up to the outer courtyard. There was no reason to hang around here guarding the car. Uncertain of whether or not he was doing the right thing, Svanberg began to walk slowly up the steps. He paused on the first step and took out his pistol. After a few moments more of hesitation, he released the safety catch and concealed it in his parka pocket. The patrol guarding the outer courtyard had taken shelter in the hut leaning against the back wall of Axel Oxenstierna's palace. There was no sign of life anywhere at all, and Svanberg could see no trace of Tragg.


Alex arrived in the inner courtyard at exactly 8:20 p.m. It was on his normal route from his apartment in Österlångga-tan to his office in the Chancery. He had eight minutes in which to shoot Greger Tragg. Military routines are locked into strict schedules, and patrols invariably leave at set times and follow fixed routes. Like the king, Alex could rely on the precision of the Royal guard.

Alex intended to devote two of the eight minutes to a calm but rapid walk down the steps to Lejonbacken and over Mynttorget before ringing the doorbell at the Chancery entrance. Within thirty seconds at most, the guard would open the door and let him into the building with a welcoming greeting rather than a security check.

The weapon he was carrying in the pocket of his fur-trimmed overcoat had been bought in Belgium fifteen years ago, and he had tested it last week from his bedroom window. It was fitted with a silencer.

Alex had allowed three minutes for talking to Tragg, which gave him a margin of four and a half, or, if worst came to worst, four minutes. With the weather like this, it would not surprise him if the body were not discovered for an hour or so: none of the patrols came past this particular spot.

Just inside the passage known as the Royal Guard Terrace, Tragg was waiting a few yards from the locked door leading to Oscar II's suite of rooms that look out over Lejonbacken. Where he stood, he could not be seen from the Royal Guard's barrack room, which is rarely if ever occupied, although it faces the terrace. Tragg's position was the most sheltered spot from which he had a clear view of the whole palace.

As Alex passed through the inner courtyard, Tragg took out the Czech pen and cocked the mechanism. He held it between the first and second fingers of his left hand, intending to take no risks: if there were any truth in Marika's warning, this would be Alex's last chance. Tragg shook off the half-melted snowflakes from his face and wrinkled his brow. It was eight years since he had last held a weapon in his hand, ready to kill. He was not a professional murderer, hence his relief when Bunter agreed to send the false telex. Tragg had no desire to take Ahmed Kassir's life, but he would have done so if necessary just as he was prepared to defend himself here and now, should it prove to be unavoidable.

Suddenly, as if someone had pulled up a blind, they were standing face to face. They both had the same thought at the same time: he hasn't changed. Neither of them offered to shake hands.

"Your method of concluding our business is unsatisfactory," said Alex.

Like Tragg, he had stepped one pace backwards, and the two men were eyeing each other warily.

"I obey orders," replied Tragg.

"It looks to me as if you're running away."

198

"I'm being recalled because I'm beginning to be a threat to you."

Alex stared haughtily at him. Tragg met his gaze, and knew what was going through the other's mind. You have always been a threat. Tragg looked away—it was not his eyes that were dangerous, but his hands. The gun was in his right-hand pocket, the safety catch was off, and Alex's finger was on the trigger; but it was pointing obliquely downwards. In his left hand, Alex held a cigarette holder complete with burning cigarette. For a split-second, Tragg wondered if he had blundered into a film from the forties; but the man in front of him was no less dangerous for striking a pose from his formative days thirty years ago. If Alex was intending to shoot through his pocket, he would first have to draw his right arm back and raise the barrel of the pistol in order to get the right angle. That was time-consuming.

"How much does SÄPO know?"

"About me, everything. About you, nothing."

"How can you be so sure?"

"We wouldn't be on our own here if it were otherwise."

"What does Sasha intend to do next?"

"I've no idea. You'll have to work out yourself how to keep the contact going in future. If there is a future, that is."

"There is for me in any case," muttered Alex, and Tragg kept a watchful eye open for any sign of movement in Alex's right-hand pocket. There was none. Alex flicked the ash off his cigarette with his left hand. There was about half an inch left to smoke.

"Have you betrayed me?"

"If you mean have I told Sasha who and what you are, the answer is no. Apart from Marika and yourself I am the only one who knows who Alex is."

"Where are you thinking of going to?"

Tragg tensed himself. Alex's almost friendly sounding question followed by his rapid, patronizing smile was a

199

warning signal. He merely shook his head and moved one pace nearer the Palace wall.

In the same split-second as Alex whipped the pistol out of his overcoat pocket Tragg flung himself sideways. His foot slipped slightly as he jumped and he misjudged his speed, so that the mercury-tipped bullet hit Alex a few inches lower than intended. At the same time, he realized with astonishment that Alex had not been aiming at him, but at a target behind his back, and he had managed to fire before Tragg's bullet felled him.

In the narrow passageway, the report from Svanberg's Walther echoed like a whip-crack. His bullet sailed up into the sky and eventually fell harmlessly in Logården. Alex had seen the young man come into the Royal Guard Terrace with a pistol in his right hand, and realized immediately he was a dangerous accomplice: he had not hesitated at all. From less than fifteen yards he hit Svanberg right in the throat without the young man knowing his life was at an end.

Tragg fell on his right side, hip, and shoulder. As he got up he felt a pain in his hip, but nothing seemed to be broken. Alex lay in a crumpled heap in front of him. Dark patches of blood formed a halo around his body. He lost consciousness just as Tragg was getting to his feet.

For the next few seconds Tragg reacted mechanically, as if programmed by some computer. He did not try to establish if Alex was dead or merely unconscious. The danger was still acute, but it no longer came from Alex; Tragg was unable to estimate the reactions and willpower of unknown men in uniform. Even before he reached Piero Svanberg, he knew what he would find.

Svanberg's death was quick but not beautiful. The bullet had split his carotid artery and drenched him in blood. His young, dark but staring eyes were directed uncomprehendingly at Tragg, who sighed deeply and resisted his first impulsive reaction to bend down over the corpse. The pistol lay a couple of feet away, and Tragg left it where it was. There was nothing he could do.

When the shrill whistle sounded for the second time, Tragg was only a few paces from the steps leading down from the upper courtyard to Lejonbacken. The sentry some fifty yards away had stepped out of his box and was standing there in confusion, his machine gun raised. Was that something moving rapidly in the shadows? It took Tragg only tenths of a second to flit across his field of vision. When questioned during the subsequent inquiry, the sentry denied having seen anyone leave the Royal Guard Terrace after the shooting.

Tragg felt the cold hand of terror as he leapt into the driver's seat. The keys! He sat motionless and felt the sweat break out on his brow. In desperation, he slowly lifted his right hand from the wheel and let it slide down into the breast pocket of his jacket. When his fingers rubbed against the smooth plastic tab and wrapped around the keys themselves, he sighed deeply and noisily. Chance, curiosity, and habit, that unholy triple alliance, had saved him. He had not in fact needed to ask Svanberg for his keys when they got to the garage. Suddenly his body felt much lighter, as if all the tension but also repugnant, bloody death had fled his body, at least for the next few hours. He even allowed himself time to light a cigarette before driving away from his parking place. A few minutes later, he had reached Slussen. Greger Tragg had started out on his foreign trip.

# ❧ XVII ❧

Events at the Palace first reached the ears of the general public in a radio news broadcast at ten o'clock. Alex was still being operated on at the Karolinska Hospital; a professor and assistant professor, both experts on bullet wounds and abdominal injuries, had been called in posthaste. The Prime Minister had been informed and was in the Chancery. He had still not received a detailed report from the Chief of Police. The Minister of Justice was forced to interrupt a dinner at the Continental Hotel with two of his closest colleagues, and was on his way to the Chancery on foot, the hotel reception having failed to get hold of a taxi.

Bengt List was sitting in his study at home, enjoying a gin and a Berwald symphony. His wife was out playing bridge, and was not due home until midnight. List did not hear about the shooting until twenty past twelve, when he was telephoned by an inquisitive but intelligent TV journalist. Two hours later, at twenty past two, he was summoned to a meeting with the Prime Minister.

Piero Svanberg's body was taken to the mortuary at 10:37 P.M., according to the register. No one thought of informing his mother until the next morning.

Tragg was just passing through Västerås when the newscaster started his bulletin with what he called "a possible terrorist attack at the Royal Palace." Public reaction was muted on hearing that neither the King nor his family had been disturbed by the events. The guard had immediately been reinforced, however. As far as Tragg could understand, Alex was still alive. Tragg had still not seen a single police car, let alone a roadblock. Two more hours and he would be able to leave the E3 highway south of Mariestad and take advantage of the chaotic road network in Västergötland. He was calm, and maintained a normal speed for a long journey. Tragg was heading for Varberg on the west coast, and he thought he had a good chance of getting there without any difficulty.

In Berlin, Ulrich Langer knew nothing about developments in Stockholm. He spent most of the evening and much of the early hours wandering about from room to room, taking a last look at the frequently worthless objects one accumulates when building up a home. They reminded him of Gertrud, but they were also jottings in a carelessly kept diary during an eventful life. The next morning he would be on a train to Munich, and from there to Basel. He felt restless and sentimental in turn, and tried to deaden both sensations with the aid of a bottle of Soviet cognac.


Cooperation between the police and the security services in Stockholm is excellent. Both parties respect each other, but they also endeavor not to encroach on each other's territory. One reason for this is that a significant portion of security services personnel is recruited from the crime section. For natural reasons, the flow of information between the two authorities tends to be one-way.

The Prime Minister concluded his meeting shortly after four A.M. Nothing suggested that Sweden was about to be subjected to a terrorist attack. The dead man had been identified as an insignificant taxi driver with no known political affiliations. Like his victim, he was a native Swede. The doctors at the Karolinska Hospital had finished operating and gave their patient a fair chance of surviving. If he did escape death, they predicted he would be a permanent invalid, probably in acute pain but in possession of all his mental faculties.

As regards the motive for the attempted assassination, the Chief of Police, the head of the criminal police, and the head of B-section, Bengt List, all declined to comment at this stage. The Prime Minister had the impression that the three men were withholding vital information, or at least, well-informed suspicions. When they broke up, he therefore stressed emphatically how important it was for him to be kept informed of developments.

The communiqué issued to the mass media that night described the incident as a pointless attack carried out by a drug addict.


Following the meeting with the Prime Minister, the three police chiefs went together to police headquarters where, with admirable speed and efficiency, they organized an inter-sectional working party. By six o'clock in the morning, the medical report was received, together with a small plastic envelope containing various splinters and foreign bodies removed during the operation. At about the same time, the technical section at police headquarters completed their examination of Alex's clothing. It was perfectly clear the bullet could not possibly have been fired from Piero Svanberg's pistol. This information led the police to draw the logical conclusion that a third person must have been involved, and that he was still alive and at large.

On going through Svanberg's belongings, List discovered two pencilled notes in a pocket book. He assumed the dead man had made the notes himself.

The first was the name of a nightclub in Düsseldorf, the Trichter Bar. The German town was wrongly spelled with two 'f's. The second note was probably a telephone number which, if it was a Stockholm number, should be somewhere in Sundbyberg. It only took the telephone office a quarter of an hour to unearth the name and address of the subscriber, and a quick check of the register showed the occupier had been sentenced for illegal gaming some six months ago.

Although the evidence was thin, events of the previous night together with the impressive makeup of the working party persuaded the public prosecutor to issue a search warrant. At a quarter past seven in the morning, a squad of some twenty policemen arrived at the square in Sundbyberg. The apartment under suspicion was on the second floor. The front door was unlocked, and the police party advanced rapidly upstairs. Once they had taken up their positions, the apartment door was forced quickly and efficiently by a special team equipped with repeater weapons and bullet-proof vests.

The apartment was empty, and showed plenty of signs of having been left without panic. Fingerprint experts were soon able to establish that from their point of view, the apartment was totally unwiped. On the other hand, there was a shortage of personal belongings, apart from a limited amount of household utensils and china, plus half a dozen phonograph records which showed their owner had a highly-developed musical taste.

Bengt List was convinced he had found Greger Tragg's hideout. He was also sure the fingerprint investigations would reveal that Tragg and Svanberg had been alone in the apartment. Svanberg was dead. Therefore the third man, and there must have been one, had to be Greger Tragg. If his victim survived, List would obtain confirmation of the alarming suspicion that had been worrying him for the last hour.

While his men were going through the apartment, List

sat down by the telephone in one of the simple armchairs. He was tired and he had a headache. He would have liked most of all to go out into the kitchen and pour himself a whiskey from one of the bottles the previous occupier had so generously left behind. That was not to be. It was against all police ethics, especially as he was being watched by a dozen or so eager pairs of eyes.

List realized his search for the master spy was over. He had been rendered harmless, but not exposed, and the would-be assassin still had to be found. The security chief assumed neither the victim nor the gunman, who had to be Greger Tragg, would admit to anything illegal. The paradoxical truth was that if the wounded man survived and in the course of some future conversation—needless to say there could be no interrogation in the usual sense—confirmed the existence of a third man on the Royal Guard Terrace, and could even identify him, then List's deductions collapsed. If on the other hand the victim, whose fate would doubtless be followed with great sympathy by the Swedish public and their sensitive press, denied all knowledge of the man who fired the shot, then List would know for certain he had unmasked the country's most dangerous spy. Know, but be unable to prove. He was not even sure he would be able to convey his suspicions to the Prime Minister: if he did, it would have to be in private.

In any case, he's harmless now, List kept repeating to himself. He derived no satisfaction from this. Criminals differ from policemen in that the former are happy when they have eliminated an opponent, whereas a policeman wants to bring him to justice. This may be proof of how good the policeman is, or it may demonstrate that the police are doing a worthwhile job.

As the head of criminal investigations sat down with List to go through the facts, the telephone started to ring. At first List hesitated—a perfectly natural reaction—but then he lifted the receiver and said: "Hello." List was suddenly wide awake.

It may have been his imagination, but he thought he could hear a quick intake of breath at the other end. "Hello."

A couple of seconds later the connection was broken. The caller had replaced the receiver. It was highly unlikely the call could be traced.

"He's still in Sweden," said List to the police commissioner. "He was calling from a public phone booth. Probably on his way to Düsseldorf. His name is Greger Tragg and I've already issued a warrant for his arrest if he tries to leave the country."

Shortly after nine o'clock a nationwide alert was sent out together with Tragg's description. Interpol was informed at the same time, and that same afternoon they circulated his personal data and appearance to all associated countries. List spoke personally to the security chiefs in Norway, Denmark, and West Germany. Within twenty-four hours of the murder of Piero Svanberg and the wounding of Alex, most of Western Europe's police forces and security services had been informed. The following morning, similar information was passed on to London and, after a certain amount of hesitation, to Finland. At about the same time, similar messages began to stream in to the intelligence services in Moscow and East Berlin, albeit by very different routes.

Greger Tragg had ceased to be a non-person.

The harbor at Varberg had still not emerged from its winter sleep when Tragg parked in the gravel courtyard outside the ferry terminal. Three trailer trucks were standing sullenly in the enclosed customs area, awaiting permission to board the ferry. The drive through Hökensås and the back roads around Sjuhärad had gone more quickly than expected, and Tragg was not sure whether the ticket office would be open yet. He left the car and went for a stroll around the castle which had once been successfully stormed by the Danes, despite its stout, off-putting appearance.

The sharp, salty sea air did him good, and when he returned to the quay half an hour later he felt alert and cautiously optimistic. All the way here, he had avoided thinking about events at the Palace. He had pushed them out of his mind and closed his brain to everything that had happened before he turned the ignition key and pulled out from the curb at Lejonbacken. Only once had a picture of Marika hovered before his eyes, but he suppressed that, too. She and the death of Piero Svanberg made a melancholy background which must not be allowed to disturb his concentrated, alert state of mind. All he could afford to think about was the immediate future, and nothing else. He was on the last lap now, and what kept him going and forced all other diversions out of his mind was not success and the money but the prospect of being able to sit back and take his first carefree breath of air. In his present situation, what some people called ruthlessness or hardened criminal behavior was for him a necessity if he was going to survive. He had learned to live with facts, and knew the past is only dangerous if you resurrect it and allow it to take possession of you.

The customs shed was beginning to show signs of life. Tragg watched from the quay as two men positioned themselves by the ramp, waiting for the first of the rumbling heavy trucks to reach the ferry. Embarkation had started. His own car was the only one in the parking area some distance away. It was partly hidden by a telephone booth. Without really knowing why, he went up to the booth and opened the door. He found a suitable coin in his pocket and pressed it into the slot. A warped smile hovered on his lips as he dialed the Sundbyberg number. The phone rang three times, then someone lifted the receiver three hundred miles away.

"Hello."

The smile faded and he sighed deeply. They had moved faster than he had expected.

* * *

The girl in the ticket office had difficulty in suppressing a yawn.

"Do you intend going ashore in Grenå?" she asked.

"Yes."

"The night ferry doesn't leave Denmark till midnight. Do you want a cabin for the return journey?"

He hesitated slightly. "No thanks," he said. "I must get going again as soon as we arrive in Varberg."

She did not even look at him as she passed over the ticket and took the money; she was just glad not to have to sit at the computer terminal and type in the cabin request. Although Tragg was the only passenger to use her ticket window that morning, she had no idea how old he was or what he looked like when she was questioned about him later. All the customers looked the same to her, unless they could be bothered to have a little chat with her, or caused her a few problems, and that happened often enough, thank you very much.

The bosun was standing by the gangway, collecting tickets.

"Oh, no," he said, "no police or customs on duty here today! That's what we call inter-Nordic cooperation!"

The bosun recognized Tragg without difficulty from the photograph he was shown when he got back to Varberg that night. Even so, he swore blind that no passenger looking remotely like the man in the picture had boarded his boat that morning. The bosun made a point of never interfering in anybody else's business, especially where passengers were concerned. Besides, he rather liked this man. In some strange way he felt as if they were on the same wavelength, even though they had only exchange a few words. The main reason why the bosun did not tell the truth is that he disliked the policeman who was cross-examining him. Some months ago there had been a scuffle on board and the captain had been forced to intervene; the bosun had been reprimanded. By denying all knowledge of Greger Tragg, the bosun felt he had managed to get his own back. Bullying and pomposity are bad tactics on the part of the uniformed police. Not everybody is scared by it.

After about two hours at sea, the ferry passed the pile of sand in the middle of the Skagerack known as Anholt. By then, Tragg had worked out his tactics. The ferry was almost empty, and there had only been about another ten passengers in the dining room for breakfast. Five of them were obviously long-distance truck drivers. They were sitting at a reserved table, four loud-voiced Danes and a morose Swede. The Danes did not even bother to look at their Swedish colleague.

Tragg was able to study the Swede from behind. He was big and strong, hardly moved, and seemed to be shy because he was in an unaccustomed, strange environment. Once or twice he half turned to the Danes, as if seeking to start a conversation or ask a question. He got no further than thinking about it, but instead resumed his favorite position, his head resting on his large, filthy right first. He sat there like that for over ten minutes, immobile and unapproachable. A man lacking in imagination, but with a difficult job ahead of him that has to be done, even though he's unhappy about it. Tragg thought he knew why.

When the Danes finally left, Tragg went to fetch the coffee pot from the self-service table.

"Refill?" he asked, and proceeded to pour without waiting for an answer.

The Swede looked up, signs of life flickering in his watery blue eyes, suggesting vague hope but also sly caution. Tragg looked around for cream and sugar, and placed them on the table between them.

"Me too," said the truck driver with an awkward smile, reaching for the cream and stirring his coffee clumsily. A thought struck him, and he produced a crumpled cigarette packet from his pocket, offering it tentatively across the table.

Tragg took a cigarette and waited for his companion to do the same, lighter poised at the ready. They exhaled more or less in unison, and nodded approvingly at each other. They had become friends.

"Where are you heading for?"

"Holland."

"First trip?"

The driver sighed and frowned. His face was once more clouded over with anxiety. "Jerker Eriksson got sick," he said. "There was nobody else to turn to at short notice, so I had to take over."

"A trip abroad won't do you any harm!"

"I've only ever been to Mallorca before. This is my first time with the truck. It's the language, isn't it? And the customs. They say the Germans are real bastards at the border."

Tragg paused, as though considering the suggestion.

"Sometimes," he said hesitantly. "Once they kept me waiting for twenty hours. But usually it's farily painless."

This comment needed thinking about. Tragg waited patiently while his companion attempted to frame questions which would not appear pushy or inopportune, but could possibly solve his problems.

"You've driven this route before, then?"

"Gave it up ten years ago. It's not the job for a married man pushing middle age."

The truck driver agreed.

"That's just what Jerker says."

They took a sip of coffee, and eyed each other in a way that suggested they were moving on to the same wavelength.

"You've got your car with you, I suppose."

Tragg smiled and shook his head. "My friend got held up, so I'm left with three days to fill in. Varberg's not much of a place at this time of the year, so I thought of taking the train to Hamburg from Grenå. It's ages since I've had a chance to paint the town red."

His companion grinned. "Reeperbahn?"

"Could be."

The driver screwed up his eyes and seemed to be thinking hard. "You know the lingo, do you?"

"German?"

"Hmm."

"Oh, yes," replied Tragg casually. "Ich spreche Deutsch."

The driver had already made up his mind, but he had trouble putting what he wanted to say into words, and he shuffled about awkwardly. He scraped the tablecloth nervously with his filthy fingernails.

"You could ride with me," he almost whispered, "and give me a hand at the border. If necessary."

Tragg's face lit up. "That would be great," he said with a smile. "I'd be only too pleased to help."

The truck driver sighed with relief and shook Tragg's hand vigorously. They had struck a deal.

Not until about midnight, when he had parked his truck halfway to Bremen and was settling down for a few hours' sleep, did it occur to the lorry driver that his companion had no luggage. He chewed it over for a while. The stranger had not said much about himself. He had not even said what his name was. But he had been useful all right.

# ❧XVIII❧

Ulrich Langer stood on the balcony enjoying the spring sunshine and looking out over the streets of Basel. Down below, the few remaining puddles were evaporating in the heat and heading for the stratosphere in thin, hazy clouds. There, they would be blown about by the winds and fall again several days later, in a new country and in a new form. Langer smiled. He had felt this voluptuous sensation of freedom taking hold of him even when he lay in the bath earlier. From now on, he was a free man. Liberated from the well-regulated but also puritanical way of life imposed on its citizens by the Republic. Liberated from the philistinism that threatened to swamp him if he had been content with the museum job in Magdeburg. Liberated from Lutz Köstner. This latter freedom was the one he prized most highly.

Tomorrow morning, he and Greger Tragg would visit the Swiss bank and go through all the formalities necessary to make them millionaires and guarantee them a financially secure future. Then—and he savoured the word—they would *evaporate* just like the water in the streets, only to materialize again in the little island republic they had chosen as their new home.

215

Others might call them deserters, and that was technically correct. Being a deserter means liberating oneself, flinging aside a framework of compulsion which has become unbearable, and seeking the freedom which can only be appreciated by a hunted man. Many people would call them defectors, but they would be wrong. A defector continues his previous existence in the same old way, albeit under different colors. He must expect to be debriefed for years in a strictly guarded, luxurious prison put at his disposal for his own safety. When at last he is allocated a new existence in a place of exile chosen for him by someone else, he is still surrounded by deceit and distrust. A defector's freedom is relative, and restricted by invisible bonds which reduce him to a cripple with no hope of ever attaining real liberation.

Some people would call them traitors, the simplest of all labels. Their treachery consisted of demonstrating against absolute power and questioning its absoluteness. Among the men exerting power, there are those who believe loyalty is timeless and inviolable. They would demand punishment regardless of cost or effort. They would be listened to with respect and mumbled agreement, and assured no stone would be left unturned until the traitors were tracked down and wiped out. However, the very first orders would entail a scaling down of the punishment. Too many people had an interest in ensuring that petty incidents like this were soon forgotten. Too many people could summon up pragmatic and dialectical arguments, suggesting all that had really happened was that two expendable comrades had managed to get hold of a sum of money which, strictly speaking, had already been stolen by unknown Algerian colleagues.

Did not Engels say every movement contained from the start the seeds of its own destruction? Langer considered the quotation without deriving much satisfaction. Treachery on a large scale had always existed, not only amongst themselves and during the last fifty years, but ever since time began. Nowadays, traitors held the reins of power. If anyone managed

216

to slip out of their grip in order to seek the voluptuous willfulness that personal freedom represents, he was not only a traitor to the cause but also to treachery itself. Even so, he would be classed quite ruthlessly as a criminal, and sentenced according to the laws of treason. The sentence was clear. He would be taken out. But if it proved impossible to carry out the punishment, he would be disowned before the infection had a chance to spread.

In the elevator on the way down to the bar, it was above all the feeling of freedom which possessed Ulrich Langer. As he sat there alone in the bar and raised his glass to the future, his expression radiated confidence, happiness, and triumph. The bartender, who had withdrawn discreetly to the far end of the bar, smiled broadly in approval. The single guest belonged to that small minority who had managed to make the world their own, and dragged themselves out of the anonymous crowds where millions of nonentities clung on to each other. This type of customer was seldom generous when it came to tipping, but that did not matter so much. These silent moments alone with a real winner were highlights of the barman's life.

The day before Langer left Berlin, he had access to all available information. On that basis he had been able to judge the situation objectively and had decided all was going according to plan. Twenty-four hours later, that claim had proved to be an illusion.

The difference between Tragg and Langer, between the tactician and the strategist, would have been clear if their roles in Basel had been reversed. Tragg would naturally have checked in at the Intercontinental Hotel, true, since the room had been booked by the travel agency in Berlin, and they were bound to check that he had arrived. But having done so, he would have left the hotel immediately and looked for a safer place to spend the night. Above all, he would have covered himself against unwelcome surprises. With the aid of solid Swiss francs, he would have made a bargain with the reception staff whereby any inquiries about him, especially if they were anonymous, would have been noted and reported to him on his return. Moreover, he would have made certain he was not followed, and that nobody took the opportunity of searching his room while he was away without him knowing.

Langer took none of these precautions. Even so, only a few hours after his arrival in Basel, he had been surprised to receive a phone call from Tragg, telling him he had been delayed. There had been a few complications when it came to getting away, but he was sure he would turn up in Basel at the time agreed.

"I'll pick you up an hour before the meeting," Tragg had ended by saying. "Look after yourself."

Langer had realized he was being warned, but had been unable to see any concrete message in Tragg's words. There was nothing in Tragg's voice to suggest problems. Of course, both of them were aware the phone might be tapped. Whatever the reason for Tragg's delay, it obviously did not mean there was any risk that the meeting at the bank the next morning might have to be postponed.

As he sipped at his second drink, Langer decided to stay in the hotel for dinner. An elderly American couple had joined him in the bar; it transpired that they were on their first trip to Europe, and were in the room next to his own on the fourth floor. They were eager to talk, and were looking for company. Langer decided to spend the evening with them. The loquacious American lady and her less talkative husband would provide perfect camouflage—Langer was just another tourist this evening, and of no interest to anyone who did not know who he was. He made sure he got a well-hidden seat in the dining room, from which he could nevertheless keep his eye on the rest of the diners. He saw nothing suspicious all evening. None of the guests were sitting on their own; small groups of vacationers were mixed up with businessmen busily talking away, and everyone seemed to have reserved a table in advance.

By about eleven, Langer's companions appeared to have had enough, and the superficial chatter dried up. If the food had not been excellent, he would have found the evening unbearable. As it was, he bade the Americans goodnight and made some vague promise about renewing their acquaintanceship the next day. Before taking the elevator up to his room, he returned briefly to the bar in order to wash down all the rubbish he had been forced to listen to during the long, drawn-out dinner. For the third time that day he contemplated buying a newspaper, but for the third time decided against it.

The shooting drama at the Royal Palace in Stockholm did not make the front page in the continental newspapers, but it was reported on the foreign pages. The accounts were sufficiently detailed for Langer to have understood the nature of the problems Greger Tragg had been facing.


Shortly before ten o'clock that same evening, Tragg reached the outskirts of the German part of Basel. He parked in the back yard of a decrepit house displaying at the front a notice saying "Zimmer frei." It seemed that travelers with no great pretentions could find overnight lodgings within its walls. The landlord was a Turkish immigrant who asked no questions once he had been paid in advance for the only free room, and he assured Tragg he could have the room to himself until the next morning.

Tragg had "rented" the car, a 1967 Volkswagen, from a Yugoslavian businessman in Hamburg whose office was a mobile home parked temporarily on a demolition site alongside some thirty or so ancient vehicles of doubtful quality. The "rent" was equivalent to the selling price of the car, and the Yugoslav was not worried about getting it back until the agreed rental period—one week—had expired. The Yugoslav had asked no questions, and took it for granted Tragg had a driving license.

219

During the course of the day, Tragg changed his plans several times. He had first intended to ask Langer to find somewhere safe for the night for both of them, but rejected the idea, mainly for fear of the telephone being tapped. After a while, he realized he was going to be very late. There was nothing wrong with the car, which chugged along merrily at about 75 miles per hour, but just outside Munich Tragg got caught up in a traffic jam which took over an hour to disperse. When he finally reached Basel, he was four hours behind schedule.

The Turk, who had arranged his guest room in lodging house style with six uncomfortable bunks, all of which brought him an income, would certainly have had no objection to Tragg's choice of overnight companion. But the thought of crossing the border between West Germany and Switzerland twice in the space of an hour with the vague hope of finding Langer still at the hotel was not particularly attractive. He thought another phone call was out of the question.

Tragg had a nasty feeling that everything was too late. He collected a night key from his cantankerous host and went out for a walk. A few hundred yards from the Turk's house, he came upon a café which fitted perfectly into its surroundings and seemed to have come through the Wirtschaftswunder completely unscathed. He went in and ordered beer and schnaps, and after a while was served with some surprisingly tasty sausages.

Tragg was a realist and a skeptic, and had little sympathy for the mysteries of this world. But he did not deny the possibility of intuition. Several times in his life, he had heard alarm bells ringing without being able to give a rational explanation either before or after. It was thanks to this sensitivity of his that he was still alive and kicking.

Of course, his mood could be explained by the nervous tension he had been undergoing these last few months. The threat to his freedom had increased week by week, and had culminated in the shooting at the Palace. The margins between arrest and freedom had shrunk progressively until they were almost non-existent. Even so, he did not feel particularly threatened himself. That was illogical, since he and no one else was the prey.

He went on drinking—in moderation—while spelling out the situation in which he and Langer found themselves. The whole of the West European security forces were searching for him, supported by the criminal police and Interpol. It was a situation for which he was prepared, and it did not scare him. He had always known he would end up in that position sooner or later. If he got caught, it would be because of his own stupidity or his inability to react faster than the opposition in some unexpected and completely unplanned situation. The money, which he counted on obtaining tomorrow, would ease the situation, making it simpler to escape and create a new existence, but even if he failed to get the money he would not regard the game as lost. The only thing that would change would be his chances of living in comfort. His greatest asset was his ability to adapt, and he sometimes regarded himself—without being the slightest bit conceited—as a person with an unusual talent for the unpretentious, when circumstances required it.

The real threat came from Köstner. Tragg assumed Köstner had heard about events at the Palace within twenty-four hours. Köstner worked with probabilities. He would soon realize the wounded man in Stockholm could well be his top agent Alex, and Köstner's informer in SÄPO would report simultaneously, or within twelve hours at most, that Tragg did the shooting. This information would be confirmed during the next day from various sources all over Europe and in Interpol.

Köstner's acute problem was money. Tragg did not doubt for one moment that Köstner assumed he was on the way to Basel to pick up the commission for himself. He was quite certain Köstner would do all he could to insure the money went to nobody but the Arabs. Normally, he had access to considerable resources, but on this occasion he was forced to act independently, without help from Sasha. His real headache was time, and the difficulty of checking the necessary facts about the transaction in Basel without arousing suspicion.

An ambassadorial post was at stake, and Lutz Köstner would certainly have been dreaming about a role which made him one of the privileged upper classes who imagine they rule the world because they are given immunity in the host country and are less susceptible to political whims or eruptions than a president, ministers, or party secretaries. Tragg's usefulness was expended, and now Alex was incapacitated he was a dangerous threat who must be eliminated immediately.

The question was: by whom?

Even if Köstner had entertained the idea of informing the Arabs and asking for their assistance, he would reject it after careful consideration. Partly because it would put him in a weaker and almost embarrassing situation if he had to admit he had been hoodwinked by one of his own men. Partly because it was unlikely anyone from Algeria could get there in time. Most planes leave during the day, and the Arab would have to change flights in Paris and perhaps take the train for Zurich. Moreover, he would have to be ready to leave immediately, and be able to reach a quick decision together with the other interested parties.

Would not Köstner assume Langer was mixed up in it? He must find it a remarkable coincidence that Tragg and Langer were in Basel at the same time. The most obvious way to get rid of Tragg was for Langer to do it, but Langer was at best a desk murderer with no practical experience for years, while Tragg had lived day in, day out with the necessity of being on his guard and ready for the crucial attack. Thirty years of close cooperation and trust could not just be ignored, either. The possibility that Langer was in league with Tragg

222

meant Köstner was forced to use somebody else. The special teams of hit men were based in the Republic. Even if time was short, there was a danger that one of them might get to Basel in time.

Whoever the assassin was, he would use Langer as bait. Tragg returned to his evil-smelling Turkish hostel for a few hours of much-needed sleep, which he could indulge in without risk of interruption. Before falling asleep, he began to feel uncomfortably aware that, despite his logical reasonings, he was still not convinced he had covered all possibilities. He still had that disturbing feeling, and the illogical impression that he was not the one under threat.

It was a standard hotel room with a narrow corridor just inside the door. The bathroom was on the right, and closets on the left. When Langer switched on the light in the doorway, he could only see half of the room proper. He locked the door carefully behind him, and fastened the safety chain. His next thought was to order a wake-up call, and find out if there were any telephone messages.

The man was standing behind the armchair to the right of the floor lamp, pointing the pistol straight at Langer's chest. He was still blinking in the sudden, bright light, and sweating profusely with tension, a fact he tried to hide behind a cold, piercing stare. It did not seem to fit in with his naturally sanguine appearance. He was in his forties, red-haired, and on the fat side.

"Sit down!" he growled, pointing with his pistol at the armchair in front of him.

"Willi," said Langer uncomprehendingly. "Whatever's got into you?"

"Do as I say!"

The pistol swayed ominously and Langer obeyed. As he flopped unsteadily into the chair, he felt the cold steel of the

223

barrel in his neck, and at the same time the first piercing pain in his chest.

"Put your hands on your knees."

Langer did as he was told, and closed his eyes. The pain in his chest had become duller, as if it were sinking into him, and he found himself fighting for breath. Not now, he thought. It must not happen now. But he realized immediately it was on its way, and nothing could stop it. He could feel the grip around his throat as if some invisible assailant were trying to strangle him, and he had difficulty in breathing in.

"We're going to have a little chat," went on the Swiss, more relaxed now. "If you just answer my questions, no harm will come to you."

Nothing. Langer could see himself through the mirror in the corner. Willi was leaning back against the wall, the pistol still pointing at Langer's neck. The pain in his chest was spreading like rings in the water. He raised his hand to loosen his collar.

"That's enough."

"Willi . . . my heart . . ." gasped Langer.

The response came like a snort.

"Sit still!"

He had managed to undo his top button, and it helped a little. But he knew it was only a temporary respite. Panic and fear were there all right, but at a distance, and Willi's squeaky voice seemed to be coming from behind a sound curtain.

"Where's Tragg?"

"Who?"

"Greger Tragg. The Swede. You've come to Basel to meet him, right? Not to have dinner with me tomorrow night."

"I don't know where he is."

Langer's voice sounded muffled, as if he had fetched it up from the cellar.

"You're lying. You might as well come clean."

"What am I supposed to come clean about?"

224

Silence. An expectant pause. Langer's chin sank down onto his chest, and his red face began to turn purple. He did not know if he would be able to stand up. The tablets were in the bathroom. In his toilet bag. "Willi, you've got to believe me. It's a heart attack."

The cold barrel of the pistol felt cool against his neck, and he shuddered when it was replaced by Willi's breath, heavy with cognac.

The Swiss had moved around the chair and was standing in front of him, looking confused. He smiled slightly, and Langer could not decide if it was with satisfaction or malevolence.

"Willi . . . ! In the bathroom. Hurry!"

Willi hesitated. Then he stepped quickly forward and pressed the pistol into Langer's stomach while frisking him with his free hand, looking for a hidden weapon in Langer's armpit, pockets, and crotch. Nothing.

Langer groaned under his captor's weight. The pain had spread right across his chest and he did not even notice when the Swiss stood up and, still pointing the pistol, shuffled backwards towards the bathroom. Perhaps he lost consciousness for a few seconds. He neither heard nor responded to Willi's barked threat:

"If you so much as move, I'll shoot you."

When Langer opened his eyes slowly, almost doubtfully, he realized he had survived. Even though the pressure and the pain in the chest were still there and although every breath was an almost insuperable effort, the first few seconds of consciousness brought with them a feeling of bliss which shut out everything else. He had survived, and he wanted to go on living.

Willi had forced the tablets into Langer's mouth, and he had swallowed them instinctively. His shirt front was soaking wet. The Swiss sat in front of him on a desk chair in the middle of the room, the pistol in his right hand. Langer looked at him as though he had rediscovered him.

"Thank you," he said, wearily.

Willi nodded, and added with a sneer: "You're getting too old for this kind of thing. It's time you retired. Tell me what you know about Tragg and I'll have a doctor here in ten minutes. Then we can get you straight to the hospital. We're pretty good with hearts in this country."

"I don't know where he is. Will you please get me a glass of water?"

Langer was trying to gain time. Something had gone wrong. Köstner must have sent Willi. But how . . . why? . . . He could see no explanation, no connection.

Willi, a Swiss field agent, who had that very afternoon been looking forward eagerly to having dinner with Langer the next night, was badly briefed. His telephone had rung at about one o'clock. It had been threatening and ruthless, and to his surprise it was not in code.

"Force Ulrich Langer—never mind how—to tell you how to find Greger Tragg. Kill the Swede before nine o'clock tomorrow morning. If not, it will be the worse for you." The voice from West Berlin had silenced Willi's attempts to protest by his uncompromising final words. "I'll call you at ten tomorrow. If you have fulfilled your mission, you can expect a reward. If you have failed, you can start writing your will."

Willi had not been told why Tragg had to be killed, but he knew that as far as he was concerned, there was no alternative. He had taken his pistol with him to the nearest café, where he had started drinking coffee and cognac. By five in the afternoon, he was convinced that even if the mission was unpleasant, it would be fairly easy to carry out and, in spite of everything, not too risky.

"First tell me where Greger Tragg is, then you can have your water."

"I've told you I don't know."

"Don't try my patience, Ulrich. You know where he is, and you're going to tell me. Now!"

He stood up and took a step towards Langer. Perhaps Langer misjudged the distance. What is certain is that he acted without the discipline needed to survive in the intelligence services. Langer did not know where Tragg was that night. He might have been able to convince Willi of the truth; that is, they had agreed to meet in the hotel lobby at nine the next morning. The Swiss must have realized the heart attack was genuine and Langer was in a fragile state, so he would not have dared to use any rough tactics. A dead Ulrich Langer was no good to Willi, whose chances of carrying out his mission would then have been virtually nil. Just at the moment, the biggest threat to Willi's own life would be the death of Langer.

If Langer had spent the night thinking and putting veiled questions to Willi, he would probably have realized he was bluffing, at least in part. Willi had never met Greger Tragg, and had only been given a vague description of the Swede. As time went by, Langer's superior intelligence would gradually have evened out the odds between them, and eventually they would have swung in his favor. When the confrontation with Tragg finally arrived—however that might come about— Willi's strong suit, his possession of a weapon, would have been reduced to a surmountable obstacle. Langer's behavior would have been so different from normal that Tragg would have been on his guard immediately, even more so than usual. It was impossible to predict the outcome, but from an objective point of view, the odds must have been roughly fifty-fifty.

The heart attack had undermined Langer's thinking. His actions were not considered, but a defiant, desperate effort to reclaim the years of peace, freedom, and comfort he had been longing for, and which he had regarded as automatic ever since that afternoon. His attempt to overpower Willi was feeble. As he was still struggling to his feet, his opponent defended himself by a swinging blow with his pistol which hit Langer just below his right ear. Death, that split-second between something and nothing, reached Langer while he was still falling, and smothered the report from the pistol which went off simultaneously. Ulrich Langer's heart stopped beating. The bullet missed Langer by a couple of inches, passing through the curtains and shattering the window. Willi was ill prepared for what had happened. For a couple of seconds, he stood by the corpse as if transfixed, but managed to control his panic. The smell of gunpowder irritated his nostrils, and he made up his mind with a toss of the head. Without looking around, he disappeared from the room. He had almost reached the bottom of the fire escape before the American woman in the next room, without makeup and looking aged in her mauve nightgown, opened her door and seemed drawn compulsively into the dead German's room, trembling but irresistibly curious. Her scream was shrill and alarming, unlike the sound of the shot and the dull thud as Langer's body hit the floor.

Within minutes the corridor was full of terrified hotel guests and fussy staff. It was half an hour before a local police superintendent arrived to restore calm and begin the inquiry. Only in the bar was there an atmosphere of feverish excitement, and when the barman was eventually able to close at about four in the morning, he noted, not without a feeling of satisfaction, that moneywise, he had just had one of the best nights of his life. He put out the lights, and saluted the dead man in silence.

# ❧ XIX ❧

The falconer was standing about ten paces behind the bunch of tourists who were staring up at the eagle in the treetops at the other side of the square. The distance to the eagle was at least a hundred yards. Slowly, the falconer took the piece of meat in his gloved left hand and turned to show it to the bird, which launched itself into a long, sweeping, perfectly timed glide less than a foot above the heads of the terrified tourists, before landing on the falconer's arm and ravenously gulping the bloody bait.

This was the highlight of the falconer's act. The golden eagle which repeated the feat several times a week was his pride and joy. One week he would never forget, it had flown over Manhattan skyscrapers, been filmed from the rooftops and a helicopter, and later admired by million of cinema-goers all over the world.

The performance always had the same effect. The tourists scattered shrieking like a flock of terrified geese, only to recover a few seconds later and, hesitantly at first but then more and more enthusiastically, to applaud in admiration for the eagle and its straggly-bearded owner. Not many of them

229

actually looked at the taciturn man with the strange foreign accent. Although he was the undisputed master of the tattered remnants of some of Europe's proudest birds, like them he was condemned to life-long captivity in the same remote corner of this island off the beaten track. Twice a day the crowds of spectators, looking like vultures, were herded into the fenced-off enclosure. Some fifty or so eagles, falcons, owls, and hawks, all chained by the foot, would sit there staring at the chattering hordes with hostility and contempt oozing forth from their poisonous, yellow eyes. The yellow poison was even stronger in the eyes of the falconer, concealed behind a veiled gaze which seemed anchored far away into the past. He was born and bred in Silesia and had come to Eire about a month after the end of the war. The only real contact he had maintained with his homeland was Ulrich Langer; he had only heard about his death a few days ago.

Tragg observed the performance from a rickety table outside the modest cafeteria. He had waited until his third visit before mentioning the password which confirmed he had been sent by Ulrich Langer and was entitled to help and assistance, but most of all discretion. The falconer had asked him to come back that afternoon, and asked only one question after listening to Tragg's story. He wanted to know how Langer had died, and received the news without any change in his expression. His only comment was, "Ulrich was a friend of mine."

While chattering tourists dispersed to the bar to sample the bitter Irish beer, the falconer paused at Tragg's table.

"Mr. Kelly will be here in half an hour," he said in his croaking Silesian accent. "You can trust him completely. The organization he belongs to is not acquainted with any traitors who are still alive."

Tragg nodded, and sank back listlessly in his chair. Never in all his adult life had he had so much time on his hands as now.

230

•   •   •

It was pouring rain early the next morning when Tragg
left the Turk's foul-smelling lodging house in the suburbs of
Basel. He left his Volkswagen behind, and joined the stream
of commuters crossing over from the German to the Swiss side
of Basel. No one displayed much interest in his German
identity card. As soon as he approached the hotel entrance,
he realized something was wrong. Several police cars were
parked outside, and although it was still early the coffee bar in
the lower lounge was quite full. Tragg sat down on one of the
bar stools and ordered coffee and a sandwich, in English. An
elderly lady looking very American turned to him and said,
"Isn't it awful! It was me who found him!"

She proceeded to talk non-stop for the next quarter of an
hour—the dinner, the shot and the dull thud in the next
room, the running feet in the corridor, the first police
questions. She did not leave out a single detail, and ended by
letting Tragg into a secret.

"At nine o'clock I'm due for another session here in the
hotel with that awful policeman. You should just hear his
English!"

She smiled at Tragg, and it was obvious she appreciated
having a listener who was considerate enough not to interrupt
her with irrelevant comments.

"I liked him so much," she blurted out suddenly, with
tears in her eyes. "He was a real gentleman, and he had such a
funny hairstyle. Like a monk."

There was no doubt at all: the dead man was Ulrich
Langer. Köstner had struck, quickly and ruthlessly; Tragg was
surprised, shaken, and afraid. Without trying to resist, he
allowed himself to sink into that remote, emotionless state
which transformed him into a pre-programmed automaton
with only one function in life: fulfilling the mission he had
embarked upon with not a hint of weakness.

231

He himself ought to have been the first name on Köstner's hit list. If he survived the next few hours, Ulrich Langer's death must have been a mistake. He had no illusions. If that were not the case, he might just as well prepare for death straight away.

Nothing happened. Tragg left the hotel and turned up at the bank exactly at ten o'clock. He used the staff entrance, and found the check waiting for him. The number code was correct. Half an hour later he had been through all the formalities, opened a numbered account and also acquired a considerable sum in cash. Shortly before twelve he was back at the Turk's, and astonished him by renting the room for another night. He slept for fifteen hours, restlessly at first, but increasingly deeply. He left Basel at five the next morning, and a month later was on the ferry from Holyhead to Dublin. He was using a Dutch passport which only an expert could have seen was false. Like the German identity card, it was a present from Ulrich Langer. It had been produced in Berlin six months ago, and was in the black briefcase Tragg had brought back to Stockholm from Müggelsee.

Tragg had changed his appearance very slightly. There is not much one can do about most things: one cannot change one's height, nor one's shoe size, and neither makeup nor false additions will stand up to close scrutiny. On the other hand, one can change the color of one's hair, change to or from glasses, adjust one's eyebrows, adopt a hairstyle which makes one's ears look different, and dress like a schoolmaster. As Tragg was sitting there outside the falconer's cafeteria, it is likely that even Piero Svanberg would have had difficulty in recognizing him, at least not until he had come within a few feet.

How much more difficult it is for a policeman, who has at best a blurred memory of a photograph to help him identify a wanted man. During the holiday season, millions of people wander apparently aimlessly all over Europe, from Gibraltar to

232

the North Cape. Only those who stand out in a crowd attract any attention at all, and Tragg avoided behavior which might appear unseemly for a schoolmaster. He ate at self-service restaurants and stayed at simple but decent middle-class hotels. Next day, no one could remember who he was. Gray, dull, and correct, once more he assumed the role of a non-person, and became nothing more than a figure in the country's tourist statistics.

Tragg occasionally came across a Swedish newspaper, and read in one of them that Alex had survived. His wound was so serious he would have to spend the rest of his life in a wheelchair. In recognition of his many years of service and his important contribution to the good of his country, the government had awarded him a special pension on top of the usual disability pension he was now getting. Even in future, the government intended to make sure of the invalid statesman's great experience, his dedicated and selfless efforts on Sweden's behalf. Unfortunately, his state of health would severely limit the extent to which his services could be used.

Needless to say, the article said nothing about the conversation Bengt List had had in private with the Prime Minister. At the latter's suggestion they agreed the discussions had been private in character, and should neither be minuted nor noted in the official diary. List had the distinct impression from the Prime Minister's concluding remarks that he might well be offered the post of Provincial Governor in Halland. If and when an official offer came, List intended to accept.

Most of the Solvalla racegoers had never heard of Piero Svanberg. They were used to scandals and newspaper head-lines, and no one thought it remarkable that the man who fired the pistol at the Palace was a bookie. Svanberg's corner table in the cafeteria was soon taken over by an ambitious young man who knew how to handle his clients and proved he could take serious setbacks in his stride. The only person to keep in touch with Svanberg's next of kin, his mother, for several months was the trainer who went on looking after his horse. Money is no consolation for a mother's sorrow when her only son departs this life, but the fifty thousand kronor brought in by the sale of the horse did help a little. Agda Svanberg always refused to speak about events at the Palace. Instead, whenever her son's name and fate were brought up she changed the subject rapidly and talked about the horse. In many circles fifty thousand kronor is a sum which silences nosy people. She never admitted, either to herself or to anyone else, that her son was a murderer. In this respect, her mother's instinct served her well. She alone knew the truth and was prepared to tell it. The small number of other people who shared her knowledge twisted it into a lie which they all took with them to their graves.

Many of the regulars in the owners' section at Solvalla noticed a change of staff at the payout window. Instead of the pleasant lady they had been used to for the past ten years, they were served by a sullen, brusque man who paid out winnings with the same supreme indifference as a bailiff taking possession of a debtor's only remaining estate. One owner happened to come across her on a beach in Yugoslavia early in July. His first impulse was to resume and possibly to develop their relationship, but he soon changed his mind. She had changed, and aged remarkably. Moreover, he did not like the company she kept. The two fawning men hovering around her would not let go of their prey without a struggle, and a gambler rarely looks for a struggle, not unless the odds are in his favor.

At the beginning of July, *Neues Deutschland* carried a report to the effect that Lutz Köstner had been made DDR Ambassador to Algeria. This piece of news never reached Tragg. If it had, he would have been able to save large amounts of money and allow himself greater freedom of movement. On the other hand, he still had SÄPO, Interpol, and the Service to contend with. Köstner's time as head of the

234

Algerian delegation was less than glorious, and he was recalled to Berlin after only eight months on the grounds that the reception he received from the Algerians was surprisingly chilly, not to say hostile. This attitude could not be attributed to any moves or intrigues on the part of Ahmed Kassir, since even before Köstner arrived in Algiers he had been banished to the remote areas near the border where Polisario was engaged in a struggle for liberation. A month later, Kassir's widow was informed in writing that her husband had been killed in a gun battle with Moroccan bandits.

As the Algerian purchasers refused to pay any commercial credit for the remaining deliveries specified by the contract with Intereloc, the company's annual revenues fell so drastically that headquarters felt obliged to make changes in the top management of their Swedish subsidiary. Tore Wattinius took early retirement, and felt he had backed a winner. In future, he could concentrate on his yacht and his stamp collection. Lars Bunter was given several months to look around for a new job, and before the year was out he was appointed sales manager of a firm delivering mechanical cranes. His impressive knowledge of Arab marketing methods soon led to an expansion and the company was able to employ an extra one hundred and fifteen men. After only a year, Bunter was able to open a numbered account in Switzerland.

For some years, the pianist from Harlem retained a preference for men of Italian origin among her white friends. There were not many Italians in Berlin, which was her next booking. One evening, she amused herself between numbers by talking to a red-haired German woman whose outspokenness and lack of prejudice appealed to her. They would never meet again. Moreover, she was disappointed when, later in the evening, she was introduced to the somewhat unsophisticated Frenchman the German woman had married. When the conversation came round to cats, she lost interest altogether.

The Nordschein Region was reorganized rapidly and

efficiently during the summer months. The exercise was supervised in detail by Sasha, who was delighted to find his mole in Stockholm had been made head of a Chancery division. There had been no real break in normal activities. The loss was significant, that could not be denied, but the new contact was doing very well. The important thing was the Republic could count on his services right up to the turn of the century.